THE CASTRATO

Music was my first love
And it will be my last
Music of the future
And music of the past
— John Mile

The castrato

Joyce Pool

Translated by *Jonathan Ellis*

Lemniscaat  New York

This book was published with the support of the Dutch
Foundation for Literature.

N **ederlands**
letterenfonds
dutch foundation
for literature

First published in the United States and Canada in 2015 by
Lemniscaat USA LLC • New York
Distributed in the United States by Lemniscaat USA LLC • New York

Library of Congress Cataloging-in-Publication Data is available.
ISBN 13: 978-1-935954-41-5 (Hardcover)
Printing and binding: Lightning Source Inc., La Vergne, USA
First U.S. edition

PROLOGUE

Florence, 1698

Heaven…Was this Heaven? Could it be anything else?

Angelic voices praised God's majesty and a bright light shone through my eyelids. Heaven.

I was taken from my sister Mariana and my aunt Ignatia to be killed. Why?

What had I done?

My head throbbed and a burning pain in my groin set fire to my stomach and thighs. I didn't know there could be pain in Heaven. Wasn't everything here good and beautiful?

Apparently not.

Another sharp stab. I doubled up in pain. My hands shifted to my stomach. And lower. To the side of my groin. To the lump there.

Carefully my hands slid across the bulge. What was it? A piece of fabric? I touched it, fiddled my fingers under it.

The fabric that had stuck to my leg tore loose and I almost screamed out loud. Thank God I was able to contain myself. Screaming in Heaven?

I clenched my teeth and waited for the pain to abate. Then I parted my legs slightly and allowed my fingers to explore further.

The angelic singing grew nearer. Suddenly I felt something or someone near me. I stiffened, my hand still on my crotch. I lay perfectly still. What would I see if I opened my eyes? Two wings spread over me? Saint Peter, ready to lead me into Heaven? Or my mother and father waiting for me with open arms?

I didn't want to see it, did not want to know for sure. I wanted to dream that I felt no pain and was working alongside my father in the tannery, scraping hides.

"*Work carefully, Angelo. Not a single hair may remain. No complaints…*"

"*Yes, Papa,*" I whispered. "*Not a single hair…*"

"Ah." I heard next to me. "Boy…are you awake?"

I squeezed my eyes even firmer together.

"Wake up, boy. You're talking nonsense."

Wake up? No. Not Heaven. Not dead. Mama, forgive me.

My mattress was pressed downwards. Somebody was leaning next to my head.

"It's me, Paolo. Your new room-mate." Fingers tapped my cheek. "Are you awake?"

I wanted to beat him off. But my hand, there in my crotch… That terrible pain!

"Good lord, you're burning! It's as if they've just taken you from an oven! Shall I let in some air?" Without warning, the blanket was pulled from me.

My eyes sprang open reflexively. A boy with blond hair was looking down at me.

"Playing with yourself?" he asked with a glance at my hand. "Can't be much fun. Just been treated?"

I shivered. Withdrew my hand. Grabbed for the blanket. "Cold…"

"Well." He flapped the blanket. "You'll have to put up with it. If I cracked an egg on your forehead, it'd fry." Cautiously, he wrapped the blanket around me again and folded the end under my feet. "So."

I tried to turn my head, to look around. "This…?"

Paolo grinned. "No idea where you are, huh? That's what they always do bring the new ones in at night. They wake us up,

8

banging into the milk churns, but they couldn't care less about that. As long as we are up and about before dawn, as fresh as a daisy. Anyway, you are in the boarding school of the oldest conservatory in Florence."

Conservatory? Arrived late in the evening? I tried to let the words penetrate my confusion.

"Not Heaven?"

"Heaven?" Paolo sniffed. "It depends on who you ask. Sometimes it seems more like the underworld here. Doesn't it, lads?"

The others could not apparently interrupt their singing, for nobody answered. But a cushion did fly at Paolo's head. He laughed and threw it back to the other side of the chamber. "And perhaps you could play the role of Lucifer, Silvio? And you could all perform a symphony of farts together."

The angelic singing was interrupted by sniggering.

Paolo turned back to me. "You look rather old for somebody who has just been treated. How old are you? Twelve? You look about the same age as me."

I wanted to answer but my tongue felt like a piece of dried meat. I stuck it out and licked my lips.

"Dry mouth? Wait!"

The song of praise continued around me, in various keys. The chamber, I saw, was a dormitory. Boys were standing beside the beds, dressed in white cassocks with dark blue choir smocks over them, and singing as they straightened the blankets. It was a strange sight: I had only seen choir boys in their proper contexts: in the nave of a church or on the way to it. Here they stood in their choral vestments making beds. If my abdomen hadn't been burning so badly and my head throbbing with pain, I might have laughed.

It wasn't long before Paolo returned. "I've dipped a rag in water;

perhaps you can suck enough of a drink from it. Crockery is not allowed in the dormitory, but you'll learn all the rules soon enough yourself." He supported my head as I sucked on the rag. "What's it like…down there? Is it burning?"

His question acted like the stab of a knife, and I immediately felt the burning pain shoot through my body. He apparently read the answer in my face.

"It will slowly grow less," he said. "It took two years in my case. I don't feel it anymore."

"What's happened to me?"

"Your unmanning."

If I had been able, I would have jumped up. "My *what?*"

"I bet nobody told you." He grinned again.

"What do you mean?"

"You have a beautiful voice, yes?"

"They said so." The maestro, the padres, and the bishop. And that skinny girl with those burning eyes, Rosa Scarlatti. They all said it.

Paolo nodded wisely. "Well, you will now keep that beautiful voice for the rest of your life. The conservatory has made sure of that. With all of us." He gestured toward the other boys, who had now nearly finished making their beds.

I lifted my head in bewilderment and looked around me. Some boys waved at me or pulled a funny face. One made a theatrical bow the one with the cushions. Silvio.

I fell back on the mattress and stared straight ahead. Had they all been through what I was feeling now? I couldn't believe it.

"Look here," said Paolo. "It's like this: With a beautiful voice, you are worth a fortune to the Church. They let you sing during masses, funerals, and processions, and they get paid money for that. Never seen a cent, I bet?"

I shook my head.

"Nobody here has. We do it all for Our Sweet Lord and the Holy Mother. But they earn a lot. And they earn most from pure boys' voices. Unfortunately for the Church, that purity changes as boys get older. Never noticed that? Or didn't it cross your mind that your father no longer has the voice of a child?"

"He doesn't have any voice anymore," I whispered.

"Dead? That's a shame."

I swallowed. "But when he was still alive, he had a deep voice."

"That's what I mean," said Paolo. "Your voice was about to change. And that, of course, was something the padres and maestros wanted to avoid. Get it?"

"How?"

"How do they prevent it?"

"Yes."

He nodded to the place under the blankets where my crotch was covered with a piece of cloth. "Can't you guess?"

My hand moved back to the same place. I said nothing. I didn't want to guess.

Paolo sighed. "Fine," he said. "Then I will tell you. Somewhere round there is a thing that influences your voice. They've cut it, ours too, and that keeps our voices like they are."

"Cut?"

"Yes, cut. Destroyed it. All for that beautiful sound from your throat."

I felt as if I wanted to throw up.

Paolo didn't appear to notice. "Very soon you'll hear what your voice will sound like. The guys in the next dormitory are sixteen or seventeen, and they tower head and shoulders above most of the old people at the conservatory. But they talk with the voice of a ten-year-old. The first time I heard it, I nearly pissed myself with laughter."

Suddenly tears filled my eyes. "But they nearly strangled me! I thought I was dying!" I searched for words. "They asked me whether I would like to attend the conservatory. That's not the same as taking a knife to me *cutting* me!"

Paolo shrugged. "You must have said something that the padres took as permission. Did you sign anything, by chance?"

"Only a document saying that they would take care of me."

He slapped his leg. "And you didn't read it, I bet. Yes, that's how those people go to work. They are supposed to get permission from your papa. But if he is no longer alive and you have a very beautiful voice…" He fell silent. "My old man thanked the Lord when they came to the door. Another one taken care of. What do you expect? One bakery and fourteen sons to leave it to…"

I crumpled the blanket in my fist. "They should have told me what they were going to do to me."

"Would you have agreed?"

I remained silent. How was I supposed to know?

Paolo lowered his voice. "And it's not only your voice that changes. But you'll see that next door "

Somewhere in the distance, a bell sounded. The singing stopped immediately and the boys rushed to the door.

"I have to go." Paolo got up. "Prayers in the chapel. I'll be back at the end of the morning."

"But "

"If I don't get a move on, I'll have to clear up everybody else's filthy mess. Don't fancy that." He turned and ran after his roommates.

I remained behind in astonishment. All the beds around me were neatly made. Nothing revealed that they had recently been slept in by boys of my age. It stank of sleep, musty armpits, and sweaty feet, but otherwise…

Had they all really gone through this, the same as me? Were they also "unmanned"?

Again I let my hand slip under the blanket. I felt the piece of cloth and under it…threads? Right through my flesh? Cautiously I rubbed it. Had they done it there, the barber and the padre?

And what did it mean, unmanned? I retained my normal voice, but otherwise? My sex had in any case not been cut off. That was clearly there next to the patch.

But what about peeing? And later, making love to girls?

I slowly sat up, supporting my weight on my elbows. There were ten beds: five on my side and five on the other. There were stools at the end of the beds, most of them bearing a folded shirt, a nightshirt, presumably.

Mine only had the white shirt I was wearing yesterday when I left Fiesole; no cassock, no choir smock. And no sign of my doublet.

Should I get up? Follow the other boys? In my white shirt?

I swung my legs over the edge of the bed and almost fainted with pain and nausea.

"Still feeling poorly?" Padre Matteo Battista was standing in the doorway looking at me. He took a few paces in my direction and stretched out his hand.

I ignored it. "What have you done to me?"

"Ensured that you will keep your beautiful voice. I'm sorry that we have had to cause you pain."

"How?"

The padre studied me through half-closed eyes. "Have you spoken to anybody?"

"Something has been cut away."

He nodded. "An unnecessary piece of your body. Surely that is all you need to know?"

"What have you cut away? And why, in God's name?"

"Be careful how you use the name of our Father, my son."

"Why?" My voice broke. "Tell me!"

"For your own good. Believe me, Angelo. You will not be troubled by it, not like now."

"I want to know what you have done!"

"Calm down," hushed the padre. "Of course you may know." He placed my shirt on the bottom of the bed, shifted the stool closer, and sat down next to me. "God has created us men in such a way that there are things down there that can affect your voice. That is true of me and of you, and it was also true of your father. These things ensure that at a given moment your voice becomes heavier, has a different timbre and cannot reach the same heights. Sometimes, I must admit, the result is a feast for the ears. But your voice, Angelo, was already so beautiful in all its youthful resilience and purity when Padre Alonso and I heard you in Fiesole! It would have been an unimaginable loss for everyone if you had lost it. So we invited you to come to the conservatory and have those nasty things removed by a barber."

"Did I ever mention that I wanted to be unmanned?" If I did not feel worse with every beat, nothing would have been able to prevent me from getting up, taking one of the stools and slamming it against a wall. Had the padres gone mad?

"Unmanned?" Padre Matteo Battista smiled. My hands itched even more. "Whatever gave you that idea? We didn't do that! You were born as a man and you will always remain a man. There's no need to be afraid of that."

"But Paolo said…"

Now he laughed out loud. "Oh, Paolo. I should have known. He is one of our best singers but also a comedian. Unmanning would mean removing your sex. Of course we haven't done that."

I calmed down somewhat. "I…I felt that. It…it is still there."

Again Padre Matteo Battista laughed. Then he turned serious. "Listen, Angelino, if we had done nothing, your voice would have certainly become less beautiful within no time. You may even not have managed the Papal Mass. Is that what you would have wanted? A screeching, breaking voice while the Pope listened? Of course not." He placed his hand on my head. "With that voice of yours, you are going to have a wonderful future, my son. Perhaps you will even sing for princes and bishops. That is not something many singers attain."

I could think of nothing more to say. I was numbed. And there was that pain in my crotch, that horrible, nauseating pain. It all proved too much for me and I tried to fight back my tears. "Make me whole again. Put back what you took away. Sew everything together again. I don't want a beautiful voice. A voice like my father's is good enough for me."

"My son," said the padre. "You don't know what you're saying."

Wasn't that something Papa used to say? I now knew for certain what I was saying, better than ever before!

"Make me whole!" I screamed.

Padre Matteo Battista lowered his eyes. "I'm sorry if that's what you want. And I'm sorry I have to tell you that it's not possible."

"What?" Finally the tears flooded my eyes. Wet streams flowed along my cheeks to my chin. "I'll remain damaged for ever?" I fell backwards and pulled up my legs. The pain in my crotch robbed me of breath and I stretched out my legs again.

"Be grateful for being chosen. You will make your Heavenly Father very happy." The padre stood up and pulled the blanket over me. "Now it is important that you rest. The wound must heal. If you move too soon, it will bleed. You may be able to walk around the room a little this afternoon, and if all goes well, you will meet the other sopranists tomorrow morning."

Sopranists echoed in my mind. Boys like me. Unmanned.

"How many of us are there?" Angrily I wiped away my tears with my arm.

"Eight the same age as you and six who are several years older. Not many, Angelo. Sopranists are rare." Padre Matteo Battista took a step back. "But you are not, in any case, the only one. And you will soon feel better and again start singing like the nightingale we heard at maestro Alonesi's."

I closed my eyes. "Go away," I whispered.

"Mind your words," said the padre.

"Leave me alone!" I struggled onto my side and pushed my face into the cushions. I was suddenly so very tired. Drained of strength.

Too weak and too nauseous to fight, to scream. I wanted to sleep and forget. Escape the pain. Go home. Just go home.

"Be well soon." The padre stood up. His voice dissolved into nothingness.

PART I

1

Fiesole, nineteen days earlier

I stared at the sparkling ray of light that fell through the church's stained-glass window. Today it was exactly a year since my mother had died. "One last time, *signori.*"

I heard the maestro's voice, but I couldn't shake off the memory. Mama, my mama, so sweet, so beautiful…Do I really look like her? With my dark eyes, big nose, and short arms and legs?

"Montegne," squealed the maestro's voice. "Am I conducting the people on the street?"

A nudge in my side. "Pay attention!" hissed Gaetano without looking at me.

I tore my gaze away from the high stained-glass window and shifted it to the maestro.

"Idiot!" a voice hissed next to me.

"Well, Montegne? Are we now paying attention?"

"Yes, maestro," I said weakly.

"I would expect such behaviour from any other of these gentlemen, but not from you." Irritated, the maestro leant over his stand. His pince-nez slid from his nose, but he caught it before it hit the ground. "You know you may leave if this does not interest you." His look pinned us down as if we were flies on a white wall and he was the fly swatter. "Victorio? Luigi? Gaetano?"

"Yes, maestro," they said in unison.

"And you, Angelo?"

I felt myself blush. All their eyes were on me. I wished I could go up in smoke. "Yes, maestro. *Scusi.*"

The maestro placed his pince-nez on his nose and looked at me for a few seconds. Then he cleared his throat. "Again, gentlemen? Concentration please." He tapped his stand. "One…"

My fingers grimly gripped the music folder. I really did want to concentrate. If only the sunlight were not so delightful through the coloured windows…if only it were not precisely one year ago today…

I swallowed. Don't think about Mama. Or about the weather. Or the sun. For eight days at a stretch, water had been raining down, without letting up for a moment. As if God had thrown open the heavenly sluices to give everything a good cleansing. It had changed the streets into streams that carried away everything in their paths: stones, bushes, the butcher's cart and even a couple of dogs.

Since early this morning, sunlight had beaten down on the water, and very soon the streams would turn into puddles which, in turn, would evaporate as if they had never existed. Just like Mama had disappeared as if she had never existed…

I bit my lower lip as hard as possible. *Stop it!*

"Two…"

Concentrate. Stand up straight. Breath. Pull back your shoulders.

I heard the boys around me take in a breath. I stared straight into the wide eyes of the maestro.

Precisely on "Three!" we all started together. From the quick smile on the face of maestro Alonesi, I saw he was satisfied. Thank goodness. If the rest went as well, he might forget his anger.

Exactly at the moment the choir master raised his right hand and described a delicate circle with his left, all the voices stopped.

Alonesi clapped with joy. "Well done, gentlemen. Today you have given me hope that it will all turn out well. Perhaps I will even experience satisfaction in this mortal life."

Around me, boys shuffled their feet restlessly, some boys

grinned in relief. This time no roaring, no cane swishing around wildly. Excellent. Alonesi's shrill voice often rang harshly in my ears as I left the church. Sometimes, as I was nearing my home, I could still feel the echo of the sounds of the cane strokes racing through my whole body. Not that I had ever felt the actual cane myself, heaven be praised! The others would sometimes have to face it, but for some reason or other he would always spare me. He singled me out by occasionally ruffling my hair and smiling at me.

I didn't like either, not that ruffling nor that smile. The other boys teased me about that. "Maestro's pet!" they would shout after me. "Maestro's little choir boy!"

Not that I could do anything about it. After all, I hadn't ask for special treatment. All I ever wanted to do was sing.

This time, the maestro did not smile at me. His gaze slid across everybody, but didn't reach me. Was he still angry? I would have to slip past him as quickly as possible and disappear.

The maestro scratched his stand with the nail of his index finger. "At half past six precisely, we shall start preparing for the mass. I expect all of you to be here in plenty of time!" For a moment, his gaze bored into the eyes of Victorio. "That includes you, *signore* Capri!" He waved his hands to signal that we could leave. "Presto, presto!"

"Good afternoon, Maestro!"

"Angelo Montegne and Gaetano Bernardi, you will stay behind."

I nudged my neighbour in amazement. "Us?"

"Why?" whispered Gaetano.

I shrugged.

"Maestro?" The dark eyebrows above Gaetano's sunken eyes arched indignantly. "Why must I stay behind? I'm hungry! I want to go home. My family will be waiting for me."

I remained silent. My stomach began to contract. Had I angered the maestro? Would he complain to my father?

"Your fault," hissed Gaetano. "All because you attracted his attention. I'll never stand next to you again."

"We are arranged by age." I didn't look at him.

"I don't care," snarled Gaetano. "I'll never stand next to you again. Look what happens. And you stink worse than a pig that's been wallowing in the mud!"

"Perhaps it's nothing." I ignored his last remark; I was used to it.

"Has he ever asked us to stay behind before? Only now, after you were stupid enough not to pay attention "

"Arrivederci!" shouted Victorio merrily as he slipped past us. "Stuff your folder down the back of your trousers, then at least you'll be able to sit down. I know what it feels like to have a black-and-blue backside. Good luck!"

"What for?" returned Gaetano. "Do you think we need it?"

Victorio grinned. "Not maestro's little choir boy, but you do."

"Silence, you little blasphemers!" boomed the maestro's curt voice. "In this sacred place we sing and converse with each other in a normal tone. Not like a group of fishwives at the market."

"But maestro," said Gaetano tremulously, "the lesson is over. Have I done something wrong?"

Was he going to cry? I turned to face him. A bead of moisture gleamed between his eyelashes. He was crying! Gaetano Bernardi, the spoilt son of the mayor, was bawling because he had to stay behind!

"Arrivederci, Angelo!"

"Ciao, Gaetano!"

The other boys followed Victorio out of the church, all carrying their music folders out into the tempting rays that set the stained glass windows aglow.

22

"Maestro," begged Gaetano again. "Please, let me go "

"Silence!" snapped Alonesi at him again. "You are no longer a babe-in-arms, signore Bernardi. Wait for me here." Without giving us a second glance, he made his way through the nave of the church, into the vestibule.

"Damned note-counter!" Gaetano flounced out of the choir stalls. He climbed onto a pew under the window and pressed his nose up against the coloured glass.

I went and stood next to him and tried to catch something of the world outside the cold confines of the church. Without success. Because of the sunlight I could see little more than a vague reflection of my own head with the small black mole just to one side of my mouth.

Papa also had a mole like that. A little higher on his cheek, but just as dark and just as shiny. "You got that mole from your father," my mother would often say as she gently stroked my birthmark. "You got your nose and legs from me. Only your voice is all yours. Nobody else is blessed with something so wonderful! Promise me you will always keep singing." And then she would look at me until I placed my hand on my breast and swore for always and ever by all the saints.

"My stomach's rumbling," Gaetano whined.

"The maestro's right," I said. "You're just like a babe-in-arms."

He pushed his fist against my chest. "Do you want a punch?"

"Quiet!" I whispered. Footsteps. "The maestro!"

Quickly we shot to our places in the choir. We waited next to each other until the short, eager steps of the choir master had reached the nave and clattered nearer over the stone floor.

"So, gentlemen," said Maestro Alonesi when he stood before us. His right hand held two music folders; his left hand rested protectively on them. "You may be asking why you had to stay behind." He tilted his head to one side and looked at Gaetano. "Or not, signore Bernardi?"

Nothing was gleaming anymore between Gaetano's eyelashes. "Yes, maestro," he answered quickly.

The maestro smiled. "I have something special and very honourable for you both."

"For us, maestro?" I asked. What had we to thank for this?

"What, maestro?" Gaetano's voice was shrill with greed. He had apparently forgotten all about his hunger.

"Yes, for you. You should know." He searched for words. "You are quite clearly the most talented pupils I have had under my wing for many years. I cannot say which of you is better. Angelo's voice is clearer and has a greater range, Gaetano's is fuller and more regular. Both of you are a gift from Heaven."

"Thank you, maestro." I took a breath in relief. He wasn't going to complain about me. Papa would not have to be ashamed of me.

"Now, please pay attention," said the maestro. "Here in my hands…" His fingers tapped the leather binding. "…I have a piece that I composed myself. In the days ahead, I want you to choose a passage and learn it, and perform it for me on Wednesday. The better of the two shall sing a solo during the visit of Pope Clement to Fiesole this autumn."

"During the visit of the Pope?" My heart swelled until I felt I was going to explode. The Pope was coming to Fiesole! That meant a festival, a great festival! With jollity and dancing and good food!

"Really?" Gaetano clenched his fists and pressed them against his cheeks. "Do you mean it? Sing for the Pope? What an honour, maestro! My father will be elated! What am I saying my whole family will jump with pride!"

Papa! I thought. Would he finally laugh like he used to during

24

the festival? Would he once again clasp me in his strong arms? If the Pope came! If I were allowed to sing for His Holiness!

"There will be no choir rehearsal on Wednesday evening. Instead, you will sing for me and I shall decide which of you is better. He will be first soloist, the other his understudy." Alonesi handed us the piece of music. "Understand how great an honour this is, and practise hard. The solos are not all that difficult, so you should be able to handle them."

"I will practise, Maestro," promised Gaetano. "All day long! And all night if need be!"

"That doesn't sound very sensible to me." The maestro smiled. "You may fall asleep over your music on Wednesday. But you may skip the rehearsals on Monday and Tuesday evening if that proves necessary." He looked at me. "Not everybody has time during the day, isn't that so Master Montegne?"

"Yes, Maestro."

I took the folder with the piece of music and opened it. The notes on the first page did not, indeed, seem too complicated. I hummed it softly and caught a satisfied glance from the maestro.

"Remember that singing for the Holy Father will bring you closer to Heaven," he said softly.

I wanted that! To be closer to Heaven. Closer to my mother.

I closed the folder and held it tightly to my chest. "Thank you, maestro. Do we now have your permission to leave?" I wanted to go home to tell my father the great news.

"Certainly."

I bowed slightly, turned round and ran out through the nave.

Gaetano followed several paces behind. "A solo, a solo!" he shouted with happiness. "For Pope Clement! Give it up, Angelo. I'm going to win this!"

"Oh yes? How do you know that?"

"Everyone knows I can sing better than you. My voice is fuller and more regular," he said, parroting the maestro. "You will be the understudy. My fine voice will take care of that if not, my father certainly will." He danced out of the doorway onto the square in front of the church, straight into the arms of his governess, Julia. "Julia! I'm going to sing for the Pope when he comes! For the Pope! Do you hear?"

"Really, master Gaetano? When the Pope comes?"

I watched the pretty governess clasp her hands against her chest in joy and felt a stab inside.

"Then we must have a new jacket made for you," said Julia. "And I shall ask madam your mother whether it may not be time for a wig made of real human hair. *Il mio cielo*! I am so proud of you!" She looked adoringly at her pupil and placed a hand on her heart.

I pursed my lips. We'd see who was going to sing for the Pope.

2

With the folder in my hand, I jogged past the half-dried puddles in the streets of Fiesole. My joy at the words of the maestro was a lot less than it was a little while ago.

What if Gaetano were right? If his father made sure that he could sing the solo? Not because Gaetano was better but simply because he had the power?

That mustn't happen!

I really wasn't dissatisfied with my life, even though my father was neither rich nor powerful. The future before me didn't scare me either; I could earn a good living as a tanner.

Our little house was right next to the workshop, where I lived with my father, my sister Mariana, and Zia Ignatia. The familiar sounds of scraping, scudding and rolling hides could be heard there from morn to night; sounds from our own tannery, but also from the others in the neighbourhood. Fine sounds. And I loved the smell of fresh leather and the freshly grated oak bark.

That people would turn up their noses when they walked through our street, or that some boys in the choir thought it necessary to tease me by holding their noses when I was around, generally did not bother me. I simply ignored it. Since I no longer attended school, I could work with my father like a good son, lugging around hides every day, and helping with the fleshing and scudding.

Until the early hours of evening, that is, when it was time to go to choir. Then I could drop all the tools, dip my hands in a pail of water, grab my music folder, and run to the great church.

Those hours at the choir school were the highlights of my day. My whole body would start to tingle when I bent over the complicated compositions. The world disappeared from my thoughts.

Except this morning. But today was a very special day.

Saturday was the only day in the week when we went to choir school in the morning. In the evening we had to sing the first mass and there was no time after that to practise in peace.

When I returned at the end of the morning, my father would often give me the rest of the day off. "Go and play with the boys from around here," he would say. He had been allowed to do that by Nonno, Mama told me. One afternoon in the week.

I never went to play. I would prefer to slip out of the town gates by myself and go into the hills. Some ways from the city was a Roman ruin. Only some parts of the old stands along with a piece of the wall had withstood the test of time. Those stands were dangerous because of the crumbling stones. As soon as you set foot on one, something rolled down to the ground. You really had to take care.

That risk was the very reason why I never told my father that I went there. He would have gone berserk. Mama had died when a stone fell from the city wall and hit her on the back of her head. She died three days after the accident. Since then, Papa was terrified of poorly maintained buildings. He hardly ever went outside because in Fiesole there were many buildings in a neglected state. If he did venture outside his workshop, he would constantly look upwards.

The old arena would have given him nightmares, but it held an enormous attraction for me, particularly because of the acoustics: there was a fantastic resonance and echo, especially when you stood in the middle. I would often scream and sing my heart out there. Sometimes from sorrow, sometimes because I was sick to death about something, and sometimes because I had had enough of the boys in the choir teasing me about the extra attention maestro Alonesi paid me. Sometimes from happiness, however, because young birds had hatched from their eggs or because I had seen an eagle soaring through the sky. And often for no reason at all. I really enjoyed hearing my voice echoing against the stands and returning to my ears as a second voice.

I could sing for ever in the old ruins. That's why I went there almost every Saturday afternoon.

I wished I was in the ruins now instead of here in this soaking wet city. I wanted to yell, scream, curse, and throw stones! That wretched Gaetano Bernardi.

I snatched up a piece of wood from the ground and flung in with all my strength against a wall.

I wanted to win and really get the better of that miserable Gaetano and his oh-so-distinguished father who always fixed everything!

I would make my father, Mariana, and Zia Ignatia glow with pride, just as Gaetano's governess, Julia, had done.

I had to be better than him. Not just a little bit better, but a whole lot better.

And I'd do it as well!

I would exercise my voice like I had never done before and only drink honeyed water. Tomorrow, after the mass, I would slip out to the ruins and listen hour after hour to my own voice as it echoed around the stands. And every time it did not sound pure or full enough, I would start again.

A burning glow started inside me. The battle was not yet over, even if Gaetano thought it was. It was only just beginning. And I knew who was going to win. The best. Me!

With new courage I jumped over the rubbish and the excrement that lay in the streets and began to hurry. Papa! I suddenly saw how he would clasp me to him with his oak stained hands. "Angelino," he would say with a voice trembling with happiness. "*Figliolo.*"

The worn step in front of our house on the Vicolo Porettana was just a little higher than a puddle. The houses were crowded so close together that sunlight could hardly penetrate the street. It would take longer here for the last of the water to dry up.

It didn't matter. I was used to it. Even when it hadn't rained, the stones were sometimes so slippery with moss that you had to be careful not to slip. Although Zia Ignatia and Mariana regularly scrubbed the doorstep, the green always seemed to return at double speed. That's why I usually jumped over the step, prepared for anything.

Just as I had taken off, my eye noticed the carriage farther down the street. The coachman was standing lazily with his back against the wall of the tannery. A customer? With a carriage?

I almost forgot to reach out my hand to push the door open as I jumped. I scraped along the door frame, and felt a brief flaming pain where it grazed my cheek. But I had no time to be distracted by something as trivial as a scratched face. Not when there were customers visiting our tannery in a carriage. They always came by foot or with carts to collect their wares. Distinguished folk who could afford a carriage went directly to the best and most expensive tanners in the fashionable part of town; certainly not to the small workshops on the Vicolo Porettana.

I reached the kitchen in three hops. Only my aunt was there, kneading a mountain of dough with her hands, sporting a white smudge of flour on her nose. I couldn't wait to tell her my big news of the day. "Zia…Zia, do you know who's coming to Fiesole?"

"*Shhh…*" She placed her finger to her lips. "Be quiet, *ragazzo mio.* Your father has a distinguished visitor in the tannery."

"Papa?" Filled with disbelief, I stared at my aunt. "Is that carriage out front for us?"

"His Lordship will have come by carriage, yes. Such high lords would not dirty their shoes for a visit to a tanner."

"Is it a customer?"

She shrugged her shoulders. "Signore Guagli, from the Saint Crispin guild."

"From the guild? What is he doing here?"

"Perhaps you would be better asking Mariana." Zia Ignatia clicked her tongue. "That cursed girl crept out of the kitchen like a cat when she heard there were visitors. It wouldn't surprise me if she were hanging around in the hall somewhere. What is to become of her?"

I had already slammed the door shut behind me.

The voices of Papa and his visitor sounded dimly from the tannery. For a brief moment, I asked myself why I had not heard them when I came into the house, but perhaps my mind was so full of my own great news that the two men's voices didn't register. Just round the corner, at the end of the hall, stood my sister Mariana. She was peering through a peephole she had made years before in the wood in the wall.

"Finally, you're here!" She could hardly bring herself to stop looking, but in the short moment that the light fell on her eyes, I saw the excited gleam in her gaze

"What's happening in there? Is that man placing a big order?"

"No idea what he wants, but it's certainly exciting."

"Exciting?" If I had been bigger and stronger, I would have pulled her away from that peephole. I wanted to stand there myself and see what was happening. "What is exciting?"

"I believe papa is going to cry."

Cry? About an order? That made no sense.

"Thievery!" I heard the heavy man's voice boom suddenly. "Your purest thievery!"

My ears must be deceiving me. Thievery?

Mariana drew in her breath sharply and her body shook. For a moment she looked at me as if to say: "You see? Didn't I tell you?"

Immediately, the maestro's assignment slipped into the background. Has this signore Guagli gone crazy? Papa never did anything that was not allowed, and he certainly never stole. If you'd asked me, I'd have said that he would rather cut off his own hand.

I pressed my ear against the wooden wall. "I have done my work as I have always done it," sounded Papa's voice. "I don't know what has gone wrong."

"You are responsible for the goods you supply, Montegne!" the visitor bellowed. "Don't try to talk your way out of it! You must bear the consequences of your failed work and pay the fine imposed! That is the only way in which we can guarantee the good name of our guild."

"Please forgive me," begged Papa. "Please, forgive me for whatever I have done wrong. I will make it up to you, but I cannot pay a fine."

"Nothing gives you the right to drag the good name of the tanners of Fiesole through the mud!"

"I have not done that, as Saint Crispin is my witness. I do not even know what you are accusing me of. Nobody has been here to claim recompense."

The visitor gave an exaggerated sigh. "No, of course not! They did that directly to the guild."

I slapped my hand to my mouth. Were there complaints? Even

though Papa always worked so carefully and I helped him so well?

"Please signore…perhaps it was one of the other tanners."

I hardly recognised my father in the pleading coming from the other side of the wall.

Neither, apparently, did Mariana. "Just throw him out of the house, Papa," she whispered. "If you don't have any idea what he's talking about."

"Who has complained?" I asked her.

She shrugged her shoulders. "What difference does that make? Do you remember hearing about the butcher who was supposed to have sold pork for beef? There wasn't a scrap of truth to the story, but the butchers' guild dropped him and he lost all his customers." She sighed. "That's how it is in this miserable city. If only we lived in Florence."

Why in Heaven's name would anybody want to live in Florence? I asked myself. According to the stories, the place was swarming with pickpockets, beggars, and swindlers.

"Have you heard any gossip in the market?" I asked.

Again Mariana shrugged her shoulders.

I had no idea who could have lodged such a complaint. As far as I knew, Papa never had problems with anyone. How could he? The suppliers of the hides and the shoemakers who came to collect the hides all treated him as their friend. I had seen that plenty of times for myself.

I bit my lower lip and tried to listen to what was going on inside. Papa's voice was shaking. The last time I had heard him like this was when Mama died. After that, his tone become flatter and flatter and the few words he spoke all sounded the same. Until now.

"Look round my workshop," begged Papa. "Judge for yourself!"

Guagli growled. "What good would that do? Do you think I

would take you for somebody who left proof hanging around? I'm not as stupid as that."

"Then I cannot prove my innocence." I imagined the slump of Papa's shoulders, his neck barely able to support his head.

"Accusations have been made by three different sources," said Guagli. "And I have seen a piece of cracking leather with my own eyes. Your guilt is as good as proven. But you can make restitution for it by paying the price I have just mentioned: fifty ducats. That will take care of compensation for the damage plus a fine."

Next to me, Mariana clasped her hand to her mouth. "Fifty ducats…that's a fortune!"

A bump sounded from the workshop.

I immediately pushed my sister to one side. "My turn!"

"Hey!"

"*Shhh!*" I peered through the hole and to my dismay I saw Papa fall to his knees. "I beg you…"

"We cannot afford mercy," interrupted Guagli. "The Saint Crispin guild has a name to protect, as simple as that. Quality must be guaranteed. If you do not pay, we will expel you from the tanners' guild and you will have to fend for yourself."

My breath stuck in my throat. Holy Mother Mary! Out of the guild? Then we would lose our livelihood and the workshop! Where would we live?

"Does he want to ruin Papa?" hissed Mariana. "The bastard! The devilish, miserable shitface!"

I hardly had time to be shocked at the swear words she used. Heavy steps left the workshop. "I shall return in two weeks to collect the debt." The door to the Vicolo Porettana slammed shut.

A groan sounded in the workshop. I crept out of our hiding place and pushed open the door. My father was still sitting on the ground, his face hidden behind his hands.

"Papa?"

He immediately turned his head away, his hand wiping his eyes.

I entered hesitantly. Should I say something? What? Could I let him know I had heard signore Guagli?

"I'm here too, Papa," said Mariana softly. "Is everything all right?"

Quickly he stood up. "I dropped a scraper but I can't see it anywhere. Can you?" A muscle twitched next to his mouth and his face was as pale as a corpse.

"We heard you had a visitor," I said. "Who was that man?"

My father shook his head.

"We heard him through the whole house," said Mariana. "Why was he so angry, Papa? Was something wrong with your work?"

"It's nothing," said my father evasively. "Don't worry." But that muscle pulled at his mouth.

"Why did he act like that then?" insisted Mariana.

"It's nothing, as I've told you." He quickly changed the subject. "Are you back from choir school already, Angelo?"

I saw Mariana's face turn red with anger at our father's obvious diversionary tactics. She knew, just as I did, that he never normally asked where we'd been. Her fists clenched and an irritated frown appeared above her eyebrows. But an explosion wouldn't help anybody right now, and my father would simply clam up altogether. So I forced a smile on my face and swallowed. "Yes, maestro Alonesi was pleased with us. Nobody got the cane this time." Not that Papa knew anything about the other times when somebody did get it. It didn't matter; he hardly heard me.

"Good," he said and pushed me to one side. "I'm hungry." He walked into the hallway without waiting for us.

Mariana looked as if she wanted to strangle somebody.

"It's nothing to do with us," I said, trying to calm her down. "Perhaps it's not as bad as it seemed."

"Do you really believe that?" She pressed her lips together in determination. "But I won't let Papa go bankrupt. What would we live on in the name of our Holy Mother? From the scraps of meat we scud from the hides? Oh no…" Cynically, she pursed her lips. "We won't even have that anymore."

I didn't have the slightest doubt that she would find out in no time exactly what situation was and who had complained. Whatever my sister put her mind to, she'd do it. Mama was exactly the same.

I made the sign of a cross behind Mariana's back and sent a short prayer up to Heaven. Hopefully it wasn't as bad as it seemed. But if that wasn't the case, we could use some help from above.

3

"So." Papa wiped his arm across his mouth, pushed his chair back, and left the kitchen. The door to the narrow hall closed behind him with a bang.

"What was the matter with his dinner?" Mariana was still in a dark mood. "He didn't even clear his plate!"

I gave her a kick under the table. "It was delicious, Zia."

"Good," my aunt said. "Then get out of my kitchen and let me clear up." She got up and began bang around the pots and pans. My attempt to distract her from the house's general feeling of doom had clearly failed.

"Mariana," said Zia, "you stay here. I need your help. The step needs scrubbing."

My sister and I looked at each other.

"Scrub the step?" said Mariana. "Really?"

"Yes. Really." As she bustled around, Zia Ignatia dropped a spoon. "*Madre di Dio!*" she cursed.

The tension in the kitchen could be cut with a knife. I got up. "I'm going to the church," I lied. "The maestro said I could practise there for this evening's mass."

"Come off it." Mariana threw me an accusing look. "Run away, go on."

"Doesn't your father need your help?" My aunt did not look at me as she asked.

"It's Saturday. Had you forgotten? We have to sing this evening."

"No, I hadn't forgotten, ragazzo mio," said aunt Ignatia. "But your father may have. Go and see him."

I nodded. I'd go to him if she wanted me to, but I hoped Papa would just let me leave. I couldn't bear the oppressive mood. Anyway, I really had to practise for the audition on Wednesday.

Quickly I took the music folder from the cupboard and stuck my head round the corner of the workshop. "Papa? I'm going to practise in the church. Will you be coming to mass this evening? You haven't come to listen for quite some time!"

"Bye," he said. I don't think he understood what I said.

It was quiet outside. Many people took a rest after lunch. Not me I wasn't tired. In fact, I had too much energy.

I slipped past the gossiping gate guards and left the city. The ruins of the amphitheatre were quite a walk from the city wall. I had come upon them by accident about two years ago, when our father had sent Mariana and me to look for new oak bark. Generally our regular merchant supplied us, but this time the man had kept us waiting, and Papa urgently needed some. The first oak trees grew close to the city and Papa knew we wouldn't need to go far from the safe settlement. But Mariana and I somehow wandered farther and farther. We climbed into the hills, dragging our cart behind us as we searched in the bushes and suddenly there it was like a large secret, carefully kept by nature the old theatre. Long branches of honeysuckle spread their sweet fragrance, hares bolted off at each footstep. All around us was the sound of birds singing and insects buzzing. Far in the distance echoed the hollow croaking of frogs.

The place looked like the paradise that our padre had once described. From the moment I saw it, I fell under its spell.

By now I knew that the shortest way to the theatre was to take the old road to the north. After a few hundred yards, I had to leave the road and find my way through thorny bushes, along overgrown wood and across grass-covered hills. It was awkward but that didn't bother me.

Today I again took the centuries-old road, sunk in thought, with the maestro's music under my tunic, close to my chest. Would we really be evicted? Where would we go? Drift around? The image of two beggars who lived in the city slums appeared before me. Dressed in rags, with smudges on their cheeks and dirty, black hands, they would hang around the church hoping for the charity of the church-goers. "*Alms for a poor wretch! Alms for a wretch!*"

It was said that some beggars actually mutilated themselves in order to receive more money. Would we sink that low? Would I be able to sleep night after night under the clear skies, even when it got colder or when it rained as it had the last few days? And would a shy and submissive Mariana be able to hold out her hand?

My musings took me so far away that I only heard the clattering of the wheels and the pounding of the horses' hooves when the carriage was almost on top of me.

"Out of the way!" yelled a voice over all the noise. "Idiot!" A whip cracked in the air.

Reflexively, I let myself fall to one side, right into the thorns of a bramble bush. "Ouch!"

The carriage did not slow down, although the coachman and his assistant did glance back. Laughter rolled across the quiet road.

"Boil faces!" Tears of pain filled my eyes. "Rat droppings. Filthy swine!"

I carefully freed myself from the brambles, hoping to avoid more scratches than necessary. There were tears in my trousers, in my tunic and in my stockings. *Cavolo*! Zia would have something to say about this! And she wasn't in a good mood at the moment.

I took a deep breath. Fortunately it was only tears and scratches. The wheels could just as easily have clattered over me, leaving me a pile of broken arms and legs. I glared after the expensive carriage in indignation. A golden crest glittered on the rear: six bulbs and three lilies.

The De Medicis. Of course, who else? Had those illustrious folk ever slowed down when they drove full tilt through Fiesole?

Apparently rules applied differently to the nobility than to ordinary folk. It didn't matter if one of us were crushed   one peasant more or less didn't make much difference. Probably we were nothing more to them than a bunch of annoying lice that you squeezed to death between your thumb and forefinger.

My thoughts once again returned to this morning. Perhaps the citizens would soon regard us as nothing more than chickens. Praise be to the Holy Mother that Mama did not live to see this.

I brushed the last twigs and leaves from my doublet and continued my journey.

After carefully surveying the surroundings to see how many new nests and holes had appeared, I sat down on a block of stone in the middle of the arena. I pulled the folder from under my tunic and studied the music. Almost automatically, my voice began picking out individual notes and weaving them into pieces of melody. Although it naturally sounded rather wooden the first time, I felt almost at once the strength flowing from the melody. There were several decorative ornaments, and the notes seemed to be at the perfect pitch for my voice. When I saw the high notes, I felt a tickle of happiness in my stomach. Hadn't Alonesi said that my voice could reach higher than Gaetano's? I would sing the notes as high as the music allowed, purer than ever before. They would echo through the church and I would hold onto them longer, until the maestro glowed with pleasure.

I hummed the melody again. I had never known that Alonesi had talents beyond directing the choir. After the high mass, when the boys' choir sang with the men's choir, he was often praised because the various voices were in such beautiful harmony. But that he could compose music himself?

Quickly, I felt out the direction in which the maestro was leading me. When I went through the music a second time, I stood up to allow my lungs to take in all the air I needed to make my voice resonate among the old stones.

I was just about to take a breath halfway through the first verse when birdsong suddenly sounded from the ash woods close to the ruins. I stopped singing in amazement. How beautiful! Melodious. Almost as if…

Was the bird repeating my singing? Was that possible? I sang the last piece of the melody again and concentrated on my surroundings.

It certainly sounded like it! A little higher in pitch, but it was the melody.

I tiptoed to the place where the sound was coming from. Still singing, I carefully bent aside some twigs. I squinted until I finally saw it: a jet black bird hiding in the shadows and the leaves. Only its bright orange beak was clearly visible. A blackbird? The creature stretched its neck and whistled its heart out. Very slowly I pushed aside some leaves to get closer to it.

But not slowly enough. The blackbird was startled and flew away. First to the top of one of the tall alders, then completely out of sight.

Idiot! Perhaps the blackbird had been a messenger from above, sent by Mama to give me courage. Why hadn't I been more careful?

But there was no sense in moping about it. I was here to practise, and that is exactly what I did. In four days, Gaetano and I would have to sing. He was going to be in for a shock!

4

As soon as I entered the church that Wednesday evening, Gaetano ran to meet me. "Give it up, Angelo," he sang in a provoking tone. "I'll be first singer, and you'll be the substitute."

There may have been four days in between last Saturday and Wednesday, but Gaetano's arrogance hadn't diminished a whit in that time. He looked impressive in his velvet knickerbockers, white shirt and with a scarf round his neck; a lot better than I did, with my grey overalls and shabby doublet. I was exhausted and it must have shown. Papa had had me scudding hides from early morning, until I got cramp in my hands. I felt utterly defeated even before I could begin. Gaetano, on the other hand, was the picture of confidence: his cheeks were red with excitement and his eyes twinkled as if the victory was already his.

"Let me pass." Furiously, I pushed him aside.

"I have practised so hard that I don't even need my music," he shouted in delight. "My mother says I have a celestial voice. So high and pure."

But not as high as mine, I thought. Even if I had to spend the next few days hoarse as a crow, I would make sure that today those high notes of the maestro came out with the purest clarity. As pure as a blackbird.

"They're all here. Papa, Mama, Julia," said Gaetano. "Nobody dares to go against Papa. If he tells the maestro I must win, then that happens."

"If you really were so certain of your victory, you wouldn't keep going on about it," I snapped. "Now, get out of the way. I want to warm up."

"Ha! I don't need to."

No, of course not. I didn't want to waste words on that show off. Nor any thoughts especially no thoughts.

Nobody was with me. Papa still didn't know about the audition. He hardly knew we existed. He was in the tannery working from early morning to late at night. And even though I worked alongside him, nothing more than "do this" or "do that" came out of his mouth. Mariana said it was as if he were tanning the life out of himself.

I hadn't given it a moment's thought to ask her to come with me. Since that visit from Guagli, her face looked like thunder. Every word she said was a snarl. And my aunt scrubbed and cooked as if her life depended on it. Actually she did exactly the same as Papa: she worked like crazy in order to cover her agitation.

I slipped into the dark alcove where the altar boys changed. The maestro wouldn't mind me preparing for the audition here. I placed one hand on my chest to feel my breathing, planted my feet firmly on the ground, and practised one scale after another. In between, I wove some pieces of the maestro's music and a few choral items, all intended to warm up my voice.

Just as I was about to take a deep breath, a clear voice spoke: "Not bad!"

"Huh?" I turned round with a start. "What…?"

Next to the piles of altar boy shirts stood a skinny child with fiery eyes in a narrow head with elaborately fashioned hair.

"What are you doing here?"

"I could ask you the same thing," she shot back. "As personal guest of the bishop, I was given permission to hang my cloak here and freshen up. I can't remember you being invited." She took a step forward, her gaze brazenly taking me in. "You are one of the boys who are going to sing for us, aren't you?"

"For you? Have you gone mad?"

She grinned. "A moment ago, you sounded just like a singer," she teased. "And it wasn't half bad. I should know." She wiggled her hips. "I know about music."

"Oh, sure." I turned my back on her.

"Don't you believe me?" she asked. "I can sing pretty well myself."

"You're a girl!" I snapped. "Girls don't sing." I forgot for the moment that my mother would sing while doing the washing and wringing, and that it always sounded wonderful.

Without hesitation, the girl began singing an *Ave Maria*. It sounded magnificent but I would rather have sunk through the ground than admit it.

"I have to go." Quickly I walked over to the door. I heard the measured steps of the maestro approaching along the corridor.

"*Buongiorno*, Gaetano," he said. "Did your practice go well?"

"Of course, maestro," answered the voice of Gaetano. "My father says you have written an excellent piece. I sang it perfectly right from the start."

"That's good, my boy."

I could almost imagine how he was smiling and stroking Gaetano's hair. I felt sick.

"Who's that?"

I jumped out of my skin. The girl was suddenly there behind me, her head just a hair's breadth from mine.

For a moment I forgot everything around me. She smelt like a bramble when the first fruits are just beginning to ripen.

"Your opponent?" And when I didn't respond: "Haven't you learned that you should always answer if somebody asks you something?"

44

"Do you always creep around like...like a cat?"

"Only when I'm hunting." She bent her hands into claws and growled. Was she crazy?

"Well?" she asked again. "Is that your opponent on the other side of the door?"

I gave in and nodded.

"Is he as good as you?"

"If you carry on nagging, I won't hear what they're saying!" I whispered.

I felt her breath against my ear when she laughed. "I'll keep quiet," she whispered.

"Papa has come as well," said Gaetano behind the door. "He is in the vestibule and would like to say hello."

"Oh. Yes...well..." said the maestro defensively. "Perhaps after your performance? Is Angelo here?"

"Yes...but maestro?" Gaetano's voice sounded disappointed, and I felt a small rush of hope. Perhaps I had been wrong in thinking that everybody could be persuaded by the mayor.

Quickly I threw open the door. "*Buonasera*, maestro. I'm here."

"Ah, good." The maestro smiled. "The two most important persons are present. We will have to wait a moment, boys." His expression had something secretive about it. "There are going to be some unexpected but important listeners." Suddenly his expression changed. He stared past me, his eyes wide.

"Buongiorno, maestro," said the skinny child, as if nothing was the matter.

"Wh-who are you?" maestro Alonesi stuttered. "What in the name of the Holy Mother are you doing in that room with Angelo?"

I was suddenly bathed in sweat. "She just appeared out of nowhere in there, maestro," I said quickly. "I don't know her."

"I am Rosa Scarlatti." The girl gracefully lifted her skirt and dropped a curtsy. Suddenly she looked a lot like Julia, Gaetano's governess.

"The composer Scarlatti? You are his daughter?"

"At your service, maestro." Again she curtsied. Dark dots had appeared in her fiery eyes. "I was coincidentally in the room when Angelo came in to practise. And since he was only interested in his sheet of music, he did not see me."

"Oh." Some colour returned to Alonesi's face. "So then…" He pointed with his finger. "In that room…"

"You do not need concern yourself. Nothing happened." She clasped her hand to her mouth and hurriedly turned away. I would swear she was trying not to laugh and felt myself getting warmer.

"Oh well, I naturally didn't think that," muttered the maestro. "The daughter of the great Scarlatti…"

I couldn't care less who that damned Scarlatti was. I was embarrassed that I had been caught in a room together with a girl who was not my sister. And a rude scallywag of a girl, at that!

The one good thing about the situation was that Gaetano apparently didn't know what to think about it either. His eyes went from me to Rosa Scarlatti to the maestro. But as soon as the maestro averted his gaze from the girl, Gaetano began to rattle on again, acting like an excited horse. "What did you just say, maestro? There are other listeners? Who? Do I know them? It will make my family prouder than ever!" He couldn't wait to celebrate his triumph in front of as large an audience as possible.

The maestro pulled thoughtfully on his jacket. "Have you brought others beside your father?" he asked distractedly.

"Do you think Mama could have stood not being at my audition?"

Alonesi pursed his lips almost imperceptibly. His pince-nez

slipped down his nose. He pushed it back and sighed. "The other guests, including this young lady, are of a completely different sort." He abruptly turned and was about to leave.

"I have also been able to practise the piece, maestro," I said calmly.

Alonesi half turned and smiled at me again. "That's good, my boy." He left and gestured to Rosa to follow him. "You boys stay here," he said. "You may practise together in that antechamber until the other guests arrive. I will send for you."

"But maestro," started Gaetano. "I don't need to…"

The maestro reacted precisely as I had expected. He turned round for a second time, as if bitten by a snake. "Gaetano Bernardi. Learn one thing today: even as an accomplished musician, you can never practise too much. Should you become first singer, then I shall expect you to spend at least one hour a day practicing in a separate room. Preferably more. Perhaps you should consider whether that is what you want!"

Gaetano fell into a dazed silence. I just caught the sarcastic wink from Rosa Scarlatti before she wandered into the nave, a few steps ahead of the maestro.

The bells above our heads had already sounded half-past five when the maestro came to get us. "We're ready," he said.

Immediately I felt a tickle in my throat. "*Ahhum*," I rasped hastily. "*Aggghem.*"

Grinning, Gaetano looked to one side. "Frog in your throat, Angelo? A little nervous?"

I ignored him. He shouldn't think I was going to make things easy for him.

"You've both warmed up?"

"Yes, maestro," we said in unison.

"Good. Gaetano, go and fetch your parents. Angelo, did you bring anyone?"

I shook my head.

"Then come with me."

A stand had been placed in the choir of the church, directly opposite the front choir pew. In the pew sat four men, three in cassocks of the clergy, one in extravagantly coloured clothes and with a high black wig on his head. I immediately recognised our bishop and my heart skipped a beat.

Rosa took a seat next to the man in the colourful clothes. Her eyes gleamed with hidden laughter, and I quickly turned away from her.

I nodded awkwardly as I passed the guests. One of the clergy, a priest with a round, cheerful face and an equally round body smiled at me. The other's expression was blank.

"So, young man," said our bishop. "We have come to listen to you." His gaze lingered on my shabby doublet. If only I had put on a clean choir shirt.

Apologetically, I smiled at the bishop.

"You must be Angelo Montegne? I know your face, but your name..."

"Yes, I am Angelo, your Eminence."

"The son of the tanner." The bishop clasped his hands on his chest. "The maestro speaks very well of you. I am curious about your singing."

My cheeks started to burn. "I'll do my best, your Eminence."

I never thought I would be pleased to see Gaetano. He entered the church noisily with his family. All attention was drawn to them and I was able to take a few steps back and make myself invisible.

Father Bernardi stamped on his fat legs directly toward the guests and shook their hands as if he were the host. It worked. The priests, who had been silent until now, answered at length his questions about the church, the weather, and the highly anticipated papal visit.

Again I thought I might just as well give up. All attention was now fixed on the show-off and his family. Gaetano himself stood beaming with pride between his parents. Governess Julia stood behind him, smiling. Two beautiful half-moon shaped dimples seemed carved into her cheeks and tendrils of raven black hair curled down beside her face. I stared from her to Rosa. The governess was a dream, the perfect young lady of noble descent. The composer's daughter with her fiery eyes, on the other hand, seemed more like a pugnacious city girl.

Quickly I turned away from them and tried to blend into the stones of the church wall.

The maestro noticed. "Come and stand here, Angelo. You too, Gaetano. We are going to begin." He gestured to a spot at the side of the choir, took his place behind the stand, and faced the assembled company.

"Your Eminence, padres, signore Scarlatti of Naples and signorina, family members: I bid you welcome. This evening, we shall be listening to the singing qualities of two of my best pupils. I am convinced that each of them will perform the piece I have written superbly, and make an excellent impression during the visit of Pope Clement. But your Eminence, signore Scarlatti, and signores of the Florence conservatory, you are not here just as listeners. You are here as experts."

I caught my breath. Were these two strange clergymen from the conservatory of Florence? What were they doing here? Had the maestro invited them? Why? Didn't he dare to make the decision himself?

"Please listen carefully. It is, after all, about the honour of Fiesole. After the performance, I shall wait in full expectation on your expert judgement. I would like to ask Gaetano Bernardi to sing the section he has chosen."

Gaetano stepped forward with a solemn face. He took his place in front of the maestro with his music folder in his hands. I saw how his eyes glazed over and concentrated on the task at hand. He nodded, and the maestro ticked one bar. Then he began. His eyes closed, his back straight, he sang as if inspired. Even I was entranced. It was almost completely in tune, although the odd high tone shook.

Was there any need for me to sing? I looked round furtively. The faces of the listeners in the front pew showed no reaction, but Gaetano's parents and his governess beamed with pride. As the last notes sounded, father Bernardi jumped up and applauded. "Bravo!" he shouted. "Bravissimo, Gaetano!"

The other family members and Rosa Scarlatti also clapped, although Rosa only used the tips of her fingers.

"Settle down," pleaded the maestro. "Please, let us not forget where we are." But he beamed with pride in a way I had seldom seen before. "Well done, Gaetano," he said. "The low and middle tones were almost sublime. But we have another candidate. Angelo Montegne, step forward please."

I felt their eyes on me but stared straight ahead at Gaetano. He stepped aside for me with a triumphant look in his eyes. I placed my folder on the desk and opened it. Carefully I flattened the sheet of music with the section I had chosen.

"Are you ready, Angelo?" asked the maestro.

Before I knew it, my glance went to the composer's skinny daughter. She winked at me again. I swallowed and quickly looked away. *Please, no frog in my throat*, I thought. *No frog…*

I cleared my throat and took a deep breath. "Yes."

"Very good." The maestro tapped the desk with his baton.

I began. *Don't look at her* said a little voice in my head. *Pretend you're in the amphitheatre and only the stones and the birds are listening to you.*

As controlled as possible, I performed an adagio from the maestro's composition. Goose-pimples appeared on my arms, my head grew hot, but my hands kept a firm grasp on the music folder without shaking. I sang as if my life depended on it and halfway through, I actually began to believe I was somewhere outside Fiesole. Among the overgrown stands of alders and oaks, with hares racing away.

Only when I had finished with a long high note did I find myself back in the church. A deathly silence surrounded me. The priests looked at me with wide eyes. Rosa Scarlatti had a broad grin and the beautiful governess pressed the palms of her hands together. The mouths of Gaetano's parents gaped open and the face of my opponent looked black. For a moment I was knocked off balance. Had I done so badly? Was it out of tune? Was my pronunciation unclear? I held my breath and had to force myself not to run out through the aisle.

Then the maestro broke the silence. "Bravo! *Fantastico*, Angelo!"

Rosa jumped up and started to applaud loudly.

Relieved I let out my breath. In any case, not everyone thought I was bad. But the maestro's applause died down quickly and Rosa's father pulled her back into her seat by her arm. Again there was a silence that could be cut with a knife. Maestro Alonesi and I stood shuffling uneasily next to each other.

Then Gaetano's father stood up. "Well done, boys, don't you agree people? It will be quite a chore to decide who was better. What say you, maestro?" He didn't wait for an answer. "I assume you will need time to deliberate. We will await your decision outside." He paused for a moment for emphasis. "And afterwards

I hope that the maestro has a moment to discuss his license for a new choir."

He left, followed by his wife and Julia. I could follow the clicking of their heels until they reached the doorway.

"Yes," muttered the maestro, a little brow-beaten. "Good, then."

The priests from the conservatory of Florence bent toward each other and spoke softly.

"Not bad, blockhead," whispered Gaetano to me.

"You weren't so bad yourself."

"A pity, though, that you weren't quite as good as me." With his head held high, he walked off after his parents.

The maestro patted my shoulder and said: "Run along with them, lad. I am going to talk with the gentlemen. It won't take long."

"Very well, maestro." As I left, I noticed the bishop giving me a friendly but searching look.

On the church square, Mayor Bernardi paced back and forth, his hands clasped behind his back. Signora Bernardi and Julia stood talking to Gaetano. As soon as Gaetano's father saw me come out the door, he beckoned to me. "Young man! Come here for a moment."

Signora Bernardi and Julia turned toward me at the same time. The governess's gaze swept over me, taking in my stained clothes. Just for a moment, but not so short that I didn't see it, she turned up her nose.

Silently, I approached Gaetano's father. "Signore?"

"Congratulations on your fine voice, lad. That throat of yours produces a wonderful sound."

I bowed slightly. "Thank you, signore."

"But Papa…"

A gesture from Bernardi was enough to silence his son.

"Do they support your singing career at home?" Signore Bernardi looked around. "Nobody came with you, I see."

I lowered my eyes. "Papa had to work."

"Oh yes, of course. What does your father do?" He sounded genuinely interested.

I hesitated slightly. Did he know Papa? Did he have contacts with the guild? "My father is…a tanner," I whispered.

"Tanner?" A pensive look slid over the mayor's face. I saw him studying my appearance. "What an honour for you," he said as his right hand inconspicuously stroked the expensive fabric of his fashionable jacket, "to be allowed to compete with my son."

Puffed up toad! Uneasily, I scraped at the sand with my foot. Just at that moment, the church door swung open.

"Papa, they're coming," hissed Gaetano.

Only one person appeared: the maestro.

"Angelo and Gaetano," he said. "Come here, please."

We looked up at him from two paces away. Could I read the result in his eyes?

"Listen, boys," said maestro Alonesi. "You have both given the very best of yourselves. And you were so good that the gentlemen and I need somewhat longer before we can make our choice. I shall inform you tomorrow morning after choir rehearsal which of you will be the first singer."

"Maestro, please," said Gaetano's father. "My wife and I are here now."

"I am sorry, mayor." Alonesi would not be swayed. "The honourable guests will return tomorrow, and unfortunately I must ask you to do the same."

Signore Bernardi raised his hands in a dramatic gesture of compliance. "Then that is how it shall be. And my discussion with you about your licence?"

The maestro smiled apologetically. "I'm sorry but that too must be postponed. We shall now continue our deliberations. You will understand that I cannot keep the gentlemen waiting."

It was difficult to suppress a grin. The mayor did not always get his own way, and the postponement meant that I had not yet lost.

"Angelo, Gaetano, I will see you tomorrow," said the maestro. "You both did very well," he repeated again. "Bravissimo!"

5

Later that evening, Zia Ignatia, Mariana, and I sat together in the kitchen. Mariana was trying to embroider by the light of some candles. My aunt gave instructions and sat nearby with mending in her hands. I was trying to concentrate on the piece of music that our choir would be performing in a few weeks, when suddenly the dull thud of the door knocker sounded.

The three of us jumped up. For a moment we stared at each other. Did this mean yet more bad news?

Zia Ignatia was the first to recover. "What on earth is this? So late in the evening?" She stood up and shuffled out of the kitchen to the front door.

"Yes?" I heard her say. "Ah, Padre."

"A priest," hissed Mariana.

"A priest?" I raised my eyebrows. "What does he want here?"

We stood up at the same time. We tiptoed to the kitchen door and peeped round the corner.

"Good evening," I heard a deep voice say. "I am at the Montegne residence, am I not?"

"Certainly," said Zia Ignatia. "Are you looking for the tanner? I shall summon him for you. Would you care to wait a moment?"

Her footsteps approached. Quickly we hid ourselves as she passed the kitchen. "Carlo, visitors!" she called at the door of the work place.

A tool landed with a bang on the table. The door to the tannery squeaked on its hinges. Papa's slow steps preceded those of Zia Ignatia down the hall. Carefully we opened the kitchen door a little wider.

"Good evening, Padre," said Papa. "Ignatia, you may leave."

My aunt returned to the kitchen. "Were you eavesdropping again like a pair of little rascals?" she grumbled softly. Of course she knew what we'd been doing. "Go on, back to work."

She remained remarkably close to the door. Mariana winked at me and inconspicuously moved her own chair a little closer to the half-open door. I just bent forward a little. Fortunately I have good ears. Was the padre here to announce a death to us? Who then? We no longer had any relations in the city, not since Nonno and Nonna had died a few years before our mother. Vaguely, I heard Papa say something.

"…help, Padre?" asked Papa.

"My son," sounded the deep voice of the priest. Not our own Padre; he spoke so slowly that you wanted to drag the words from his mouth. "I wish to talk to you about your son, Angelo."

Immediately I felt Mariana's finger dig into my chest. "He's after you, little brother," she hissed.

What was there to discuss about me? Had I done something wrong? Had I forgotten to confess? I racked my brains. As far as I knew, I went to confession last Friday after choir, just like usual.

"Perhaps they want you to enter the monastery," whispered Mariana. "So you can become a priest."

"Why would I want to do that?"

"The honour, little brother, the honour." Although I did not look at her, I knew she was grinning. Since the tailor's son who lived just down the street had entered the monastery, he had changed from a party-goer who danced at the front of every carnival procession into a sour-faced young man with an eternal frown on his forehead.

Never in my life would I want to follow him. And Mariana knew that all too well. I was going to be a tanner, just like papa.

"My son?" Papa's voice sounded surprised. "Should I be anxious?"

"No, not at all," I heard the voice say. Until my aunt closed the door.

"So," she said. "At least we now know that no-one has died. That's the most important thing. We may hear the rest later from your father."

"Zia Ignatia…" I begged. "It's about me!"

"We don't eavesdrop on a priest," she said hypocritically. "Angelo, get your music, and Mariana, you've got a lot to do with your embroidery."

"But Zia, aren't you curious?" persisted Mariana.

"Doesn't matter," she answered. "You heard me." She poured two mugs of thin beer and placed them in front of us. "If there's nobody else to bring you up properly, I'll do it myself."

"Ridiculous." Mariana threw her piece of cloth onto the table and folded her arms indignantly. Both of us clenched our teeth for several minutes. Occasionally I threw a glance at my aunt which hopefully expressed my rage. Why didn't she just let us hear what we could hear? Nothing ever happened in this house, and now this.

"Are you sure you haven't been up to anything?" said Mariana after a while. She picked up her piece of cloth again and pushed the needle through it with knitted eyebrows.

"Yes, I agree." Zia Ignatia lowered her needlework and grabbed me by the ear. "What else could it be? You've done something wrong!"

"Ow," I yelped. "Ow…No!"

"Must have," said Mariana.

"Honest!" I pulled myself free. "I've no idea what the padre wants to talk about. He isn't even from our own parish. Didn't you hear that?"

"Now that you mention it." Zia Ignatia, who just like most of the women in Fiesole visited the church almost every day to light a candle, looked thoughtful. "I didn't recognise him either. Okay then." She sought comfort again in her repair work. "As I said before, we'll hear about it later."

But Mariana didn't give up so easily. "Did you recognize his voice then?"

"Perhaps." I had heard it before. But where? Or was I imagining it?

She looked at the folder in my hands. "Does he have something to do with the choir?"

I narrowed my eyes. Was that it?

"Or did you see him in the work place? In the street? In the church?"

"If I knew, I'd tell you!" I snapped.

But Mariana kept her questions coming. "Did you get in his way? Were you rude to him? Did you take something that didn't belong to you?"

Now tears sprang up in my eyes. "Just stop it! The visit has nothing to do with me! At least." I slapped my hand against my head. "Not that I know of."

Yet I couldn't prevent my stomach feeling as if there were hundreds of ants crawling around in it. Why had the visitor mentioned my name?

What did he want with me?

The waiting seemed to last for hours. I had to force myself not to disobey Zia Ignatia and press my ear against the door. Mariana had again laid her embroidery to one side and was pacing back and forth. All the while, she cast nervous glances at the door, behind which a soft mumbling could be heard. Zia Ignatia's watchful glare kept us in check. *Do not attempt to eavesdrop on a man of God,* her eyes flashed at us.

Finally, we heard something. The priest's voice got louder and there was a knock on the kitchen door

"Angelo?" asked the priest. "Are you there?"

"Yes, Padre." Before I could do anything, Mariana threw open the door. I recognized him at once: the fat father with the round face from the Florence conservatory.

"Did you want to talk to him?" asked my sister.

He gave her a friendly look. "Thank you, my daughter. Are you his sister?"

"Yes, Padre. His elder sister."

"I can see that." His eyes sought mine. "Angelo, I would like to say once more that you sang beautifully this evening. You are blessed with a heavenly voice; we all agreed on that."

"Thank you, Padre." I felt Ignatia and Mariana give me inquisitive looks.

"I hope to see you again very soon," continued the priest, undisturbed by the uneasy silence that suddenly fell. "As far as I'm concerned, you are the one who could best perform the solo."

"Angelo?"

I looked up. My papa was standing in the doorway, looking at me.

"Good evening, Padre," said Papa. "My sister will show you out. Angelo, come with me into the workshop." It sounded like an order and I winced.

"Yes, papa," I said timidly.

"Ooh," whispered Mariana.

The priest gave me a brotherly wave and then allowed my aunt to show him out.

With lead in my shoes, I went into the tannery. Papa's hands were leaning on the work table. His eyes closed and his shoulders taut as if he had been nailed to a plank. "Papa?" I asked softly.

"What did the padre want?"

Slowly he turned toward me. "Why didn't you tell me you were auditioning?" Disappointment sounded in his voice. "Why did I have to hear it from somebody else?"

"Audition?" I hadn't noticed Mariana had come in behind us.

"Don't interfere," said Papa.

I lowered my eyes. Could I say I had kept silent because he had so many other things on his mind? Because he always hid himself away in his workshop and didn't speak to me?

"Well? Why?"

"I'm sorry, Papa."

He placed his hand to his forehead and closed his eyes for a moment. "Why?" he repeated.

I took a deep breath and looked him straight in the eye. "Because Mr Guagli was here when I wanted to tell you. That audition no longer seemed all that important."

Papa allowed a silence to fall. "Next time I will decide whether I think something is important or not," he finally said.

"Yes, Papa."

He took a piece of hide and examined it. "Well, tell me more about your audition," he said without looking at me. "Did you put up a good fight against the mayor's son?"

I smiled. "I think so." I almost confessed that I had practised at the amphitheatre and that a bird had imitated my song. But my father's attention seemed far away. "They clapped loudly," I finally added.

"Good." He picked up a tool.

"What did the priest want?" asked Mariana.

"My permission to school your brother at the conservatory of Florence," said Papa.

"Schooling? At the conservatory? Me?" I almost collapsed.

"That won't happen, of course," said my father, immediately dispelling my dreams.

No, of course not. Who would help him in the tannery? Who would look after him and the women later on? The conservatory was no place for a tanner's son. Everybody understood that.

"But why not?" asked Mariana. "I don't know anybody who attends a conservatory. What exactly do you learn there?"

I shrugged. I didn't really know. "Singing, of course. And perhaps conducting like the maestro."

"You don't need to know about it because you won't be having anything to do with it. It won't happen," repeated papa.

But Mariana insisted. "Papa, the conservatory! What tanner's son ever gets such a chance? Mama would..."

Mama would have been delighted, I thought. Hadn't she made me swear that I would always keep on singing? But she had also made me swear to be a good son to papa. Could the two go together? I sighed.

"You don't know what you're talking about, Mariana. What's more, you know as well as I do that I can't do without your brother's hands. And now get out of my workshop." Papa turned round and shifted his concentration to the hide. His shoulders seemed more obstinate than ever.

"But " Mariana tried again.

"And close the door behind you."

6

"When will you hear whether you've been chosen?" asked my father the next day. I was rather pleased he hadn't forgotten.

"I have to be in the church at half past five. First, we have choir practice."

"If only I could be there." He rubbed his eyes. The circles around them were almost pitch black. "But there are too many hides to be rolled. I can't just leave them."

He wouldn't have gone anyway. But that didn't matter.

"I can go with you," offered Mariana.

"Nobody needs to come," I said. "I'd just as soon go alone."

"No." Papa placed his hand on my sister's shoulder. "Mariana, you go along with him. And ask your aunt as well. The mayor mustn't get the idea that your performance doesn't mean anything to us."

"So that's settled," said Mariana.

"As long as you keep your mouth shut," I said.

"I won't say a word," promised Mariana.

"And don't forget that I have choir practice first," I said again. "Don't get there too early."

"Don't worry," said my sister. "We'll wait at the door until you come and get us." She looked as if she was gloating at the idea of getting a look at my opponent. As long as she didn't work off her irritations of recent days on Gaetano.

The choir practice proceeded as usual with some grumbling by the maestro and some of the boys acting up. Time seemed to creep by. At the end of the rehearsal, Victorio suggested walking home with me.

"Can't," I said. "Gaetano and I have to wait for the maestro."

"Why?" asked Victorio. "What have you been up to? You had to stay behind on Saturday as well. You weren't there on Monday and Tuesday, and yesterday "

"Pope Clement is coming to Fiesole," I said. "One of us will sing a solo during his mass."

"Really?" yelled Victorio. "Man, what an honour!"

Gaetano came and joined us. "And now we'll see which of us is the best."

Victorio shook his head. "I don't need any trial to know that, and I don't think the maestro does either."

Gaetano narrowed his eyes. "What do you mean?"

Victorio grinned. "Friend, you sing beautifully, but Angelo does his name proud. He sings like an angel, straight from the heavenly choir."

I curtsied like a girl. "*Grazie, amico.*"

"You're only saying that because you live close to each other." Gaetano's face was dark with rage.

"Believe me, Gaetano," persisted Victorio. "You both sing better than the rest of us, but nobody sings as well as Angelo. Have you never noticed how the maestro gives all his attention to him when we practise?"

"Wouldn't he do that if Angelo sang out of tune?"

"I've never heard Angelo sing a wrong note."

Gaetano growled. "You're biased. I should have known "

"What? That " Victorio stopped abruptly. His eyes widened. "Who is that?"

Gaetano and I turned our heads at the same time in the direction of the main door…just in time to see Mariana looking around in the rear pews.

Gaetano hissed through his teeth. "Amore…"

"My sister," I said. "Mariana. Don't you know her?"

Gaetano grabbed my arm. "Your sister? Introduce me to her."

"No, me!" cried Victorio. "I'm your best friend, Angelo!"

Introduce them? To Mariana? What was wrong with them? I looked in amazement from them to my sister. She had put on one of Mama's dresses and coats, and they made her older than she was. More feminine. Was that why Victorio and Gaetano reacted like that?

At that moment, she saw me. "Angelo!" Her skirts rustled back and forth as she walked toward us. "I said I'd wait, but it took so long. Zia is still waiting at the door."

Before she knew what was happening, Victorio had grabbed her hand and planted a kiss on it. "Victorio Capri, at your service."

Mariana looked in astonishment from him to me. "Mariana Montegne," she said. "Who are you?"

"Your brother's friend. Has he never mentioned my name?"

"Oh." I read the thought on her face. "No." She looked at me. "Angelo doesn't talk very much."

"Disgraceful!" Victorio gave me a shove against my shoulder. "He doesn't deserve my friendship, that boy. Probably thinks I'm too old to call me his friend." He tapped his breast. "I'm two years older than him."

"And this is Gaetano Bernardi," I said quickly. "He's the other singer."

Gaetano did not say a word but tried to grab my sister's hand. He had apparently forgotten that she too was a tanner's child who could prove smelly.

But Mariana did not want his attention and quickly took a step backwards. "So," she said. "You are Gaetano. I hear you can sing rather well." Her voice sounded so cold that even Victorio grimaced.

64

Hesitantly, Gaetano sought support from me. "Uh, yes. But not as well as your brother, I have just been told."

I felt a gust of laughter coming. Quickly, I hid my face behind my music folder.

"He is right about that," said Victorio without blushing. "In some ways, this lad is pretty smart. But not in everything! I, for example "

Mariana giggled.

Maestro Alonesi came into the church, followed closely by Zia Ignatia. "Boys, will you come this way?"

"I think I will stay and listen for a while," said Victorio with a sideways glance at Mariana.

"Come along, Mariana," said Zia in a shrill voice. "We will sit right at the front. I want to be able to follow everything."

"I don't know whether we will have to sing," I said. "The maestro has said nothing about that."

"Doesn't matter," said Mariana. "We are here to support you."

"Precisely," agreed Zia Ignatia.

We walked in single file to the choir of the church. The priests from the Florence conservatory were again sitting in the pew. The plump man who came to our house yesterday smiled at me and waved briefly at Mariana. The composer and his daughter were also sitting in readiness, Rosa Scarlatti on the edge of the pew.

"Ciao, Angelo," she called through the cavernous nave. This resulted in an admonishing look from her father and caused my face to burn. Why do girls always make so much noise?

Gaetano's father was there as well, of course. He shifted restlessly in his place. Only the bishop was missing; such a high dignitary was probably too busy to come here again this evening.

"So, boys, sit down." The maestro took his place behind the lectern.

"Aren't we going to sing?" I asked.

He shook his head. "We have heard enough. You are here to learn our decision."

Gaetano shifted next to me. He clenched and relaxed his fists. "Me!" I heard him whisper. It sounded like a prayer. "Me."

I would only believe that when I heard it from the mouth of the maestro himself. He looked at us in turn. "You have both done very well, boys. You do know that, don't you?"

"Yes," we said together.

"We would prefer to let both of you sing a solo for the pope, but we only have one. Whoever is not chosen will be given a prominent role in the choir during the high mass."

Just say it, I thought. My stomach began to protest again. But the maestro wasn't through with his speech.

"We all hope, the four of us, signore Scarlatti, Padre Matteo Battista and Padre Alonso from Florence, and I, that you will remain good friends."

Behind me, I heard a splutter from Victorio.

And despite the tension, I could barely contain my laughter. Good friends? Gaetano   the one who pinched his nose when I approached   and me?

Gaetano nudged me. "Of course. Why not?" He looked at me. "Isn't that so, Angelo? We'll remain friends, won't we?"

"Yes," I said. I heard Mariana sniff. Despite his fine words, she understood that the posh Gaetano assumed he had won the battle.

"Angelo Montegne is the winner," said maestro Alonesi, just like that. "He shall sing the solo during the mass in the presence of Pope Clement."

Me!

I wanted to spring up, to shout with joy and pride. But it felt as if I were glued to my seat. I couldn't move and no words came out of my mouth.

On my behalf, Mariana cried out: "Bravo, Angelino! Bravo, *fratello!*"

Applause and congratulations sounded from the direction of Rosa Scarlatti and her father.

Next to me, things remained strangely quiet. I saw that Gaetano had half turned toward his father, who also said nothing. Father Bernardi bit his lower lip, his fingers drumming on his belly. I was asking myself whether the message had got through to him when he suddenly jumped up. Without saying anything and without even giving me a glance, he stormed past me, grabbed his son by the hand, and dragged him through the church and out of the building.

7

"And?" My father actually poked his head around the corner of his workshop when he heard us come home.

"Victory!" cheered Mariana.

"Good." He came into the hallway. "So my son is going to sing for Pope Clement?" He lowered his eyes and took a deep breath.

Wasn't he pleased for me?

"Angelo was clearly the best," Zia Ignatia added quickly. "The maestro said so after the mayor had left. He and his son weren't very good losers."

"You should have seen the face of that loud mouth when his father dragged him away. What a sissy!" giggled Mariana.

I hadn't said anything yet. Desperately I tried to gather my courage. "Papa…" I started hesitantly. "Why won't you let me go to the conservatory?"

Mariana crumpled the pinafore her aunt had given her. "The priests from Florence have just spoken to Angelo again about it," she said.

"They said that it would make God happy if I went, and Mama in heaven as well. I would be famous in the whole of Tuscany and they want to bear the costs of my training themselves. I can honour God until I am old and my voice starts to give out. Papa, I can go on and earn money with my voice."

"I've already said I can't do without you," said Papa. "*Basta.*"

Zia Ignatia shuffled uneasily through the kitchen.

"Father Matteo Battista promised to solve the problem for you, Papa," said Mariana. "The conservatory will hire a boy for you at the tannery if you give your permission."

"Those people from Florence don't need to give me anything!" My father turned his head away. "The price is too high; it's not going to happen!" With that, he returned to his workshop.

I bowed my head.

"What would you do in a tannery with a voice like yours?" the padre with the plump face had asked me.

"Tan hides, of course!" I had said. What else? Just like Papa and Nonno. I had been used to the idea from my earliest childhood. That's how it was: you became what your father was and married a local girl.

"The Lord would weep at such waste!" The padre's face had fallen. "And your mother, who is seated at his side…"

Promise me that you will always keep singing, I suddenly heard her voice in my head. *By all the saints! Promise me!*

And then I understood. God had sent the padres to ask me to go to the conservatory so that I could keep my promise to my Mama.

"Perhaps Papa just needs to get used to the idea," said Mariana, trying to comfort me. "You know that he doesn't like things to change." She looked straight ahead, thinking.

Zia Ignatia placed a mug of thin wine on the kitchen table and gestured to me to sit down. "Accept things for what they are, my boy. Tanning is a good trade. You'll be able to earn a living for you and your family."

"Family!" I felt myself getting nauseous. "If Papa loses the tannery, I'll never have a family!" I threw down the music folder and ran out the door.

Nobody stopped me when I passed the city gate and stormed off to the north like someone possessed. I fell down in the old amphitheatre on a stone and took my head in my hands.

Why couldn't I? Why didn't Papa even want to talk about it?

Didn't he want me to keep my promise to Mama? Was he jealous of my new opportunities?

Suddenly I couldn't control myself any more. Tears sprang into my eyes and before I knew it, I was crying like a small child.

A long time passed before my head gradually cleared. Lord in the heavens, what have I done? Allowed some priest from Florence to talk me into dreaming? Was I really so stupid that I didn't know that dreaming wasn't meant for simple people like us?

My future was decided. I would become a tanner and help Papa keep the guild off our backs. And was there anything wrong with that? Of course not! This was the role I had been assigned since birth. What else could I do but accept it? I should think myself fortunate that I had been chosen to sing for Pope Clement. How many people would love to change places with me?

8

The word "conservatory" was not mentioned again in our tiny house on the Vicolo Porettana. Nor in the workshop, where Papa and I prepared the new hides next to each other.

Even though he never said a word about it, I knew Papa was extremely anxious about the words of signore Guagli. He worked like a man possessed, grim and determined.

The tension had also taken hold of me; I tried my best not to complain and to work hard. Silently I scoured the hides as I had been taught, even when my hands were completely cramped around the scudder. I scraped until not a fibre of fat could be found on the inside of the hide, and before Papa asked me, I had made sure there was a new store of oak bark from which he could make the tannin.

My father himself took care of scudding the tanned hides, his face a mask concentration. Every time I looked up, his head was hovering just above the leather, searching through squinting eyes for any imperfections that may remain.

When Mariana came to tell us that our food was on the table, I dropped the scudder with a sigh. Would I ever be able to stretch my fingers again? They were so cramped that jolts of pain shot through my arm. "Ah, good," I said. "Food. Papa? Are you coming?"

"No," he said without looking up. "Ask your aunt to put something aside for me. The cobbler has already been here to ask when I can deliver his hides. I haven't got time to come to the table."

My father had never skipped his meal. It was usually a welcome interruption of the heavy work, a moment of rest. Beads of sweat stood out on his red forehead.

"Then I'll stay too." I stretched my fingers a couple of times, shrugged my shoulders, and picked up the scudder.

"No, you won't," said Papa. "Go and eat. Do you think I want to get in trouble with your aunt?"

I quickly swallowed back a retort: that Zia Ignatia would also be annoyed if he didn't come to the table. But it wouldn't have done any good. "Very well, Papa," I said and put down the scudder for the second time.

"Where is your father?" Zia Ignatia asked immediately, as I had predicted.

"He wants to keep working," I answered.

"All because of that visit from that Guagli." Mariana placed the dishes noisily on the table. "Since then, we don't exist for him."

"But he did ask about my audition."

"*Pffft*..." she huffed. "Mama would have wanted to hear everything, every detail. And then she would have run to the padre to ask what he thought about you going to the conservatory."

I closed my eyes for a moment. I didn't want to think about that any more.

"God keep the soul of your dear mother," said Zia Ignatia. "And leave your father alone, Mariana. He works hard to give you this meal! And it's no business of yours which decisions he makes."

"But he's missing out on this delicious food," grumbled Mariana.

"I'll take it to him later," says Aunt.

The meal continued in silence. The problems our tannery was facing hung heavily over our heads. In another week we would have to pay the fine to signore Guagli.

Immediately after the meal, our aunt sent Mariana outside to scrub the encrusted dirt off the walls.

"Again?" asked Mariana.

"Now that the water has gone, it's high time to clean things up properly," said our aunt. "Nobody has to see on the outside that we have debts here. And you, Angelo, go to your papa and make sure he stops working. I'll bring his meal as soon as I've heated it up."

I was already standing next to my chair. In some way, I felt a little guilty that I had left my father to work on his own, even though he had told me himself to go and eat. How could he handle the work if he didn't rest now and then?

I noticed how quiet it was when I took the first step into the hallway. No scraping, pressing or scudding. Had Papa stopped after all?

I pushed open the door. "Papa?" He was nowhere to be seen, not at the scudding block and not at the tanning barrel. My heart began to beat faster. Had Papa gone out? He hardly ever did that.

Slowly I entered the workshop. I could now feel my heartbeat in my temples. All my senses were alerted.

The door to the street was closed, but light shone through the cracks between the planks. In one of the beams of light, I discovered Papa's feet. They were sticking out from under the work bench, the toes turned up.

"Papa." I knelt down next to him. He was white as a sheet, his eyes were strangely turned away. "Papa…oh, Papa." I pushed his shoulder. "Papa, wake up…"

No reaction.

A burning feeling started behind my eyes. "Mariana! Zia! Help!"

The door crashed open against the wall. Legs rushed toward me.

"What? What in the name of heaven?" Then Mariana's eye fell on Papa. "Papa...?" She sank to the ground. The rag she was holding in her hand half slid over Papa's chest. Her hands flew to her face, covered her cheeks. Nails scratched her skin. I saw it, but at the same time, my glance did not leave my father's frozen face. "Papa...papa!"

"Madre di Dio!" exclaimed Zia Ignatia. "Angelo, the surgeon! Quickly!"

I jumped up and ran from the workshop. The surgeon. Where did he live? Surely I knew that! Why was my head so empty? I ran along the Vicolo Porettana but then halfway down, I decided I was going in the wrong direction. I ran back. I didn't know which way to go.

"Angelo?" One of the other tanners had just come out of his workshop. "What's the matter, lad?"

"Papa..." I grabbed at my head and felt my knees shake.

"What's wrong with your father?" Signore Luigi stood still for moment and then started running toward our house. I rushed after him.

Mariana and Zia Ignatia were kneeling next to Papa. Mariana was crying, stroking his head and arms. Aunt was muttering prayers, her hands folded.

Signore Luigi pushed my aunt to one side and placed his fingers against Papa's neck.

I could hardly move. Was this my fault? Because I had nagged about going to the conservatory, while my father had so many other things on his mind? Had I driven him to despair?

At the same time, a feeling of disbelief came over me. This couldn't be true   this couldn't really be happening. Not after Mama. It must be a dream...a crazy, terrible nightmare.

Signore Luigi bowed his head. "He has followed his wife into eternity," he said softly. "How terrible..."

Mariana jumped up. "No! No! No!" She began to pull at her hair like a savage. "No, that can't be! What are we to do?"

Sobbing, Zia Ignatia got up. She threw her arms around Mariana. "Quiet, Mariana, quiet now. It is God's will."

Signore Luigi took things in hand. "Mariana, go and fetch my wife and your neighbour across the way, mistress Constanza. Your father must be prepared."

"No…Papa, no."

"I'll go." I turned round, relieved that I could flee the terrible scene.

The two women only needed half a word to understand what had happened. They tied on their aprons and rushed to our house.

"He was so busy," I heard mistress Constanza sigh. "Didn't that awful man from the guild visit recently? He never means any good. Never, I tell you!"

In the workshop, she walked straight over to Mariana and took her from Zia Ignatia. "It is a tragedy, my dear." Her thick arms almost crushed my sister to dust. "But what has happened has happened. The only thing we can do for your father now is to prepare him well and respectfully. Do you understand?"

"I was just about to take him his meal," sobbed Zia Ignatia. "Carlo, my only brother."

"Somebody must fetch the priest," said the wife of signore Luigi. "Shall I go?" She was out of the workshop before I could say anything.

"Good," commanded mistress Constanza. "Now, you men must leave to our duties. Mariana, will you help me lay out your father? Ignatia, where would you like him placed?"

I stood there and heard everything, but I could hardly take it all in. The whole world had become a misty haze and I could do nothing but float along in it.

9

For the second time in hardly a year, I cleaned our cart until it shone. A local carpenter had made a simple coffin from a few rough oak planks. My father would have liked it.

I had told signore Luigi that I wanted to push the cart to the church on my own, but it was too heavy. I couldn't manage it for more than a few steps.

Signore Luigi saw me struggling. "Let me drive him to the church," he said. "Then you can help me and the other neighbours carry the coffin into the church. Okay?"

Not really, I wanted to say. But I was too young and too small, and I didn't have the strength. So I walked alongside Mariana and Zia Ignatia behind the cart.

The mass itself was modest and short. Another two funerals were waiting after Papa's, and the priest made a mistake with Papa's name. Yet people had come to pay their respects and I was pleased about that. Even though he had hardly set foot out of the house after Mama's death, Papa had clearly not been forgotten. In addition to the pallbearers, I saw almost all the other workers from our neighbourhood, and at the back of the church, lonely and alone, I even recognised signore Guagli. He obviously thought that, as representative of the guild, he should attend. As far as I was concerned, he could go to hell.

Only Mariana, Zia Ignatia, signore Luigi, mistress Constanza and I were at the burial in the cemetery behind the church. And of course the priest and two altar boys. The priest censed and blessed the grave and gabbled a hasty prayer. Then he had to rush to the next requiem mass and we left the cemetery. I turned my head one last time to look at the place where my father's body would lie for ever, and saw the gravediggers coming out of their shed at the back of the grounds.

A few hours after Papa's funeral there was a knock at the door.

"Montegne?" sounded a heavy voice. "Are you there?"

"Open the door, Mariana." Zia Ignatia sounded drained. The three of us had hardly eaten, although signore Luigi's wife had brought us a stew with freshly baked bread and smoked garlic.

"Good evening, donna Montegne, *giovane uomo*." Signore Guagli stood on the threshold of the kitchen. His wig of long, dark hair hung in waves over his collar. "I hope you do not mind letting me in, Mariana." He didn't wait for our reaction. "I come to give my deepest condolences. Although signore Montegne and the guild recently had some problems, I am extremely sorry that he has been so suddenly called away by God."

He took a step into the kitchen. Mariana remained in the doorway, her head bowed. Probably she hadn't even heard what Guagli said.

Zia Ignatia didn't seem very interested either. "We thank you, signore," she said. "But if you do not mind "

"I have come with a proposition," signore Guagli interrupted. "May I take a seat?"

"A proposition…" Zia stood up and pulled back a chair. "For us?"

"I am asking you to hear what I have to say and think about it," said Guagli. "There is no need to answer immediately."

Papa lay less than half a day in his grave, and already the vultures were circling. Although I didn't have much understanding of business dealings, I immediately understood that the proposition must have something to do with the tannery. I caught a glance from my aunt, which said I should remain quiet. There was no need for her to worry. What would I say?

"Are you aware of the problems?"

It was as if my sister woke up at that moment. "Problems? No," she said with a steely face. "How would we know that? The tannery belonged to our father, God bless his soul."

"What problems?" I asked, adding my two cents worth.

Guagli began shifting back and forth. He clearly felt assured by our denial, undoubtedly feeling he could deal with us easily. "Oh," he said, "business matters." He waved his hand. "Nothing of interest to you. The point is that the Guild of Saint Crispin recognises that your father has not left a fully-fledged successor." He turned to me. "With all respect, giovane uomo. You are still too young to take charge of a workshop."

"Continue," said my aunt, coldly.

"We wish to buy the tannery and the house from you," said signore Guagli, throwing all his cards on the table. "The workshop is not worth enough to pay off the debts, we know that. So this offer would seems more than fair, wouldn't you agree?"

Mariana's mouth dropped open; Zia Ignatia pressed her lips together.

"And what about us?" I asked. "Where are we to go? Are we to go and live on the street?"

He threw us a smile. "Of course not. You will receive a fair amount for the workshop. You would be able to buy a small house farther down the Vicolo Porettana, or somewhere else if you prefer. And you, young man, you may be able to find an apprenticeship in the tannery. I cannot guarantee anything, but I shall do my very best to assist you."

My aunt's face was pale. "The proposition from the guild is inconvenient," she said. "I would like you to leave."

The colour faded from Guagli's face. "The board of the Saint Crispin guild felt it would be good for you to know that you need not worry about the future."

My aunt stood up. She straightened her back and seemed taller than usual. "It is none of your business whether we are worried," she said. "For the moment we are mourning."

A felt a warm pride for my aunt come over me.

"I shall return one of these days to learn your answer." Without saying farewell, signore Guagli left our house.

"*Pfft*." Mariana sat down at the table and laid her head in her hands.

"Well done, Zia," I said.

"Have they gone completely crazy?" she snorted. "Your dear father is not yet cold in his grave…"

"He's right, though." Mariana's voice could hardly be heard. "You know that, don't you? What else is there to do but sell the tannery?"

"We don't have to concern ourselves with that yet," said my aunt. "The neighbours will support us in the days ahead. Then we will see what happens."

"The neighbours are not rich either and the guild has imposed an impossible fine on us," said Mariana.

I didn't want to think about it, but I knew she was right. We had to think about the future.

"There's nothing else to do," whispered Mariana. "Perhaps we can negotiate the amount of the buyout. Signore Luigi can advise us."

"Not now," said Zia Ignatia. "Today we mourn. Tomorrow we shall see."

"Then I will go to our neighbour tomorrow." My sister turned her head away from us.

79

That night, I heard Mariana tossing and turning on her straw mattress. She obviously couldn't sleep. Neither could I. I kept thinking about Papa in his coffin. Would he feel cold? Had he found Mama in Heaven? Was Mama angry with me? Did she blame me?

"Angelo?"

"Yes."

"I keep on thinking about your audition."

That was the last thing on my mind.

"Do you remember how that fat priest asked you to go to the conservatory?"

"Yes." Suddenly I understood what she was getting at. "Forget it, Mariana. I won't leave you and our aunt alone."

"If a tanner were to accept you as an apprentice, you will probably never become more than a servant. You'll never have your own tannery."

"Papa didn't want me to go to Florence. He thought the price was too high."

"The situation has changed." She fell silent. "That no longer applies."

I didn't know what to say. Was she right? Was the price no longer too high? And what exactly had Papa meant by that?

If only I could ask him.

"Go to the conservatory, Angelo. If the offer still holds, do it!"

"And what about you two?"

"Is there any choice other than to accept the offer from that creep?" She sounded bitter. "We shall have to leave behind everything that is dear to us, but the money he offers is our only chance for a decent life." Tears sounded in her words. "Zia and I will manage, Angelo. We can set ourselves up in service. I can be a serving girl, or Zia and I can become washer women or something."

I turned onto my side. "I don't want to think about it, Mariana. Go to sleep."

But the next morning, my sister returned to the matter immediately.

"Do it!" she said insistently. "Go to maestro Alonesi and have him send a message to the conservatory."

To my utter amazement, Zia Ignatia agreed with her. "The priest from Florence promised you a beautiful future. Grab the chance."

"But Papa didn't want me to!" I protested again. "He wanted me to become a tanner, just like him and Nonno!"

"Well," said my aunt, "I don't really know why my brother was so strongly opposed to that conservatory of yours. I have never seen him refuse something so vehemently. But alas he is no longer alive and our future has been turned upside down. I have no idea what the future holds for Mariana and me, but it would give me peace if I knew you were being cared for."

"We'll go into service," said Mariana. "Or perhaps I can buy wool and spin it into thread."

Slowly I felt myself becoming desperate. "I don't want to leave you alone! I'm the only man in the house!"

For the first time since Papa's death, I saw a shadow of a smile slide across Mariana's face. Was she laughing at me?

"Your sense of responsibility is admirable," said my aunt. "But we may be able to look after ourselves better if you are not around. And you can come and visit us now and again, no?"

"But "

"Go to the maestro, *Angelo mio*," she said gently. "And don't put it off too long."

10

Maestro Alonesi received me with open arms. But when he heard the reason for my visit, he was less happy. "Do you understand that you will give up your chance of singing for the pope if you leave for Florence?" he asked.

That hadn't occurred to me. "Why?"

"The leadership of the conservatory will want you to come immediately and not in a couple of months' time," he explained. "Think about it, Angelo. Of course I understand why you want to seize this chance." He paused. "It is terrible about your father, but at least here "

"It is exactly because of what has happened to my father that I must go, Maestro," I interrupted. But once again, I was filled with doubt. Singing for the pope…wasn't that the greatest opportunity of a lifetime?

"On the other hand," said the maestro slowly, "the Florentine conservatory frequently accompanies masses attended by high dignitaries. You may get a new chance to delight the pope with your voice." He grabbed my hand and pulled me to a chair. "Listen, Angelo Montegne. I would hate for you to leave, and for my own selfish reasons, I wish you to remain here. But as a music lover, I must admit that the experts at a conservatory would develop your beautiful voice more completely than this simple maestro ever could. You will learn to perfect the way you use your voice you will move a thousand hearts, my boy!" He patted me on the head. "Don't let me hold you back. Go!"

I felt a lump in my throat. "I will miss the choir, Maestro. And you as well."

"And I will miss you and your formidable voice. Now, get up and go and do what you must. I will send the priests from the conservatory a message saying they can come and get you."

"Congratulate Gaetano for me," I added. "He'll be beside himself with delight."

"And so will his father." The maestro grinned. "He was so angry that his son came second!" He once again placed his hand on my head. "Farewell, my boy."

+++

Precisely one week later, the plump priest from Florence stood outside our door.

"Good evening! May I come in?" sounded his jolly voice.

My heart missed a beat.

"Quick, open the door," hissed my aunt. I rushed to the door.

"My boy, I am so pleased to see you again so quickly." Padre Matteo Battista stamped into the kitchen. "What terrible circumstances, but what a joyful reunion."

"Hello, Padre," said Zia Ignatia.

"Where is your dear sister?" the padre asked me.

"At the market," my aunt answered for me. "She will be back soon."

"Good." He bent over toward me. "You understand that I'm here to take you away?"

I nodded.

"Good. Then we shall first deal with some business." He pulled a piece of paper from his pouch and placed it on the table in front of me. "Here is the official document in which the conservatory promises to provide you education and offer you food and lodging. Can you write?"

"Of course he can write," said Zia Ignatia quickly. "His father had him attend school for four years."

The padre smiled. "Then it will not cause you any problems to place your name under this."

He pushed the paper toward me and I signed it at the place he indicated.

"So." He grabbed the document almost from under my hands and immediately returned it to his pouch. "I have some business to attend to this afternoon in the city, so I shall come for you early in the evening. Agreed?"

Again I nodded. Now that the time for departure was at hand, doubt took hold of me for the umpteenth time. What was I doing?

But the padre gave me no chance to change my mind. "Take the time you have left to say farewell to your loved ones, Angelo. Of course you will be given the opportunity to see them, but some time will pass before then."

My aunt pushed my doubts aside as well. "My nephew is really looking forward to his new future. We shall miss him terribly, but I'm sure that he will be in good hands."

"But of course," said the padre. "You need not doubt that. From this very moment, Angelo is completely under the safe-keeping of the Florentine conservatory. I guarantee that we shall make his name famous and you will be prouder of him than ever."

That evening, the knock on the door came far too soon, to my mind, but my aunt jumped up to answer it. Mariana, who was sitting next to me, seemed first to stiffen and then grabbed my arm.

"Little brother, I suddenly have such a strange feeling," she said with a hoarse voice.

"Me too." I constantly had to resist the urge to wipe my sweaty hands on the fabric of my trousers. "I am still thinking of Papa and how opposed he was to it."

"But only because he wanted to keep you in his workshop," said Mariana. "Not for any other reason." She sounded as if she were trying to convince herself as well.

Why had Papa opposed it, I asked myself yet again. Was I doing something wrong by going to Florence?

Too late. Padre Matteo Battista came in. "So, young man," he said, "your future is about to begin. Coming?"

"I'll fetch my pouch," I answered softly.

"Little brother." Mariana held me as I passed her. "You will return as often as possible? Promise me that!"

"As often as I can."

"That is good," said Zia Ignatia. When I had thrown my pouch over my shoulder, she quickly gave me a cloth-wrapped bundle that smelled of freshly baked cake. "For the road." She had tears in her eyes, and I quickly lowered mine. "Angelo, bring honour to the name of Montegne," she whispered quickly in my ear. "Whatever you do."

"I shall, Zia," I said. "Goodbye, Mariana."

I left the house ahead of the padre. If I had stayed any longer, I would either have burst into tears or grabbed hold of somebody. I wanted to do neither.

11

"So," said Padre Matteo Battista once we had mounted the carriage waiting for us. "We must first pay a visit to a barber who will check whether you are healthy."

"Why?" I asked. "Nothing is wrong with me."

He gave me a friendly smile. "Do not worry yourself about it. He will measure your height and feel your joints. It will be over before you know it."

Something didn't seem right. Did the padre think that there were terrible diseases in our workshop because it smelled so strange? Did he not trust me?

I pushed my back against the bench and pressed my lips together.

The barber was in a back alley somewhere on the other side of Fiesole. I knew the man. Papa always went to him if his hair grew down over his shoulders and he was fed up with his beard. The barber was a kind, talkative fellow.

"Padre!" He knelt and kissed the hand of Padre Matteo Battista. "Hello, Angelo!" Cheerfully he punched my arm.

"This is the boy I spoke about," said the padre.

"I know him. The son of the tanner Montegne." The barber laughed. "His father had the strongest hands in the whole village. We used to play together, if our fathers let us out, that is. I always wanted the young Montegne on my side if we were ever in a scuffle with the other boys. Nobody could stand up to that one. Came from all that work in the tannery, of course. Let's see." He took my hands and studied them. "If you ask me, you're just as strong, aren't you?"

"I used to help my father in the tannery," I said.

"Yes, I can see that." He narrowed his eyes and look inquisitively at me. "Has the padre told you what is going to happen?"

"I will be examined," I answered. "But that isn't necessary because I am completely healthy."

The barber exchanged a quick glance with the padre.

"The conservatory has so many boys, from all over the place," said Padre Matteo Battista. "You must understand that we cannot take any risks."

"Yes, but…"

"Listen, Angelino." The barber placed his hands on my shoulders and gently squeezed. "There's no need to be scared. We are going to measure you, your arms, your legs, your whole body. Then you will be given a bath." He pointed at a shallow bathtub in a corner of the room which was giving off steam. "All the dirt that may be on your body without you knowing it will be removed here. Then, you will go off to Florence with the padre. Is that clear?"

I was too astonished, too indignant to object. Dirt? I washed myself now and again, like if there were streaks on my face or if the tannin on my hands left stains before I had to go to choir practice. I washed myself precisely as Mama had taught me. And just as often. And because I was leaving, I had even scrubbed my hands this afternoon. And why did they need to measure me? Did it matter that my arms were rather short and my legs were firmly planted on the ground? With a shrug, I turned to the padre who was still looking at me calmly. Why didn't he say that everything at our house was neat and clean and that a bath wasn't necessary? My gaze went to the door. I had to get away from this barber!

Padre Matteo Battista's hand went slowly to the latch on the door and closed it with a grating sound.

Why did he lock the door?

What was happening here?

"I want to go home." I tried to sound as controlled as possible, but nobody could fail to notice that my voice shot up and down. "I think I would prefer to be a tanner's servant. I'm sorry that you have come here for nothing, Padre Matteo Battista. You need not take me home. I can find the way myself."

The padre came over to me. "Be quiet now. You're just a little tense, Angelo, my boy. This fussing really isn't necessary. This…" He gestured around him. "…is all in your best interests. In an hour we will leave for Florence and then you will have forgotten all about the examination."

"No!" Wildly, I began to shake my ahead around. I really wanted to go home, to Mariana and Zia Ignatia. "Let me go. Please!"

The padre didn't listen. Instead, he grabbed my arms, pulled them back and clasped them in an iron grip. "Go ahead," I heard him say to the barber.

"Please!" Tears flooded my eyes. "Padre…"

The barber ran a tape measure along my legs and noted the measurements on a paper roll. He did the same with my arms. I tried to pull free, but the padre was stronger.

"Calm down, Angelo. Calm down, boy…"

"Let me go!"

But the barber continued unabated. He measured the width of my shoulders, placed the tape around my neck…

"Don't be afraid," he whispered in my ear. And even as he said it, he began to tighten the tape.

Tighter and tighter.

"No," I wanted to say. My fingers spread, I wanted to grab at my neck. Free.

I had to get free.

From the corner of my eye, I saw the padre's face close to mine.

"Padre…" I opened my mouth as wide as possible and gasped for breath.

I felt how my tongue was pressed outwards. "Help…"

"Quiet now."

No, I thought. *No. Mama.*

The world became hazy, faded. Short of breath. No air. I suffocated. My legs. Everything was slackening. I was lost.

12

Florence, several days later

The wound of my castration became a festering inflammation. I had a high fever, began talking nonsense and, according to Paolo, for three days I hovered between life and death. He also told me that Padre Matteo Battista had visited me every day, placed his hand on my head, and fetched wet cloths to cool my skin. And he had hung a small cross on a leather cord above the head of my bed.

I only saw that with my own eyes when I started to get better. Gregorio, one of the servants in the boarding school, somewhat slow of mind and as bent as a hoop, had apparently stood by my bed every day and had taken care of me as if I were his own child. He moistened my lips, fed me small mouthfuls of fruit puree, and bathed me. When I had recovered a bit, I only remembered the kind, friendly words that he would keep whispering in my ear. The weak-minded servant gained a special place in my heart.

When on the fifth day I became a little aware of my surroundings, Padre Alonso was sitting next to my bed. I had not seen him since that day in the church of Fiesole when maestro Alonesi told Gaetano and me the result of the competition. But now he was suddenly here. He looked down at me with knitted brows. I turned my head away and tried to ignore him.

I did not know much about the time that lay behind me, but I had not forgotten that the pain in my crotch was thanks to him and Padre Matteo Battista. And I was not grateful to him for that.

I spent the best part of my days in bed. As time progressed, it no longer felt as if knives had been plunged into my groin. Instead, it burned constantly, as if somebody was pressing a red-hot poker against it, and that scorching pain spread through my stomach and my legs. But fortunately it grew a little less each day.

When the other boys left the dormitory every morning, singing, I remained behind alone. Once a day, Gregorio would bring me food, often broth with some breadcrumbs in it and later a thin porridge of goat's milk. He helped me relieve myself on a sort of dish which he slid under my hips. He changed the bandage in my groin and spread some ill-smelling ointment or other on the wound.

Padre Matteo Battista also frequently appeared. His visits always proceeded in the same way: I kept my mouth shut and refused to look at him while he pretended not to notice my rejection and tried to convince me that a time would come when I would thank God for what had happened to me.

What further consequences my castration might bring, besides its effect on my voice, was never discussed. Neither did Paolo mention again what he had said on that first day. I think Padre Matteo Battista had forbidden him to do so. He always asked particularly whether Paolo had visited me, so I had the feeling it would be better to deny it.

I did not forget the horrible thing for one moment. Every time I closed my eyes, I felt it all again: the hands of the barber and the tape measure…the glistening eyes of the two men when the barber slowly tightened the tape. The air I felt escaping, my hands that were held trapped in an iron grip even though they wanted to claw their way to my throat, to pull away the tape, to save my life.

That memory alone was enough to make me open my mouth wide and try to suck in as much air as possible. As if I could save up an extra supply inside, just in case…

At night, too, I would suddenly sit up to grab at the tape around my throat. When I slowly became aware of the room and the sleeping boys, tossing and turning around me, I would ask why they had done this to us. Were our voices worth so much pain and misery?

And would the barbers sometimes go too far? Were there boys like me who had died because they didn't release the tape on time?

Then, when I was awake, my thoughts would always turn to Papa. Had he known what was awaiting me? Was that why he had tried to stop me? Why hadn't he just told me what they wanted to do? And would I still have gone off with Padre Matteo Battista?

Surely not.

But at some moments, I was not absolutely sure of that.

"How are you, young sir?" asked Paolo on the sixth day. When the boys came into the dormitory in the evening, they were given a few minutes to take off their cassock and choir smocks and fold them up before Gregorio came in to check whether everything was quiet. Gregorio, so caring and friendly toward me, was severe with any disobedience. When a cassock or smock was not folded up neatly, he would have the boys get out of bed. But today, during the evening ritual, Paolo took the time to come and sit with me. He was the only one who took any notice of me; the others simply ignored me as much as possible.

"It hurts," I said.

"It will for some time," said Paolo. "With me, it took about three weeks before it was over."

I hesitated before asking the question that constantly ran through my mind: "The pain...is it worth it?"

He raised his eyebrows. "If you survive...then, sure."

I was startled. "So it sometimes goes wrong?"

He nodded. "But once the boys have been brought to the boarding school, they almost all survive. It's just..." His eyes narrowed until they were almost shut. "We are almost never as sick as you were."

So I almost died, I thought. That beautiful voice that they so wanted to retain, they had almost lost it. I clenched my hands into fists. Almost...

"I'm getting better," I whispered.

"I know." Paolo took hold of himself again. "You'll survive."

"What else changes, other than my voice?"

Paolo was confused for a moment by this unexpected question. "What are you talking about?"

"You said that yourself. That other things will change."

"Ah!" He began to grin. "So you remember that."

"What do you think?"

"Okay, listen." Paolo placed his mouth next to my ear. "Have you discovered that your willie can grow?" I felt myself getting warm.

Paolo grinned again. "Shy, are we? You'll quickly get over that. We know everything about each other: who does what, how often he does it and when, who needs a lot of time for it..."

"Is that all you've got to tell me?" I interrupted. "Then just shut up."

"No, no...the good thing is that everything still works. You can have a lot of fun with yourself. But the nasty thing is..." Now he pressed his mouth right against my ear. His breath ticked, but before I could push him away, he continued. "You can forget about making children. I hope you don't have your eye on a girl."

I lay back in astonishment. If there was one thing I hadn't considered, it was having children.

"Wait!" Paolo listened to hear whether Gregorio was on his way. Then he whispered: "If you want to know whether it was all worthwhile, you should get up early tomorrow and go to the hall of the older castrati. They look a bit odd, but their voices…" He thought for a moment. "…are overwhelming. Magnificent. I can't describe it. You have to hear it."

"Tomorrow morning?"

He nodded. "The seniors sing God's praise when they get up, just like us. You don't need to go far to hear them. This whole floor is for the castrati. One dormitory for the seniors, the other for us. By the way, make sure you never use the word "castrato" when somebody in charge is around. They don't think that's polite. The proper word is *sopranist*." He turned back to the other boys. "But that's what we are, my friends. Castrati. Half men, aren't we?"

"You, maybe," said one, stopping what he was doing. "Nobody calls me a half man!" The boy provocatively pulled up his nightshirt and showed his privates. "Well?"

There was loud laughter.

I couldn't handle the light-hearted mood in the room. Not yet. The shock of learning that I'd almost died becoming one of *them* was still too raw. Confusion and anger still had the upper hand with me. Particularly the latter. "You sound as if you're pleased with what happened," I said grumpily to Paolo.

"Oh yes," he answered at once. "I am, too. Otherwise I'd be a servant in the bakery. With my older brother as my boss." He turned up his nose. "Why would I want to spend the rest of my life sweating in front of those hot, stinking ovens?"

"What's wrong with being a baker's apprentice? I would have been a tanner. It's a good trade."

Again, Paolo turned up his nose. "Don't tanners always stink as if they've spent hours wallowing in cow shit?"

"My father made the best leather in all of Fiesole!" I said defensively.

"Fiesole?" he teased. "Where's that?"

"Bed!" Suddenly the Gregorio's deep voice thundered through the dormitory. "Vespers have been sung; eyes must now close."

"Don't forget that your willie needs some rest for the time being," whispered Paolo quickly. "Later you can play around with it as much as you want." He wandered over to his bed.

My eyes didn't close. On the contrary, I lay there with my eyes wide open, listening to the voice of Gregorio as he doled out some reprimands. Tears pricked behind my eyes. Papa had that same deep voice. After a day spent hanging the hides, he would take a moment to drink some beer in the kitchen. The sweat poured off his arms and face, and dark streaks from the oak stained his cheeks. And that deep voice carried within it the sound of safety and security.

I would never have one.

Nor would I have children. I had always assumed that they would come along once I had grown up. Every married man had children with his wife, didn't he? That's the way things are.

And now.

No children. Ever.

Would I never have a wife? No girl? No family?

"May the angels watch over you," said Gregorio as he did every night when he blew out the candles.

13

Again the next morning, I felt a little better. My head felt a little lighter and my groin was much less painful.

My fellow students were already up, singing as they made their beds, when Paolo threw me a glance. "Well, Angelo?" he asked. "Do you want to hear the seniors? If you turn right in the hallway, you can't miss them."

I pulled on the shirt that was still there on the stool at the foot of my bed. Nobody had bothered to provide me with anything else to wear. So be it. The shirt hung down below my thighs.

Unsteadily, I shuffled to the door. The other boys stopped and stared at me as if seeing me for the first time. They didn't interrupt their singing for a second. Perhaps Gregorio was in the hallway listening to make sure the boys did what they were ordered. I couldn't care less, I thought rebelliously. Let them expel me!

I dragged myself through the door, down the long hallway with its white plastered walls. Almost immediately I was overcome by a cacophony of sound; it seemed to be coming from everywhere at the same time. For a moment, I did not know where to focus my attention. Then I became aware of high, clear voices that sounded some fifty paces down the hallway.

"That's them," whispered a voice behind me. "The older castrati."

I hadn't heard Paolo following me, but it didn't startle me much.

"That way," he pointed. "Just a few more yards."

"What are those other voices?"

"You mean from downstairs?" He pushed out his lower lip. "Normal students. Baritones, tenors, basses, instrumentalists, composers…They are not castrated."

"Are all those here as well?" I looked at him in amazement.

"What did you expect?" he answered impatiently. "This is the conservatory's boarding school. All sorts of young musicians live and study here." He pointed at the stairs. "The normals have their dormitories on the lower floors. We are allowed up here because it's better for our voices. Warmer."

Had the warmth something to do with our voices? Just as I was about to ask Paolo that, I heard an abnormally high, pure sustained note which lasted for seconds.

"What did I say?" Paolo beamed. "Ever heard anything like that?"

Shaky step after shaky step, leaning on Paolo's shoulder, I approached the dormitory of the senior castrati.

"Are you sure there aren't any women in there?"

Paolo grinned. "Women? Except for the kitchen maids, you won't find a single woman within these walls. What you hear here…" He waved proudly in the direction of the door. "…is our future. And you aren't even hearing everything they are able to do."

Somewhere below, I heard somebody call out. "Hurry up, young gentlemen! High time for lauds!"

Paolo threw a glance over his shoulder. "We have to hurry," he said. "Once Gregorio has been to the lower dormitories, he will come upstairs with his bell. Come on!" He almost ran the last steps. I clenched my teeth and tried to follow him.

"My elder brother is here. If we try not to stick out, he'll let us in, I'm sure."

So he had a brother at the boarding school. Hadn't his brother

97

warned him about what lay ahead? Or had Paolo wanted the castration himself? I couldn't for the life of me imagine that.

Paolo set the door to the dormitory ajar, peered through the crack and beckoned to me to enter. I crept into the dormitory behind him. It was about half the size of ours and there were only six beds, three on one side and three on the other. And on the foot end of each...

I was so startled that I had to reach for the wall for support. The castrati were the strangest human creatures I had ever seen from close by. They were tall, at least a head taller than my father. Almost all of them had arms that reached down to about six inches above their knees, and their legs, too, seem to have grown too long. Their faces looked as if one person had pulled on their chin while another had pulled on their hair, and their skin was as smooth and rosy as that of a girl.

They looked as if they should be at the fair, as clowns or fools.

Was this my future? Would I also become such a freak? I pushed my fist into my mouth to stop myself screaming.

One of the boys interrupted his singing. "Paolo," he whispered. "What are you doing here?"

"*Buongiorno fratello*," answered Paolo. "Angelo is new here. Still weak from his operation..."

Paolo's brother smiled and I immediately saw the likeness with his brother. "Ciao, Angelo," he said.

"He wants to hear your voices," said Paolo.

Again his brother smiled. "Then I shall do my very best," he said. He stretched his back and opened his mouth to join in the singing of the others.

Sanctus, Sanctus, Sanctus
Dominus Deus Sabaoth
Pleni sunt caeli et terra gloria tua

Heavenly! I couldn't say anything else. Pure and full of vocal decorations. I forgot their strange appearance and forgot the time. With a dry mouth, I leant against the wall next to the door, listening to the magnificent sounds. After a while, my legs grew weak. I wanted to sink to the ground, close my eyes and to listen forever to that angelic singing. God must at this moment be listening with enormous pleasure. Could people really produce something like that?

Hosanna in excelsis

Benedictus qui venit in nomine Domini

Hosanna in excelsis

Would I learn this? Was this why it had happened? Could it be worth it after all?

"What are you doing here?"

We hadn't noticed that the door had opened. Padre Alonso was standing behind us.

"*Scusatemi!* I'm leaving." Paolo tried to slip out of the dormitory behind him.

"No. Stay where you are, you two!" The padre's firm hand grabbed my shoulder and Paolo's choir smock. "Well? What are you doing here?"

I suppressed my aversion to the man. "It's my fault, Padre. I wanted to hear what they sounded like."

"Who? The sopranists?" His face softened somewhat.

I pointed hesitantly at the boys who stood watching with their long, expressionless faces. "I have never before heard of…such sopranists. I had to know. I am sorry, Padre. Punish me, not Paolo."

"You should both be caned for leaving your dormitory," said Padre Alonso. "If you do not keep to the rules, there are consequences. You know that, don't you?"

How on earth could I have known that? Had anybody told me?

There I stood, in nothing more than my long shirt, before an angry priest and six silent deformed creatures.

"I am sorry." But I wasn't at all sorry. I wanted to return to my bed to take time to think about what I had seen, the boys with their elongated limbs, their bare chins, and those remarkable voices!

"Come on, Padre," said Paolo. "This is the first time Angelo has been out of bed since his operation. He had to hear what it was all for."

"I am happy to see you up again." Padre Alonso sounded less severe. His gaze rested on me. "So, what do you think of it all?"

"Beautiful."

"In a time, your voice will be just as beautiful. We chose you because your voice has something seldom heard: absolute purity."

The older castrati began shifting around. Immediately, the padre turned toward them.

"Are you already jealous of him? Good, because you have every reason to be. The voice of Angelo Montegne can measure with the best of you. Although…" He assessed me with his eyes. "This little nipper will first have to grow quite a bit. I shall see to it that you receive a healthy meal today, Angelo. And have you already be given your cassock?"

I shook my head.

"I shall have Gregorio bring it to you. Very well then." He placed his hand on his habit. "This time I shall overlook your transgression, novices, but the next time you won't get away with it so easily."

"Fine," said Paolo. "Then we will be getting back, before Gregorio wants to give us a beating. Ciao, Padre! Ciao, fratello!" He grabbed my arm and dragged me out of the dormitory.

PART II

14

Florence, four years later

In the middle of the Piazza Angelico, Padre Matteo Battista slowed down. His hands were clamped on our shoulders. "You know what is expected of you, my boys?"

"They didn't cut away my wits, padre," said Paolo. Nobody every laughed at his well-worn remark. Certainly not me.

The padre was hurrying to the stately mansion at the end of the drive, the high windows of which were shut off with dark curtains.

"Not bad," said Paolo assessing the house. "Is this where we're going?"

"The residents belong to the richest family in the city," said the padre.

"The De Medici family?" My heart began racing. Everybody knew the family by name.

"The lady of the house is a sister to the prince," acknowledged the padre. "The youngest, to be precise."

That explains why he had immediately grabbed us by the short hairs when the unfamiliar priest had turned up. There was undoubtedly a lot to be had in that house at the end of the drive.

Padre Matteo Battista half closed his eyes. "If we are fortunate, we are the first. If it is God's will, of course..." He made the sign of the cross.

"Shouldn't we get a move on then?" Paolo threw a spiteful glance over his shoulder. "If those people from the Bartolomeo Conservatory get wind of it, they'll rush here as if their pants are on fire."

This earned him an irritable glance from the padre. "Know your place, Paolo Brunetti. I have hurried here because I know the family needs comfort." He raised a pedantic finger to the sky. "If another in the name of God can offer such comfort, then I am also satisfied."

Of course. That's why he was hovering around the house like a famished falcon who had spied a mouse between the trees.

"Remain behind me," commanded the padre. "And make yourselves invisible." Still it seemed as if Paolo's remark had awoken something in him, and he walked hastily along the drive, his fat body swaying at every step.

Paolo and I grinned at each other as we pulled the hoods of our dark cloaks over our heads and followed the padre at an appropriate distance. After all these years at the conservatory, we understood the hierarchy better than they realised.

The door to the mansion was opened by a servant girl with a pale face. Soft, reddish hair slipped involuntarily from under her bonnet. But that was not what fascinated me most. That honour was claimed by her eyes. Tears glistened on the light brown pupils, and flowed along a tiny nose and freckled cheeks, leaving black tracks down her skin toward the collar around her neck.

Suddenly I felt the almost irrepressible urge to go over to her and take her in my arms. I wanted to comfort her, to wipe the tears from her cheeks, hold her and cherish her. And feel how her breasts and hips pressed against my body. She looked soft. Round.

"God bless you, sister," said Padre Matteo Battista, moved.

The young woman gave a tiny curtsy.

"We have come for signore Verde."

Without saying a word, she turned and shuffled down the corridors before us with bowed head. Again I had to suppress the urge to grasp her narrow waist and pull her against me.

"Who has actually died?" whispered Paolo. I shrugged.

"Perhaps the prince's sister herself?" Paolo let out a hopeful gasp. "That would mean that they would all be coming here. All the De Medicis." He clasped his hands together before his mouth and stared thoughtfully into the distance. "If that happens, I am going to do my rotten, stinking best to sell my voice. That's for sure!"

It was pointless to remind him that our contract still had several years to run and that under penalty of a large fine we owed the conservatory obedience and service until the very last day. In the meantime, there could be no talk of his own career. Not even at the court of a prince, a princess, or a De Medici count. Unless, of course, they placed a large sack of money on the table for us.

"Keep your head down!" I whispered to him.

"I know." He sighed.

We were led into a reception room and the servant disappeared, again without a word, to announce our visit to her master.

"*Pfft*," say Paolo teasingly. "I think I'll take the weight off my feet." He pretended that he was about to place his bottom on a velvet covered chair.

"Don't you dare." The padre lifted his hand to box his ears, but Paolo sprang away with a grin.

"I'm sorry, Padre," he said theatrically. "But if you rush along like that, my calves start complaining. Growing boys like me often suffer from that. Perhaps you can still remember what that was like?"

Padre Matteo Battista's shoulders raised and fell while he awkwardly tried to remain calm. He had learned over the past few years that it was sometimes better to ignore Paolo's pestering remarks. Yet I had frequently enough witnessed an outburst of rage by the padre, which often led to Paolo receiving a beating.

Paolo was sent to the most deserving wakes along with me

because of his amazing voice, his light blond curls, and his bright blue eyes; but his behaviour was anything but angelic. At the conservatory he would pursue the kitchen maids and youngest servants; he would confront teachers and padres with his caustic remarks; and he would often intentionally ignore orders. The man in angel's clothing was, in reality, a devil who would have been kicked out onto the street long ago if his appearances and voice had not been so valuable.

Although my curls were darker than Paolo's, my nose large, and the birthmark on my cheek shinier than before, I too would often get comments about my beauty. Of course I was happy that my teeth were not crooked, that my arms were not as long as those of some castrati, and that my legs were not as short and plump as they had been when I was a child. And it was a fact that our appearance, together with our voices, brought in a lot of money. People were prepared to pay a lot to have us perform at wedding masses, services, processions and funerals. In exchange for all the florins our performances earned, Paolo and I and the other sopranists were given food, education, and lodging.

Today we had been summoned for a wake: that much was clear. The dark curtains, the tears in the eyes of the serving girl…they said enough.

The girl. I felt a slight tingling in my stomach when I thought of her. God, I longed to take a girl of flesh and blood in my arms, to feel her, to stroke her. The girl with the shameless speckled eyes and the slim, agile body, for example, who regularly appeared in my dreams. Rosa. Rosa Scarlatti…Where would her father's career have taken her? Our ways had never crossed since that time in Fiesole; I only met her now in my dreams. And in the moments between dreaming and getting out of bed, when the dormitory was in deep slumber but my body was as fully awake as it could be.

I swallowed my desires and started looking round the salon. I did not often enter such a fine house as this; I would do well to take it all in. Perhaps the negotiations would fail and we would have to leave before the representatives of the other conservatory arrived at the door.

The reception salon was high and richly decorated, with the most wonderful paintings and sculptures on tall plinths. The paintings in particular exercised an irresistible attraction on me. I tried to recognise the Biblical scenes from the stories we were told during our religion lessons. Not a difficult task, as they were familiar scenes. The crucifixion of Jesus, the dramatic beheading of John the Baptist, David and his fight against Goliath and, above the fireplace, a life-sized image of a heavenly Madonna with baby Jesus in her arms.

The man who lived here was most certainly devout. And enormously wealthy to boot. Who else could afford such large works?

I turned on my heels and discovered another painting, smaller than the rest, next to the door. It was the only work in the room that was not a Biblical scene; instead it was a portrait of a young man in a gold embroidered jacket. Without doubt, a member of the De Medici family; the coat of arms was conspicuously worked into the frame.

I took a step toward the painting. This close, I noticed that the man portrayed in his tall black wig looked arrogant. His head was sunk into his neck and his fist pressed into his thigh as if he wanted to say: "Come on then, you plague-ridden cur! I'll take you on, whoever you are."

Which De Medici was he? The Grand Duke of Tuscany? His son, the prince? Somebody who had died long ago?

Padre Matteo Battista had also noticed the painting. He came and stood next to me and ran an avaricious finger over the gilded frame. He must be calculating what he could ask for our services. More than the usual three florins a small fortune perhaps.

Paolo showed no interest in the many precious items. He stood against the wall, picking at his nails in boredom. And when he thought nobody was looking, his finger disappeared into his nose.

Just at that moment, the door next to him swung open.

"*Oof!*"

I suppressed a grin. With a pained expression, Paolo pulled his hood further over his head.

"Padre!" A man dressed in a black housecoat walked to Padre Matteo Battista with an outstretched hand.

"As soon as your house priest told me of the disaster that has befallen your house, I came straight here." The padre grasped the hands and clenched them firmly. "God's ways are incomprehensible. We, mere humans, are often incapable of understanding them."

The man sniffed loudly and raised a hand to his face. "No, I do not understand it at all," he mumbled subdued. "My only surviving son, my heir. Only ten years old…"

"Place your faith in God, brother. He must have had some plan." The padre laid a comforting hand on the head of the mourning father. "He is with you in your sorrow and suffers with you. The Lord be praised."

"Hallelujah," muttered Paolo next to me.

"Amen," I added.

I felt Paolo's elbow in my side and took a deep breath. I was genuinely upset by the statement of the master of the house. A child. They were always the worst wakes. With screaming women, fainting, and hysteria. With a dead child, you immediately saw whether the sorrow was genuine or feigned. You saw it in the eyes of the mourners, in their jerky movements. You heard it in their voice.

The padre's sympathy in any case was not genuine. He spoke the words that were expected of him as priest, but in the end for him it was all just business. He wanted to be the first who came to the door with two castrati, and he wanted to sell us as expensively as possible. If he didn't succeed, he would turn his cassock and his shiny, polished shoes implacably toward the door, sorrow or no sorrow. Those emotions were secondary for the conservatory.

Money.

Everything in our world revolved around money.

"The child is laid out in the side room," said signore Verde. "Follow me." He led Padre Matteo Battista through the hall, at the end of which a light shone through a half-opened door.

Without saying a word, without allowing our soles to clatter on the marble floor or even to breathe audibly, we followed the master of the house and the padre. Until now, we had managed to remain invisible; nobody had spared us a glance, nobody had addressed us.

The elegant room to which signore Verde led us was, it appeared, normally used as a dining-room. A massive wooden table had been pushed against the wall. On it stood heavy silver candlesticks with flickering candles. The candlelight cast a ghost-like glow on the face of the child lying on a silk-covered bier.

I swallowed. Although I should by now have been accustomed to the stiff, dead bodies for which we had to demonstrate our art, each time my thoughts would go to my parents.

Padre Matteo Battista, however, bent forward to inspect the little boy.

"I hope the padre will get a move on," whispered Paolo in my ear as soon as the attention of the two men were no longer directed at us. He shuffled his feet slightly on the marble floor and rubbed his hands. "It's as cold as a tomb in here. You look as pale as a corpse!"

What did he know of my sorrow? I placed my finger on my lips. "Quiet…" It was not without reason that Padre Matteo Battista worked at the conservatory. His hearing was sharp and practised.

"Once again, my sincerest condolences," said the padre at that moment. "What did the child die of? I see no blemishes or blisters in his face."

"It was not the pox," said signore Verde. "The surgeon could not explain where the fever came from and why it became so virulent. Some mysterious disease or other."

The padre made the sign of the cross. "May God protect the rest of this household."

There! I'd wager my head that the padre had furthered his own advantage with that remark.

It was as if he had heard my thoughts. Slowly he straightened himself with a triumphant look on his face.

"His name is Innocentio." The voice of signore Verde was drenched in tears. "He was my eldest son, since the others…" He fell silent.

"The innocent soul of the child Innocentio will ascend to the kingdom of God," said the padre piously. Immediately he added in a business-like tone: "And none of those present has caught the fever from the boy? You will understand that I would, with all love, have him watched over, but I cannot run the risk that they will become ill."

"I would almost believe him," whispered Paolo.

Again I pressed my finger to my lips, a little more agitated than before.

"They do not run any risk," said signore Verde. "I asked the surgeon especially about it. Padre Matteo Battista, I beg you, allow the angelic voices of your sopranists to accompany the soul of my child on his final journey. I am prepared to pay ten florins instead of the usual fee."

"Did he say ten?" murmured Paolo. "Really?"

I nudged him roughly. He'll go and mess up everything.

"Ten florins…" said the padre. "Well, but the risk…"

"Twelve!" replied the father immediately.

"Do you hear that?" hissed Paolo. "Twelve! And how much of that will we see?"

At that moment, the padre apparently noticed something. I felt his inquisitive glance on us. "Everything all right, boys?"

"Yes, Padre Matteo Battista," we said politely.

After a warning click of his tongue, he turned back to the mourning father. This time he lowered his voice and turned his back to us. I could no longer understand him and there was nothing left but to wait until the padre and signore Verde had agreed on a price and what was expected of us.

Not much later, the voices became louder again and the padre half turned toward us. I just caught a glimpse of the purse that was pushed under his cassock. The deal had been made.

"Very well," said Padre Matteo Battista to the father. "I will have them collected again at ten o'clock this evening, and tomorrow these same boys will sing during the funeral mass. They are the best we have. You will be comforted by their presence."

"Thank you, padre." The father clasped the hand of the priest between his hands and shook it, clearly moved.

"Angelo and Paolo," continued the padre, "you will each take a position on either side of the bier for the rest of the day. Tomorrow you will attend the funeral and sing during the mass for the departed."

"Very well, Padre Matteo Battista." Now we were allowed to be visible. Simultaneously, Paolo and I threw back our coats.

Signore Verde showed out the priest and beckoned for us to follow. "You can change in the servants' quarters," he said. "Be quick about it; I'm paying a lot of money for your services."

"He took a very different tone with the padre," complained Paolo as soon as the man had left us alone.

I shrugged. "He is grieving for his son."

"If he treated him in the same way, I can understand if the boy chose a life in Heaven."

"Be careful what you say, Paolo. God will punish you for your mocking."

"Whatever." Paolo's voice was muffled as he pulled his choir smock over his head. "My sin will hardly be worse than that of our parents when they gave us to the church."

I turned my back on him. My father hadn't wanted to give me to the church; that had become clear to me in the past few years.

And I still regretted that I had gone. I couldn't never visit the ruins again, I missed the good care of Zia Ignatia, the talks with Mariana.

I doubted that either of them understood why I never got in touch with them.

15

Despite everything, the past four years had flown by. But I had never found peace with the operation. On the contrary, as the years passed, I felt more and more ashamed about what had happened to me, particularly when I thought of Mariana. How could I ever face her again? I was half a man, I would never father children. The name of our father would die with me.

I had followed the growth of my body with fear in my heart. I watched obsessively for any signs that my arms and legs were misshapen. Were they becoming abnormally long? Was I getting an elongated head like the older castrati?

Fortunately, the Holy Mother was merciful to me in that respect. The stocky build I had as a twelve-year-old did grow to an above-average height, but remained shorter in comparison to those of my roommates. And my face too remained relatively normal except for my big nose, but I'd had that even before I was cut.

In the beginning, I hardly felt like singing. I cursed the pure vocal sound that put me in this predicament.

Eventually, I had rediscovered the pleasure of singing, and expected my days to be filled with song for days on end. I imagined that I would learn the most beautiful music pieces and would be able to perform in the churches of Florence. But the training at the conservatory turned out to be much more. Each week, we spent hours on the rudiments of music, on breathing exercises, on improving the colour and the volume, the range and the vibration of our voice. When it was time to sleep, I would fall down on my bed, exhausted and longing for home. All this was certainly true for the first two years, but after that it became easier. At night, I stared into the darkness, seeing the faces of my parents and Mariana in my mind's eye, but as soon as the day broke, they disappeared into nothingness. Homesickness became a vague feeling that was part of me, but which no longer upset me.

The moments of insomnia also had another cause: every night, sighing and excited groans would surround me. Sometimes I saw boys leave their beds to slip into that of another, after which the volume of the groans increased.

During that time, I got to know my body better: the skin on my chest that felt so smooth, my member that grew when I simply thought of it or when the sounds in the dormitory excited me. Almost every night I fell asleep with my hand in my crotch. Before my eyes, beautiful girls would appear, smiling seductively at me, displaying their half-naked shoulders, or beckoning to me to follow them to some hidden spot. I dreamed of dark, provocative eyes, of arms around me, of hands caressing me. The tips of my fingers tingled when they slid downwards over my chest, and I imagined that they were the fingers of somebody else discovering my body. Life revolved around my studies during the day and around desire at night.

Perhaps it was that desire that coloured my voice into the purest the conservatory had ever known. Without boasting, I could say that the maestros would hang on every note when I sang a solo. The padres would openly thank Mother Mary and all the saints for my divine voice. I was chosen more frequently than the rest for holy masses, and when the conservatory received a visit from some rich benefactor or other, I was almost always pushed forward to demonstrate the qualities of the training. That didn't make me particularly popular in the dormitory, but there was little jealousy.

The boys accepted me as somebody who half belonged to them and half did not. They had other things on their mind not being caught during their forbidden games, for example. In those first four years, various boys had been expelled from the conservatory because Gregorio had entered the dormitory at the wrong moment. Once, Damiano had been so engrossed in his noisy masturbation that he didn't notice Gregorio until he was standing next to him.

In the dressing down that followed, Padre Alonso bellowed that spilling your seed was in God's eyes a sin for everybody, but that it was totally unforgivable for sopranists. In a single stroke it undid our most important virtue, our trademark: our innocence.

Most didn't bother about the sermon, and shortly afterwards, two of my roommates were caught. They were lying in bed together, grunting and prodding when Gregorio entered with a glass of thin beer for a sick boy. If the consequences had been less terrible, we would most probably have laughed ourselves silly: Gregorio who opened his eyes wide, then placed the mug on the nearest table and pulled the blankets from the pounding boys. Their astonished faces, raised nightshirts and those white naked buttocks...

They were expelled next day.

16

When Paolo and I were hauled from our beds by Gregorio on the morning of the burial of the little Innocentio, it was still too early for the morning games our roommates played. Nobody moved, and for a change we dressed in silence. We would have to use our voices enough today: from lauds until the moment the coffin was brought to the cathedral of Florence, we would stand there singing in the funeral parlour.

Yesterday we did not have to use our voices. Once Padre Matteo Battista had left and we had changed, we were posted next to the tiny coffin to keep vigil. Innocentio looked beautiful in his simple white shirt. His face pale but relaxed, his hands folded around a rosary. In the course of the day, women arrived who draped his head with flowers.

The mourning was restrained, quite different from the other times I had stood vigil for a child. Then there had been loud weeping, even screams of despair.

In the Verde house, the women their heads covered in black lace cloths sobbed softly and dabbed their cheeks with delicate, strongly perfumed handkerchiefs. The men who came to say farewell to Innocentio were all absorbed with themselves and quickly left the funeral parlour. For the best part of the time there were no visitors and Paolo and I stood alone next to the coffin.

Although I ran up and down the stairs of the conservatory every day and was in fairly good condition, my calves still hurt from all that standing.

At this time of day, only a few early tradesmen were out and about, the odd baker and a traveller who wished to reach the city gate before the sun was up. Otherwise an unearthly quiet hung over the room, and even Paolo kept his mouth shut. Perhaps he was still half asleep; on any normal morning he would have to be shaken as many as three times before he opened his eyes. Now it was hardly light.

I couldn't care less. I enjoyed the song of the gulls and the other birds who had begun their day long ago.

"What time is the requiem mass?" asked Paolo when we arrived at the end of the drive.

"The coffin will be taken at ten o" clock." I had heard signore Verde say that. "I think the funeral mass will take place at eleven."

"Good," said Paolo. "Then we'll be finished early. An awful time otherwise, don't you think?"

I smiled and said nothing. In the distance, a young falcon flew through the air.

A few carriages were standing halfway along the drive. Servants were polishing away the dull spots; horses were being groomed. Farther away, at the side of the house, a simple black hearse was waiting. The coffin of the young Innocentio would soon be laid in it, never to return.

I shivered. I never grew accustomed to the moment of farewell. We regularly sang at funeral masses for the departed of all ages, but the moment that the coffin was screwed shut and we took our last glimpse of what had once been a living body, about to embark on its last journey; I found it increasingly difficult. Was that because of my own parents? Because I had said farewell to my sister?

"Hey! Watch out!" The soft body of a large and apparently powerful horse brushed past us. Probably Paolo had been daydreaming. Like me, he was a little unsteady on his legs. The beast snorted and wildly reared its head.

119

"Will that beast be pulling a carriage?" muttered Paolo. "It will be a miracle if no accident occurs."

I didn't worry about it. We would be walking on either side of the hearse and singing soft prayers during the procession to the cathedral. If a horse played up, it wouldn't bother us. What's more there were more than enough experienced coachmen, drivers and servants around to keep things in order.

The door to the grand house was wide open when we arrived. The same serving girl as yesterday met us in the hallway. Again she did not speak a word, but seemed a little more in control of herself. There were no tears in her eyes and no traces of sorrow on her sunken cheeks. Her face looked grey.

"*Buongiorno, prediletto.*" I gave her an elegant bow.

"May I also bid you good morning," said Paolo as he tapped the side of his head.

"Can you perhaps tell me where we can change today?" I gave her my friendliest smile, hoping to get her to say something. Ah, for a kind word from this pretty serving maid!

The sweet girl turned round without giving us so much as a glance.

"What a misery," whispered Paolo.

I merely shrugged. Who could say what sorrows her life might hold?

"And now?" whispered Paolo behind her back. "Follow her?"

I raised my hands to the sky.

"Signore know-it-all doesn't know," teased Paolo, who suddenly appeared to be wide awake.

"Oh, shut up." Without giving it any further thought, I followed the footsteps of the girl into the kitchen. Despite the early hour, it was already a hive of activity. People were at the tables, cutting, grinding and mixing. Round loaves of coarse bread, with golden crusts, were being thinly sliced, barrels of wine were ready to be opened.

"Are we supposed to change here?" Paolo pulled in his stomach for a fat kitchen maid who wanted to pass, her arms laden with cheeses, and then had to step to one side for a porter with a barrel on his shoulder. "Very suitable."

A young scullery servant was polishing glasses with a soft cloth. "Back again?" he asked.

"Whatever gave you that idea?" asked Paolo. "We are ghosts, only visible to the corrupt on this earth." He bent his hands into claws and slashed them through the air.

"You may not be ghosts, exactly…" The boy stopped his polishing, his eyes taking us in. "But you have to admit, there's not much difference. Half men, but twice as big."

I sighed. It was still difficult to deal with the strange ideas some people had. Paolo was better at it. He punched the boy's arm.

"Feel it?" he asked.

"Ouch!" He dropped the cloth. "Are you mad?"

"No, not really," said Paolo, a satisfied grin on his face. "But if you don't get back to your work, I'll let you feel that my muscles are more masculine than yours." He clenched his fists provocatively.

The boy quickly picked up another glass and turned his back on us.

We sought out a quiet spot in one of the darkest corners of the kitchen and took our choir smocks from our pouch.

"Watch out!" bellowed a new porter. "Clear the way!" The contents of the barrel on his shoulder splashed around audibly as he cleared a path through the crowded kitchen.

"More wine," hissed Paolo to me. "I thought they were here to bury someone. What do they need with all that rotgut?"

"Sopranists!" echoed through the kitchen. "Are you ready?"

"Almost," called Paolo.

Quickly we pulled on our clothing and prepared to escape that madhouse.

Another maid led us to the funeral parlour. Her pitted cheeks made her was far less attractive. But she did speak. "Here, this room. Hurry up, I've got things to do."

"Are all the girls here so charming?" asked Paolo. "Are you selected for it?"

"Are all sopranists so ugly?" she snapped back.

"Ugly?" I cast a glance at Paolo. Seldom were we called ugly. Angelic. Supernatural. Gracious. All of those.

"Could it be that you have no taste?" There was a serious tone to Paolo's voice. "We are always complimented on our appearance."

"Oh," she said cattily. "Then other ideals of beauty must apply to you than to normal people."

"Ha!" Paolo placed his hand on his hip and moved his hips effeminately. "That's told us, Angelino. We are not normal people."

I smiled. That remark didn't bother me in the least. It was a fact.

Without looking at the impertinent girl I stepped past her into the funeral parlour. A woman was seated on a chair at the head of the tiny Innocentio, a woman I had not seen the day before. A black cloth hung around her shoulders. She kept her eyes closed. Had she noticed that we had entered? With one hand the woman stroked the chest of the dead boy, the other she held clenched against her breast. Softly she muttered prayers.

"What should we do?" I whispered to Paolo. "Can we disturb her?"

"Signore Verde has paid us to sing here, hasn't he?" said Paolo. "So it's up to him."

"Yes but…" This must be the mother or grandmother of Innocentio. Could we take away her last moments with the boy?

But the woman had already noticed us. "Come in," she said. "Sing my son to Heaven."

And so we took our places at the head end of the bier and sang our first notes. After a while, the woman arose. She stroked Innocentio's cheeks and kissed him on his forehead. Then she threw the cloth over her bowed head and left the funeral parlour.

A short while later, signore Verde came in. "Stop," he said to us. "It is time."

We stopped singing at precisely the same moment. It was a relief to stop, for my mouth was dry.

"Here." The fat kitchen maid held up two goblets. "I'm sure you'd like some thin beer."

"Grazie."

"Listen!" One of the kitchen maids pointed to the stairs. All the footmen and maids stopped their activities and listened carefully to the hammering above our head. "There goes our little boy," said one girl quietly. The others all looked downcast.

"He has a beautiful coffin," said a footman. "I saw it when they delivered it. Made of sycamore from one of the family's estates."

The others nodded.

"Have they been able to get in touch with his godfather?" asked someone behind me. "He was in Venice, I heard from the major-domo."

"They probably didn't reach him in such a short time," said the fat kitchen maid. "Prince Ferdinando will tear his hair out when he hears the news. Centio was the apple of his eye."

Again there were nods all round.

"It is not your fault that this is such a sad day, boys," said the fat kitchen maid to Paolo and me. "Your singing will convince our dear Lord to place the boy at His right hand."

"We'll do our best." Paolo threw a wink at the impudent maid who had shown us to the funeral parlour. She turned away.

Silently we sat among the kitchen maids and footmen, all sunk in their own thoughts.

I stared at the beautiful, silent girl opposite me who had taken a seat on a low stool. Bending forward, she crumpled the white apron tied around her waist in her hands. Poor thing. If only I could find the right words. If only I could lean her against my shoulder.

Ah well, I knew that was only a dream. But dreams were what kept me going, most days.

A knock sounded on the door behind us. It opened immediately, without waiting for an answer.

"Good day to you all!" said a cheerful voice.

I immediately turned around. I knew that voice!

"Shhh!" it said.

"Renato and Marcello!" said Paolo, confirming my fear. "What are you doing here?"

"We were sent here," whispered Marcello.

"Why?" I hissed.

"Be quiet, little castrato," whispered Renato. "Padre Matteo Battista sent us here to follow the hearse. Obviously the two of you aren't men enough for that."

I held my tongue. The baritones, basses and tenors, and we, the sopranists, were caught in an eternal struggle. We were strictly segregated at the conservatory. Sopranists were given new choir smocks more frequently, we slept with fewer in one room, and we had warmer lodgings. We even ate in different rooms since the ordinary singers had rebelled because our meals were more elaborate than theirs. But our singing voices also raised more for the school.

Marcello bowed toward me. "We're not here to sing," he explained. "That's your job. We will simply be following the hearse. The client wanted four boys in choir robes around the carriage, for the sake of appearances."

I sighed. Couldn't the padre have told us this before we left? I turned away and concentrated once more on the sound above us: wood on wood, hammering. Various women around me crossed themselves.

"He was a sweet boy," muttered the fat kitchen maid without taking her eyes off the stairs.

"Our darling," said another.

"Don't forget he could fly into a rage," said a footman. "Do you remember that time when he had to attend some official occasion or other and he absolutely didn't want to go? You could still hear him at the end of the driveway."

"He was no goodie-goodie,' said the kitchen maid.

"No, no goodie-goodie…" agreed the footman.

Again there was a silence.

"Who has actually died?" asked Renato softly. "The nobleman's son?"

"Yes."

"Oh." Leisurely, he looked round. "Posh do. You getting anything to eat?"

"I would change if I were you," whispered Paolo. "I don't think there'll be much time for that later."

Renato threw him an annoyed glance. The "normal" singers didn't like taking orders from castrati. And Paolo's words sounded suspiciously like an order.

"He's right," said Marcello, the more level-headed of the two.

"Let's get changed."

Several moments later, doors outside slammed against the wall. There was a shuffling of feet.

"Hello, boys…"

The kitchen maid and a few others wiped their faces with their aprons. The silent girl's fists had turned white, so tightly were they clenched. A footman cursed.

Footsteps approached. "Sopranists!" called the major-domo. "You are needed again! Have the other boys arrived?"

"Yes, signore." Marcello and Renato rushed forward, half dressed, from the corner of the kitchen. Paolo and I grinned at each other. That was touch and go.

Quickly, I poured the mug of beer down my throat and led Paolo and the other two upstairs, along the corridor, and outside. The sober coffin was just being placed in the hearse.

We waited next to each other in silence until everything had been arranged and the major-domo gave us a sign. Then Paolo and I took our place on either side of the carriage, and Renato and Marcello went and stood two or three paces behind us. The coachman cracked his whip on the horses' flanks. "Hup!"

Solemnly we walked beside the carriage, our hands clasped together, our faces sombre as we had been taught.

The funeral had now started. Although I could not see them, I heard several carriages pull away behind us. They must be for the family and guests.

A few stable-boys stood along the drive with other staff members in the house's uniform. It was deathly quiet at the moment we passed. All that could be heard was the clattering of the hooves and the rattling of the wheels on the cobblestones. Occasionally the horses snorted.

That was all.

17

It wasn't far to the centre of the town, and very soon the hearse was driving past the first few houses. More and more people gathered respectfully along the side of the road. Probably the news of the death of the small Innocentio had spread through the streets like wild fire. The size of the coffin, clearly visible behind the glass of the hearse, showed that a child was being buried.

Women in particular reacted emotionally: some wiped their cheeks with their skirts or allowed their tears to flow freely. The odd small child who did not understand what was the matter loudly asked questions of the woman holding his hand. Otherwise, nobody disturbed the sadly peaceful mood of the procession.

Until somewhere in the distance, the sound of galloping hooves was heard. They raced across the cobbles, approaching so quickly that we figured it must be a racehorse coming closer.

The procession grew restless around us. I had to suppress the urge to turn round and look, particularly when the people along the road all started pointing at something behind me.

"Dio Santo," I heard Renato call. "Out of the way, Angelo!"

Paolo was staring at me through the windows in the hearse, his eyes wide with amazement. "What?" he signalled with his hands.

"Don't look round!" I gestured back. That was what Padre Matteo Battista would have told us to do, I was certain of that.

The piercing whinnying of the horse that must be right behind us sent shivers down my back. Would I be knocked down? Dashed against the carriage? Involuntarily, I pulled up my shoulders and tensed my muscles, prepared if necessary to break my fall.

Horses at the rear of the procession answered the excited whinnies. The coachman on the hearse looked around in confusion.

I tried to control myself, to pretend that nothing was the matter and the funeral was simply taking its course. But when the galloping hooves stopped right next to me, I had to admit I was scared out of my wits. Wild eyes stared from the large horse's head, as it snorted and sputtered, spraying threads of saliva at me.

"Stop! Stop, I say!" So much for maintaining my calm stance. Surprised and somewhat indignant, I turned to face the horse's rider. He shot fiery glances at the coachman.

"What?" stammered the coachman.

"Stop the damned cart!" Shocked, the man obeyed.

A dishevelled man sprang from the sweating stallion. He pushed me so roughly to one side that I swayed and had to grab at the side of the coach so as not to end up on the filthy cobblestones.

"Signore, watch out!" I heard Renato shout out. He rushed forward to support me.

What on earth is happening? I wondered as I gripped the baritone's helping hand. I gestured to Paolo and Marcello on the other side of the coach to stand still and wait. Once Renato stepped back to his place behind me, I took a deep breath, straightened my back, raised my head, and resumed my unruffled pose.

But it proved difficult. From the corner of my eye, I saw how tears were flowing down the noble gentleman's cheeks.

"No," he sobbed. "No…" He pulled open the glass door, half crawled into the coach and pressed his wet cheek to the coffin. "Not Centio, not him…"

Paolo studied the scene with narrowed eyes. Behind me, the other coaches were slowing down. Signore Verde leaned from the window to see what was happening. The gentleman was still weeping, his legs dangling outside the coach and his cheek against the coffin as if he would never release it again.

"Signore…" I tried. "Signore, excuse me. We have to move on. The bishop is waiting for us…"

With a vacant stare, the man turned toward me. "Let the damned bishop go to hell! Centio was too young to die! He…he…" His voice broke. His hands stroked the coffin. "My godchild… so talented. He could have honoured the Lord in other ways than with his death."

"Noble signore…" the coachman said from above us. "You are holding up the procession."

The man did not hear him or pretended not to. In any case, there was no reaction.

Behind me came the sound of running footsteps. Signore Verde hurried up to us. "Ferdinando!"

With a start, the nobleman turned and threw himself into the arms of the mourning father. "I came immediately. It is so…" He shook his head wildly. His hat fell to the ground. "…terrible…I cannot believe it."

"It is God's will, Ferdinando," said the father softly. "We have to accept it."

"I…" began the nobleman, but his voice broke again.

Renato crept toward me. "The Prince De Medici," he whispered excitedly. "I know him. He once visited our village."

"Get back!" I hissed. I avoided looking at the scene any longer. If this man were indeed a member of the powerful De Medici family, he was not acting very nobly.

Around us, people did their best to hear what the gentlemen were saying to each other. They pushed forward and pressed me closer to the carriage.

Fortunately, signore Verde also saw it. "Come," he said to the prince. "Ride with us." He gave the footman on one of the coaches the reins of the stallion and led the prince to his own carriage.

After a little while longer, order was finally restored and the procession could proceed.

18

Two hours later, the coffin containing the body of little Innocentio was carried into the cathedral's crypt. The procession of sorrowing relatives moved off to return to the house of the Verde family.

The four of us were left standing at the entrance to the crypt. Nobody had told us what was expected of us and so we waited patiently until somebody came to tell us what to do.

"There's our answer," I said, pointing.

The major-domo of signore Verde was coming straight over to us. The candlelight from the great chandeliers reflected beautifully on the silver buttons of his livery.

"You lot, come with me."

"To the house?" I asked.

"Yes, of course." The major-domo turned around, impatient again. "What did you think?"

"What should we think if nobody tells us anything?" grumbled Paolo.

"Your work is not yet done." The man frowned. "Did you not know that more is expected of you?"

We looked at each other. "What do we have to do then?" Paolo and I asked in chorus.

"What you're good at, of course. Singing."

"Where is Padre Matteo Battista?" asked Renato.

Yes, where was he? Generally he stayed around when we had to perform anywhere. He made sure that payment was made and that we did not do more than agreed. He parried difficult questions and arranged a pause now and again in which we could rest our voices or relieve ourselves. Such a guardian was necessary because all too often our employers would try to take advantage of our services.

"I couldn't care less where your padre is!" snarled the major-domo. "My master has bought your services and that's why you're coming back to the house. *Basta!*" He grabbed Paolo by the arm and began to drag him out of the cathedral.

"Hang on!" Paolo pulled himself free.

"Do you not understand?" I tried to calm down the major-domo. "This is all news to us. We are unprepared."

The man's face turned red. "I have no time for this fooling around!"

"And what about us?" Renato took a step forward. "Should the baritones come too?"

"All of you! And if not, we'll sort it out when we get inside."

"Holy Mother Mary," whispered Paolo. "We have been sold, body and soul."

The bishop approached and joined in the discussion. "Do not worry, my friends. That is how things are in aristocratic families. After a funeral mass, a reception is held where you reflect on the death of the departed and make a toast to life. Your singing is apparently indispensable." He gave a friendly smile. "I can imagine that. Your voices…"

A toast to life. That was of course the reason why so much was happening in the kitchen, I suddenly realised. While the boy was being laid to rest, the staff were already making preparations for the festive meal.

"Off you go now," said the bishop. "I shall be along later."

"But they're still treating us like slaves," whispered Renato.

Paolo kicked a column. "I hope that we can first drink a litre of wine. Perhaps then I'll be able to manage something. My throat feels like a scorched piece of meat. I wonder what that old Padre Matteo Battista is charging for our services, by the way."

"That should be quite a fee," I said. "We've already been working for the family for two days."

"What on earth are we supposed to sing during a mourning reception?" asked Paolo.

"Save your voice." My thoughts had already returned to the sad servant girl. I would be seeing her again, and she would hear me sing! Would I be able to win her over with my voice?

The major-domo ran ahead to the simple cart that was awaiting us. We didn't hurry. I was too caught up in my dreams to make haste, and for the others it was probably an act of protest against the way things were unfolding.

Although the major-domo's face had returned to a more normal colour, there was an angry curl to his mouth. He didn't look as if he had everything under control.

When we returned, the Verde mansion looked completely different from when Innocentio's coffin has been borne away. Carriage after carriage drove up to the front door, depositing elegant ladies and gentlemen still in mourning, of course, but chatting and laughing.

We drove past the house to the servants' entrance at the rear. The major-domo stood up before the cart drew to a halt. "Wait here!" he shouted. He jumped from the cart and rushed inside.

"Of course," said Paolo as he climbed out of the cart and leant defiantly against it. "Fine."

"He's got a bit too much on his mind," said the man on the box, trying to placate us. "Signore Barsi can be a bit much sometimes, but I have never seen him as agitated as he is now."

"That's not our fault," grumbled Renato. "That's no excuse for making us the victims."

"Oh, in what way?" asked the driver. He jumped down from the box and began wiping down his horse.

"It's like we're being kidnapped," said Renato.

Paolo punched his shoulder. "If you carry on like a damsel in distress much longer, I might fall in love with you and give you a kiss!"

Renato clenched his fists and raised them to his chest. "Don't even think about it, mate. I'll beat you to pulp!"

"Where on earth is the padre?" I asked. "That is perhaps the biggest riddle."

"Yes," said Marcello. "Where is the damned man?"

"The padre?" The driver threw us a glance. "What does he look like?"

"Smart question" said Paolo mockingly. "Let's see, what does a padre look like? Cassock, white collar, tonsure."

I nudged him. "There's a lot you could say about Padre Matteo Battista," I said. "He is short and round, and his face is round as well. His cheeks glow as if pork fat has been rubbed into them."

"Does he wear spectacles?" asked the driver.

I nodded.

"Have you seen him? asked Marcello.

"Certainly." The driver spat on the ground before continuing further. "Before the mass, I was standing near the entrance to the cathedral. In no time, it was completely full, and anybody not belonging to the Verde or De Medici family were being prevented from entering. When the clergy saw that others were being turned away, they remained outside to pray with the onlookers. I think that padre of yours was with them."

Paolo and I looked at each other. Had Padre Matteo Battista given up his place to care for the crowd outside? Not at all like him.

"Aha," said Paolo. "He was being sanctimonious and showing off for the other priests."

Renato grinned. "He wouldn't have liked having to miss such a posh funeral."

"Excuse me sir," I suddenly thought of something. "Can you show us the way to the kitchen so that we can get something to eat before performing again? My stomach's groaning!"

The man nodded toward a door, about twenty-five metres away. "Go through there, down the stairs, and you'll be in the cellar. Carry on a bit, then up three steps and you're there."

"I could have told you that," said Renato. "That's where they sent Marcello and me this morning."

"I prefer to hear it from him. Thank you, my good man," said Paolo happily.

"I'll do anything for castrati." The man held up his thumb to us. "You've got enough problems as it is."

19

Chaos still reigned in the Verde kitchen. The same kitchen girls who were there this morning were hurrying around with chargers and bowls.

A footman was pouring wine into glasses. Dirty dishes were piling up against a wall.

Paolo looked around. "So," he said, "they know how to celebrate life."

We pushed our way through the staff. Nobody paid us any attention. They didn't have any time for that because orders were continuously being shouted through the kitchen. The maids and footmen constantly wiped the sweat off their brows.

"Come on," Paolo said to us. "I'll serve you." He walked over to a tray filled with delicious looking salmon-coloured snacks. Without bothering about the cooks and servants around us, he took a few. "Look here."

"Mmm, delicious, my good man," murmured Marcello. He popped the morsel into his mouth and closed his eyes in pleasure. "Not bad. Is this the sort of food distinguished people eat? You should know, Renato. You're from a well-to-do family, aren't you?"

"We ate splendidly every day," answered Renato, "but if there was a party, our cooks did their extra best, and then…" He stared ahead, dreamily.

I took a bite. I had idea what it was, but it was soft and creamy. Much better than what they served us at the conservatory, although we didn't have reason to complain there either. Certainly not compared to the food Renato and Marcello were given.

"Some more?" Paolo held out the tray to us.

Then it was my turn to choose something. I found a tray holding little shells of dough, filled with pieces of squid and pickles. I was just about to choose the best-looking snack when a shadow fell across the table. The silent maid! Her sudden appearance, exactly at the moment that I sneaking food, startled me so much that I dropped the whole tray.

"Hey," shouted Paolo behind me. "What a waste!"

I couldn't say a word. I stared at the girl with her ginger hair, which again was poking out from under her cap. Her cheeks were red from her efforts. Without saying anything, she bent down and began sweeping up the remains of the fish snacks.

"Hey, Carola," grumbled the fat kitchen maid who was passing at that moment. "Making a mess again?"

No! It was all my fault! I wanted to protest, but I still couldn't find my voice.

The girl looked at the kitchen maid and pulled a sad face. She made a gesture with her hand.

"Whatever," said the woman gruffly. "Clear it up. Sometimes I think there's more wrong with you than just losing your voice."

What? I had to grab the edge of the table. *Just losing your voice?* Is that why she didn't answer? Suddenly I looked at her through different eyes.

"Come on," Paolo said to me. "Forget about the food. We have to get something to drink. It won't be much longer before that overworked major-domo comes to get us."

In the darkest corner of the kitchen, where sunlight would never penetrate, stood jugs with sweet-smelling wine and thin beer. Marcello grabbed four mugs from a shelf and filled them.

"Here."

But I couldn't tear my eyes away from the little serving girl who was just getting up and throwing the remains of the squid in a bucket. Was it a hint from God? A boy who lived from his voice and a dumb woman? Had He brought me here to meet her?

"Take this, Carola!" I heard the fat kitchen maid snarl at her as she pushed a new tray of snacks into her hands. "Take these inside and this time, for goodness sake, hold on to them."

I wanted to push the tray into the fat maid's stomach. How dare she!

But Carola didn't show any emotion. Without giving me a glance, she disappeared from the kitchen.

Not much later, the major-domo came storming through the backdoor. "So you're here." He clucked impatiently. "I have searched heaven and hell to find you. As if I haven't enough to do. Now, hurry up. Put down those mugs. The sopranists are expected in the reception hall."

"And us?" asked Renato.

"You?" He pulled a thoughtful face. "The baritones? They paid for you, or so I understand, but there is no need for you to sing. Take off those shirts, put on an apron and start doing the dishes."

"Dishes?" stuttered Renato in disbelief.

Paolo grinned. "You heard him," he said. "Do what the signore tells you. And get a move on."

Paolo and I laughed as we followed the major-domo into a large hall where he planted us near an open window.

"So," said the major-domo softly. "Sing your hearts out, for the guests want to be entertained."

The guests want to be entertained. This must be the most bizarre funeral of my whole life: a girl that was more alive than in all my dreams, soft and round as a ripe pear, a nobleman who wept unashamedly in public, and a funeral that ended in a party.

"Just begin," whispered Paolo.

"What with?"

"I'll think of something." He took a breath and started a piece we had regularly practised. It sounded much too happy for the circumstances, but what were we to do?

The whole afternoon, we performed compositions, each one even less suitable than the last. Paolo led, I followed. The guests did not, as we were accustomed, stop to listen to us and pay us attention. We had to do our best to sing in tune above the gossiping guests.

Just as we finished our umpteenth piece and I was asking myself what else we could do, the bewigged gentleman who had almost run us down with his horse came over to us. The prince De Medici had changed, I noticed. His dishevelled clothing had been replaced by something more fitting his position: a half-length green velvet jacket with embroidery along the cuffs and a large lace collar half spilling over it.

"So, my dear boys." His slurring clearly indicated that he had had his share of wine.

Paolo and I bowed deeply. *"Buon pomeriggio, nobile signore,"* said Paolo.

"Are you not the ones who were walking next to the hearse this morning?"

"Indeed, nobile signore," I said.

"I recognise your sound," he said to me. "I have rather good hearing, you know." The nobleman flicked some hair of his black wig back with his index finger. "Cut, are we?"

I said nothing.

"Indeed," said Paolo, with his head held high. "Didn't you hear that from our singing?"

The prince smiled. "Yes, of course. And I can see it. You're a head taller than most people here. At least…" His eyes slid challengingly over my body. "You're not that tall. Are you sure?"

I felt uncomfortable under his gaze. Something in his eyes displeased me.

"He's cut too," said Paolo on my behalf.

I was surprised that this nobleman, who a few hours ago could not say a word because of his sorrow, could now smile and make small talk. Perhaps the wine did work miracles.

"I have actually not had the opportunity of listening to you properly," said the prince. "But I am very interested in everything to do with music. Would you not sing a song especially for me?"

"With all respect, nobile signore." Paolo fluttered his blue eyes innocently. "We have been hired by signore Verde. He would not be pleased if we were to neglect our duty to him. But we would also be pleased to perform for you on another occasion should you so desire."

Clever, I thought. Clever to angle for an invitation from the Prince De Medici.

Prince Ferdinando smiled again. "I think you are making a mistake, young sopranist. But you are right of course. You were hired to commemorate my dearest godchild." Again something unmentionable crossed his face. His eyes wandered through the room and fixed themselves on the ceiling.

Immediately he had himself under control again. He raised the beautiful glass with its ruby-red liquid. "The Almighty Father shall enjoy my godchild," he called. "I give you a toast." Again he looked up to the ceiling. "Salute, my Father in Heaven! Enjoy the magnificent gift that has come to You this day!"

Everywhere, people turned round to see what was happening. Paolo and I carefully shuffled away from the prince. Finally we had the attention we deserved, but in a different way than expected.

"Please continue singing, my boys." Before I understood what was happening, Prince Ferdinando threw his arms around me and pressed his lips to mine. I couldn't prevent myself closing my eyes in amazement and disgust. "Sing, beautiful boy," whispered the prince in my ear.

"And you too." He bowed toward Paolo. He seemed less shocked by the over-familiar nobleman. With gleaming eyes, he accepted the embrace with pleasure. "Thank you, nobile signore." He bowed deeply.

"I will listen to whatever you sing. And I shall consider an invitation," said Prince Ferdinando before taking a step backwards and observing us. We were still the centre of attention. The faces of some of the spectators expressed curiosity, others jealousy and in others I saw reflected my own feeling of distaste. I struggled to control myself as the perspiration broke out all over me. "Thank you, nobile signore," I said.

Paolo announced the title of the piece. I swallowed, took a deep breath, and started.

I still felt the lips of Innocentio's godfather brushing against mine.

20

Just as we had all but given up on him, Padre Matteo Battista showed his face toward the end of the afternoon. He acted as if he had not left us to our fate for hours on end and offered no explanation. "So boys," is all he said. "Just one more piece and then you're done."

Although I was pleased he had come to relieve us, he arrived at a most inconvenient moment. As the crowd of guests slowly thinned out, I increasingly caught a glimpse of Carola among those still present. Despite her long skirts, I could see how pleasingly she walked and how her hips swayed. Many of the guests were looking at her.

Throughout the afternoon, I had tried to devise an opportunity to talk to her, but the arrival of the padre put an end to that. My only hope was that he would mingle for a while with the guests and forget that our performance was nearly over.

After the last note, I saw that he was engaged in conversation with Bishop Urbanio and had just taken a fresh glass of wine from the tray.

"Go on," said Paolo. "I'll keep him busy for a while when he's finished with the bishop."

"Huh?" I looked at him in amazement.

"Did you think I wouldn't notice how your eyes were constantly on her? You were just a hair away from losing it altogether." He gave me a pat on the shoulder. "Go on, before the padre thinks it's high time to go back to the conservatory. Presto, presto!"

At that very moment, the Padre Matteo Battista started looking round. Paolo was right: not a moment to lose. I ran out of the hall. Carola was just coming out of the kitchen with a tray loaded with glasses of wine and fruit juice.

"Carola!" She couldn't talk, but I had the impression that she could hear. And indeed she turned round when I said her name. "Carola, can I see you again after today?"

She immediately turned away from me. She lifted the tray high into the air and rushed off in the other direction with short, angry paces. Was that because of the fat kitchen maid? Was she urging her to hurry up? My desire for the girl grew. I wanted to hold her against me and protect her from everyone who was nasty to her.

I caught up with her in a few strides. "Carola, I would really like to meet you," I said. "Outside this house. Will…will you…?"

"No…" Her voice sounded strange but clearly comprehensible. Carola shook her head. The glasses on the tray shifted and clinked together. Wine splashed over the edge.

I put out my hand and helped her balance the tray again. "Why not? Are you scared that you are not allowed to?"

Again she shook her head. "No!"

"Leave her alone!" sounded behind me. "How on earth in the name of the Holy Virgin can she explain? She does not have a voice!"

Behind me stood the pockmarked serving girl. Her eyes flashed and her arms pressed an empty platter to her breast.

I stiffened. "I…I'm sorry…I wanted "

"You've got a nerve!" she thundered. "Shall I answer for her?"

From the corner of my eye, I saw Carola rush off.

"She doesn't want to! Ha! What could you mean to a girl?" mocked the serving girl. "You're not a man. You'll never marry… no decent girl would want to meet you or any other of unmanned freak. Don't you get it?"

It was as if a bucket of ice-cold water had been emptied over me. I flinched, my legs shook. I wanted to disappear in a puff of smoke!

There was whispering around me. When I turned round, I saw the serving girls and footmen staring at me. Some had pity on their faces, others indignation. Right at the end of the corridor stood Renato with an apron around his waist. A triumphant grin was on his lips.

For a moment, I was engulfed in humiliation, then I ran out of the first door I could find, chased by those terrible words.

And from whom? From a serving girl! A common, petty-minded serving girl who put me in my place. I, a singer who was praised by the bishop for my voice, my volume, the wonderful trills that came from my throat...

No girl wanted me. Because I couldn't wed. Why couldn't I wed? Who said so?

I flung open doors, pushed people aside, and stormed out of the house.

Padre Matteo Battista, Paolo and the others would be looking for me. I couldn't give a damn.

21

I wandered through Florence as it gradually grew dark. Through streets and alleys, past bakers, butchers, and smiths. Randomly I walked down streets. What difference did it make where I was? Nobody wanted me. I was a beast. A monster.

Without actually heading there, I suddenly found myself in the district with the tanneries. Near the entrance to a workshop, the odours of untreated hides and oak invaded my nostrils, and suddenly I understood why the boys in the choir in Fiesole had pinched their noses. The stench of unprocessed leather upset my stomach. Retching, I dropped to my knees and burst into tears.

Regret, anger, desperation all swept through me. Why had I not listened to my father? Why, after his death, did I allow myself to be so easily persuaded? Certainly, my departure had been a solution to the mess in which Mariana, Zia Ignatia and I found ourselves. And as a reward for my so-called self-sacrifice, I now had a wonderful voice but a life without love. A future without soft arms to embrace me. Without a wife.

I wept, my back against a wall, my head feeling like sand, my heart filled with unbearable pain.

After what felt like hours later, I finally struggled to my feet. A couple of small children standing some way down the street, stared at me with their dirty faces. They said nothing, just gazed at me with wide eyes and gaping mouths.

Tanners' sons?

Had I been like that? Had I also played in front of Papa's workshop, my face dirty, too young to help him?

I wiped my elbow across my nose and noticed that my choir vestments bore filthy, brown smears. Gregorio would have something to say about that.

Well, he could go to hell! And the rest of the conservatory with him!

Nevertheless, I pulled the cassock and the choir smock over my head. Better to walk around in my vest than in that symbol of my misery.

Although I was slowly calming down, there was no way I wanted to return to the conservatory. I just couldn't bear the idea of coming under the scrutiny of Padre Matteo Battista or one of the other priests. What they had done to me could never be reversed. Or forgiven.

I really wanted to walk home to Fiesole. I had no idea how long it would take me, but I desperately wanted to see Mariana and hear how she was getting on. To be at home.

But it wasn't possible. I couldn't face them.

What's more, I would be expelled from the conservatory if I went off without permission. And what would I have then? Would I have to take over papa's tannery after all?

For a moment, I entertained the idea. Could I? Conceal that I had been castrated and return to Fiesole? I'm sure I would be able to get used to the stench of the tannery.

And then? Without a wife? Without children?

Again I was overcome by dark thoughts. What was there in Fiesole for me if I could never start a family?

I couldn't go back.

When, despite everything, I returned to the conservatory, the darkness had already descended and the evening lessons were over. I saw the tenors, baritones, and basses walking to their rooms on the ground floor; the instrumentalists stood around in small groups. Paolo and the other castrati were running up the stairs.

Before I had a chance to turn the first corner, someone grabbed my arm. "Where did you come from?" barked Padre Matteo Battista.

I tried to push him off. My anger was not far from the surface, and I had to get away from him, for his own sake as much as mine.

"Stay here!" The padre gripped my arm harder. "Who do you think you are?"

"Let go!" I heard the threat in my voice. My hands clenched into fists and my muscles tightened.

"Dear, dear," sounded a teasing voice. Paolo was leaning over the banisters, grinning. "Didn't she want you, my boy? Didn't she want half a man?"

"Keep out of this, Brunetti!" yelled the padre. "Otherwise you'll be in trouble too!"

I couldn't care less that Paolo was standing there. I couldn't care less that more and more boys were gathering around us, listening with excitement in their eyes. How they loved watching a castrato getting his comeuppance!

"I'll ask you again: where have you been?" Boiling with rage, Padre Matteo Battista's face contorted. "Tell me, you ungrateful cur! Then I'll teach you to run away!"

Strangely enough, those last words calmed me down. I relaxed my hands and directed my gaze at a point just next to the padre's head. I placed my fate in his hands. Even if he punched me in the face, kicked me down the length of the hallway, I wouldn't give a damn.

"You won't get anything out of him," said a voice that I immediately recognised. Renato was standing there, looking at me with that same triumphant smile he had worn this afternoon. "Angelo looks as if he won't say a word."

I didn't interfere. Let them get on with it, I thought. Why had they done this to me and why was a rich kid like Renato shown mercy? Who had I angered so much that I had to be punished with castration and doomed to spend the rest of my life alone?

God, how old would I be? Fifty? Sixty? As far as I was concerned, it could end tomorrow. I could make an end to it myself, I suddenly thought. I could walk into the Arno and swim until my body sank into eternity.

That thought made me even calmer. There was a way to escape loneliness. Better to die young than old and alone, waiting for death.

Maestro Perro breezed into the hallway. His cap slid from his head. "What is going on here?"

"This," began Padre Matteo Battista, "is a student who is not worthy of enjoying the best singing tuition in Florence. This is a deserter."

Maestro Perro looked at me in amazement. "Angelo, you? I can hardly imagine that."

"But he does have long legs," teased one of the basses. "Bet he can run fast on those."

A gust of laughter rose in the hall, and even the other castrati joined in. Everyone was enjoying this interruption from the daily routine.

I'd had enough. With a tug, I pulled my arm from Padre Matteo Battista's grip. "I'm going upstairs. You won't have any more problems from me. And if that isn't enough for you, I'll leave altogether. Forever."

The maestro threw a shocked glance at the padre. He placed his hand on my shoulder and shook his head. "Now, now lad…"

"Perhaps it's better that you leave," panted the padre in fury. "Don't think we can't do without you!"

"No, Angelo," joked the bass again. "Don't think that."

"Let's not be hasty," the maestro said soothingly. "I suggest we discuss this elsewhere." He nodded to the boys who were listening in the hall and on the stairway. "The performance is over. You can go to your dormitories. Come along, Angelo," he said to me. "Come with me. First some food. I imagine you haven't eaten yet?"

"Sure," sneered Renato. "If we run off, we can forget all about staying here. But if it's one of those castrati…"

Wasn't he the one who had helped me this morning when the prince pushed me away? The same Renato?

"The proper word is sopranist, Renato! We do not talk about castrati here!" snarled the maestro. "And get off to your room if you don't want to be doing extra scales tomorrow." He waved to the others. "And that applies to all of you. Be gone, and quick about it!" He turned to face Padre Matteo Battista. "And you, come with me and Angelo. Paolo Brunetti, fetch some bread from the kitchen for your friend."

Before I realised what was happening, I was pushed into the first room we came to. Padre Matteo Battista folded his arms threateningly and stood behind me.

"Sit down, Angelo," ordered the maestro. "Padre, I would appreciate it if you would first fetch Rector Orvieto before we start this conversation."

That didn't look very good. Why should the rector be here? Did this really mean an end to my studies? Wasn't I pleased if that were the case?

Without saying a word, the padre left the room. I was rather surprised that he had obeyed the maestro. I had always thought that the priests were higher in the conservatory hierarchy than the lay-people.

"So, now, just between you and me," said the maestro once the padre had left the room. "What's the matter?"

Even though I normally liked maestro Perro and he always gave me a lot of attention, I wasn't about to tell him anything at all. He wouldn't understand it anyway. He wasn't mutilated for the rest of his life. Outside the conservatory he had a wife and a bunch of children. The man was good to me because of my voice, not because of me, personally.

"Did somebody do something you disliked? Did somebody hurt you? Insult you?"

His gaze cut into me like a knife. I couldn't bear it and turned my back on him. Too bad if I insulted him.

"Stop it!" He pulled at my shoulder. "Don't you take me for a ride, Angelo Montegne! You are the pride of this conservatory! I will not accept you throwing away your career for some obscure reason or other, do you understand? Come…" He placed a finger under my chin and forced me to look at him. "You never behave like this," he said, a little calmer now. "And this storm will pass by, I assure you. But it would be much better if it happened before you were dismissed from training." His nose almost touched mine.

Still I remained silent.

"Listen to me, Angelo. I won't beat about the bush. You are a gold mine for our school. There is a lot to be earned with your voice and Paolo's. But to develop a magnificent career as singer demands more. Everyone knows that Paolo has a difficult character, and it is highly questionable that he will manage it. But you…" He lowered his eyes and shook his head. "This is the first time that you have acted in such an impossible fashion. I ask you, beg you, to get over it, whatever it is that is troubling you."

His hand stroked my arm and I suddenly broke down, wanting to weep like a small baby. But just at that moment, the door opened.

"What's this I hear, giovani Montegne? You ran away?" Padre

Orvieto, the rector of the conservatory, came in with Padre Matteo Battista on his heels.

"He needed some time for himself," said the maestro in a conciliatory tone. "Don't we all have that sometimes?"

"But run away…?" Padre Orvieto did not need any angry words to get to me. The tone of his voice was enough to make me want to crawl away.

If only I could believe that my castration had simply been the will of God. All my brooding about it had brought me nothing but trouble. Had it softened the terrible pain deep inside me?

I kept on seeing those money-hungry priests before me and the thought that they had misused an innocent child in the most terrible way forced its way into my mind. And why? Simply to make money!

A sigh escaped me. The operation could not be undone.

"I'm sorry," I said, forcing out the words.

I saw relief in the maestro's eyes.

"You'd better be," thundered Padre Matteo Battista behind Padre Orvieto. "You're not above the rest, do you hear me?"

I felt a giggle forming. Padre Matteo Battista could not have chosen his words more unfortunately; even though I was not as tall as most castrati, I was still head and shoulders taller than the rest of the gentlemen in the room because of what they had done to me.

"Silence," said Padre Orvieto, and he turned a serious face toward me. "Angelo, my son, it is true what the maestro says. At the age you are now, we all lose our way for a while. It is clear to me that God the Father has brought you to us to have your voice sing His praises. But you must make your own choice. Will you be led by the Heavenly Father or do you choose a different road? We cannot bind you or force you to sing. But if you wish to keep singing, you should do it here. That is in the contract you signed before you came here." He threw me a benevolent glance. "Sleep on it, my son, and then make your decision. If you stay with us, then you must submit to the obligations that entails."

I didn't need to sleep on it. What else could I do? Hadn't I been sick this afternoon at the smell of all that had been familiar to me?

"Run off to bed, lad," said the maestro. "We will talk again tomorrow."

Padre Orvieto nodded at me. I only wanted to get out of there. So I turned and left the room, without thinking of the meal Paolo had been sent to fetch me. It didn't matter; I wasn't hungry.

On the top floor, things were restless. Just ahead of me, I saw boys slipping into dormitories. There was whispering and boys would stare at me. As soon as I entered my own dormitory, an expectant silence fell. Paolo and the others were sitting on the end of their beds, staring at me intently.

"Well?" I said grumpily. "Say it."

"What are you going to do, mate?" asked Paolo. "Stay or leave?"

"What's it got to do with you?"

"A lot," said Josepho, one of the youngest students. His voice broke with agitation. "If you go, I've won."

I closed my eyes and sighed. Of course. When I was downstairs with the maestro and the padres, the others had made bets about what I would do. Paolo hadn't had any time to fetch the bread for me.

"What would you win?" I asked Josepho.

"If you leave, Paolo owes me his meat for a week. So?" He looked at me in anticipation.

So Paolo thought I would stay. Why?

"Well?" asked Paolo.

"I'm going to sleep," I said. Without adding anything or giving them a second glance, I took off my shirt and breeches and threw them on the stool behind my bed. I couldn't care less if Gregorio had a fit of rage. One argument more or less made no difference to me at this point.

"You see?" I heard satisfaction in Paolo's voice. "I told you so. He's staying."

"Dammit!" grumbled Josepho. As if that were a signal, all the boys stood up and started getting ready for the night.

"You can all go to hell," I mumbled. Once my head hit my pillow, I was dead to the world.

22

The following morning it was as if nothing had happened. Nobody spoke about my absence; everybody left me alone. The only thing I noticed was that, during lunch, Paolo grabbed the meat from Josepho's plate as soon as the backs of the padres were turned.

That lunch was not yet over when one of the kitchen maids reported to Padre Orvieto. Everybody followed the maid with their eyes. Not only because she was new and had a beautiful figure, but because normally nobody would dare interrupt the almost holy meal. The meal was a moment of peace amidst all the sounds of singing and instruments that filled the rest of the day. No words, other than grace and prayers, were spoken, not even by the padres and maestros who sat on a dais near the door.

Most visitors knew that they were not welcome during lunch, and when anybody knocked on the door, they were asked to return later.

But today, a maid actually dared go onto the dais and whisper something into the ear of Padre Orvieto.

Most students were so amazed they forgot to put their spoons in their mouths.

Paolo bent toward me. "You can't say that nothing ever happens here. First you, now that wench." His eyes didn't leave the curvy body in its black uniform. "Hmm…I think it's time for me to pay a visit to the kitchen."

I continued to eat   one of the few who did   but I couldn't fail to notice that everyone was keeping an eye on the dais.

Padre Orvieto allowed the girl to finish speaking, pushed a final morsel into his mouth and stood up. "Please continue with your lunch," he said.

The hum of voices filled the room. The other padres and maestros also turned to look questioningly at each other.

What exactly was going on was something we did not learn during the meal. But as soon as we entered the singing room that afternoon, maestro Perro beckoned to Paolo and me.

"We have just received a messenger from Prince De Medici," he whispered. "He has invited you to his villa in Pratolino."

"He has invited us?" I looked to one side. "To Pratolino?"

"It worked!" Paolo beamed. "You see, fortune favours the bold!"

Involuntarily, I touched my lips.

The maestro's eyes gleamed. "The prince heard you yesterday at the Verde mansion. Apparently you pleased him. Hardly surprising, of course."

Blissfully, Paolo pressed two hands against his chest. "We're going to Pratolino, Angelo."

"No, no," interrupted the maestro hastily. "He has invited you, but that doesn't mean you'll be going."

"What? Are you refusing…" Paolo turned as white as a sheet.

"Can't we go?" Did that make me happy or disappointed? I wasn't sure.

"Of course you may not go," said the maestro. "But that's neither here nor there. An important man has shown interest in you! And not just any important person. Prince Ferdinando De Medici! Somebody who is famous at home and abroad as a great music lover, and who has contacts everywhere. Vienna, Madrid, Paris." His eyes seemed to look into the distance; he shuffled to his chair and sat down. "Never before have we supplied singers to the court of the prince. This could very well mean the start of a magnificent career for you. What an honour for us all!"

"The start of a career which we are not allowed to go to," muttered Paolo in disappointment. "What good is that?"

"Is it a matter of money? Isn't the prince prepared to pay?" I asked.

Impatiently, the maestro clucked his tongue. "You do not understand. Of course money is important, but that's neither here nor there. Your voices are still developing. Every day they are shaped and formed here. Only when you have been trained in every aspect can you go into the world to give concerts. The more people look forward to hearing you, the better. You can rest assured that the world will hear that the prince has invited you!"

"By the time the conservatory is prepared to let us go, the prince will have long forgotten us." Paolo was clearly upset.

"Of course not, my boys. You may be the first students to receive a princely invitation, but you are not the first with a great talent… " The maestro grinned elatedly. "Just you wait and see. You have a great future ahead. All signs points to it!"

But Prince Ferdinando De Medici didn't let the matter rest. The following day, exactly between two lessons, we heard the rumbling of a carriage through the open window. The carriage stopped at the gate of the conservatory. "What's going on now?" asked Josepho.

We all hung around outside the classroom where we had a composition lesson. Long enough to see from the balcony on the first floor a man in a beautiful suit entering the building.

"I'll be damned!" gasped Paolo. "It's him. You see that? Himself!"

"The prince," I whispered. "What's he doing here?"

"What do you think? He's come to get us, of course!"

Was that true? For the first time since I had run off, I didn't think of the rude rejection by Carola. Did Prince Ferdinando really have such an interest in Paolo and me that he came to get us in person?

"The rector," we heard him command. The girl who had run to greet him curtsied, turned around, and ran away again.

"Inside!" shouted the composition maestro. "We're wasting our time out here. Hurry up!"

But once in the room, nobody could concentrate on the lesson. After half an hour, the maestro sent us packing. "And you lot want to become professional musicians?" he shouted after us. "Forget it. First-class amateurs. That's what you all are!"

His cursing left us cold. With the other sopranists on our heels, Paolo and I rushed through the corridors looking for a sign that the prince was still in the building. But we did not find him.

So we went off to Maestro Perro.

"Buon pomeriggio, maestro," we said, trying to put him in a good mood.

"Boys," he said curtly.

Paolo placed his hands on his hips. "What's going on?" he asked directly.

"Yes," said another sopranist in support. "What did the prince want?"

"The staff has agreed not to say a word about this," said Maestro Perro.

"Maestro!" pleaded Josepho. "Tell us!"

"What are you not going to say anything about?" I tried. I felt Paolo's elbow in my side. *It'll be fine*, it said.

As if I didn't understand that myself.

"You know very well." The maestro fiddled nervously with his shirt.

"How are we supposed to know?" said Paolo in a challenging voice "Nobody ever tells us anything."

For a moment, the maestro seemed of two minds. Then he hurried to the door and looked round the corner to see whether there were any normal students around.

"They've all left," I said. "They wanted to see all the splendour of the prince."

He nodded, shut the door quietly, and quickly beckoned us to follow him into the antechamber.

"It is, after all, about you," he whispered. "Listen, the prince does not accept the rector's refusal. He came here today himself and has offered the conservatory a very large sum of money if you go to his estate in Pratolino."

"All of us?" asked Josepho.

The maestro shook his head. "Your time will come, Josepho. Now it is about Paolo and Angelo. Their voices are more mature."

I could hardly believe maestro Perro.

"How much did he offer?" asked Paolo.

"Twenty-five florins per day for each of you." His eyes glistened. "That is a fortune for two singers. He will have you fetched and returned and he has guaranteed that both you and your voices will be looked after properly."

"Per day?" I repeated. "How many days are we to spend on his estate?"

The maestro shrugged his shoulders. "I don't know. But probably three."

"Oooh!" Josepho bowed his head with jealousy.

My excitement grew with each word the maestro said. "Three?"

Paolo and I looked at each other. Three days away from the conservatory, away from the boarding school, on the prince's estate!

"And...and...now there's a chance we will go?" Paolo stuttered.

The maestro lowered his eyes. "You know what the school

158

thinks about it," he said. "But I can tell you there is considerable discussion among the members of the staff."

Because of the money, of course. That was such a juicy carrot that even the most principled opponent should be persuaded. Seventy-five florins for three days…times two. A fortune for the conservatory!

"All the padres and maestros will be meeting this afternoon," said Maestro Perro. "And then we shall see."

"So there's still hope?" asked Paolo.

The maestro smiled. "Most certainly. Some who were fiercely opposed at the start are now leaning toward acceptance. No matter what." He took a deep breath. "The prince will send his aide tomorrow to learn our answer."

"Make them give their permission," begged Paolo. He almost got down on his knees. "Maestro, please."

"Just be patient." He walked past us and disappeared down the corridor.

"Stinkers," grumbled Josepho. "It's not fair!"

"Head up, boy," said another castrato. "You heard what Maestro Perro said. Our time will come. And if these two are out of the way, a couple of us will have to take over their parts in the mass. I tell you, this will be our breakthrough."

The comforting words appeared to have no effect on Josepho. His face looked like thunder.

23

That evening, Paolo and I were summoned to rector Orvieto.

He gave us both a friendly nod, and then he turned to me. "So, giovani Montegne, you look a lot better than you did two days ago."

I bowed my head. Although I was not ashamed of what happened, I didn't like being reminded of it. But the rector walked over to me and touched his index finger to my cheek. "Tell me honestly, are you feeling better?"

"Yes, Padre," I said. I was anxious to know why we were here. If it was only about me, Paolo had no need to be here. I heard him shuffle his feet next to me.

"Hm." The rector held me in his gaze. "Does this mean that you have considered your future and have reached a decision?"

I pulled myself up to my full height and looked him in the eye. "I shall finish my training, Padre."

A satisfied smile slid across his face. "Good," he murmured. "Excellent." Then he turned to Paolo. "And you are well, giovani Brunetti?"

"Certainly, Padre," he answered quickly. "Very well."

But the rector was not in a hurry. "Good." He walked over to a large armchair and, as he sat down, he kept us firmly in his gaze. "I have not, as you may have been aware, summoned you just to discuss your state of health."

"No," blurted out Paolo. "I hope not."

The maestro chose to ignore his rudeness. "The school was honoured this morning with a visit from somebody of noble birth." He paused.

"We saw the Prince De Medici arrive," I said.

"Indeed. In fact, he came for you," said the rector. "To invite you to visit his estate in Pratolino. He heard you sing several days ago at a funeral."

"He really does want us!" said Paolo, rashly.

"He knows how reluctant we are to accept such invitations," said the rector. "Countless days away from your studies…" He shook his head. "That is extremely bad for your progress."

"We could practise there, couldn't we?" I feared the worst, and suddenly I was certain I wanted to grab this chance. I wanted to go to Pratolino! To sing for the prince, together with Paolo.

"There is no singing tutor in Pratolino who is familiar enough with the vocal development of sopranists," said the rector. "At least…"

Paolo and I would have liked to drag the words from his mouth.

"At least…" Paolo encouraged him with a trembling voice.

This time the rector did not overlook the matter. "You forget your place, Brunetti. You are verging on rudeness."

"He's sorry, Padre," I said quickly. "And I am too, should I have said something amiss. But we are so anxious to learn what you have decided!"

The grimace around the rector's mouth relaxed a little. "I can imagine you are, my boys. We have never had such a noble visitor before. And yet…voices like yours are a rarity." He stroked his chin thoughtfully. "The staff of the conservatory will announce the following to the prince's representative tomorrow: you may leave for his estate in Pratolino, on the condition that maestro Perro accompanies you."

"Yes!" Paolo jumped for joy. "We can go! We can go!"

"Thank you, Padre," I said. My insides were on fire, with a heat fiercer than any I had ever felt. Not even when I was chosen to sing for Pope Clement, so long ago. We were going to Pratolino!

24

The carriage with the golden coat of arms stood waiting for us at the main entrance to the conservatory.

"Signori?" said the footman who held the door open for us.

I suddenly remembered the carriage that had run me down so many years ago on the outskirts of Fiesole. Had it been this carriage? And was this the same coachman and footman who had then laughed at the little boy who had ended up in the brambles?

I could not suppress a grin. Who would ever have thought that I would ever sit in a carriage like this?

"Thank you," I said. The footman threw me a strange look.

"There's no need to thank him," hissed Paolo. "I bet the people he normally carries hardly know he exists."

I shrugged. No matter how high I may reach as singer, I would never forget I was born in a tiny house, the son of a tanner who had worked himself into his grave for his family.

During the trip, I pressed my nose against the window. The fields, the lonely farms, farmers and their wives travelling with their goods. We galloped past everything so quickly that we barely saw the expression on people's faces. Only now did I understand that the coachman may not have noticed me at the time, or in any case until it was almost too late. But that didn't explain why they had laughed when I landed in the brambles.

The trip flew by and we soon arrived at the city gate of Fiesole. I felt a lump in my throat when I saw it. My town! I was born here. I had played and worked here. This was where my sister and my aunt lived. I tried to take it all in. Wasn't that the wall from which the stone fell that killed my mother? Wasn't that the place, just round the corner, where Padre Matteo Battista took me to the barber? I could hardly breathe.

Paolo nudged me. "Hey Angelo, isn't this where you come from?"

I nodded, scared that I wouldn't be able to say a word.

"Seems a nice enough town," said Paolo. "Not as fine or as large as Florence, but still…"

Shut up, I thought. I wanted to be left alone with my thoughts, with my memories. I had not been this close to my sister in four years. Mariana. How was she? Would she want to see me? Could she forgive me?

For the second time in just a few days, I had the burning desire to see her and Zia Ignatia. To feel their arms around me just for a moment. To be at home…

Did I dare? Inside, there was a fight raging between my fear of my sister's reaction and my desire to see her. But if I didn't try now, would I ever try again? Would I have to accept for eternity that I had not only lost a part of my body but also my sister? On the spur of the moment I turned and tapped on the window. "Coachman!"

The footman turned round. "How can I help you?" he shouted above the clatter of the wheels.

"Can we stop here?"

"Stop?" Maestro Perro peered at me. "Do you not feel well?" he asked anxiously.

I did not reply. My throat felt the pain caused by the lump in my throat, almost cutting off my voice.

"You are expected in Pratolino," shouted the footman.

"This is his hometown!" yelled Paolo.

The footman consulted for a moment with the coachman and turned back to me. "Very well!"

Immediately the coachman pulled at the reins. Once he had stopped in a shady square in the middle of the town, I jumped out of the carriage. "My sister lives here," I explain. "I have not seen her nor my aunt in years. We will soon be near their house. I wish to visit them now that I am here."

"We don't have much time," said the coachman grumpily. I had clearly reminded him that I was not of the rank to which he was accustomed.

"Oh come on, man, let him have his way," said Paolo, butting in. "What difference does half an hour make?"

The footman shrugged his shoulders. "The horses could do with a rest." He threw a questioning glance at the maestro, who until now had said nothing.

"Well," he said now. "These young men are special guests of the prince. I should imagine he would like their wishes to be granted." He threw me a wink. "Such a visit need not take too long. I would also like to stretch my legs and give my stomach a rest. All that bouncing around..."

The coachman sighed. "Then I would suggest that the young man climb up here beside me to show me the way. You..." He pointed at his footman. "...you can take your place at the rear of the carriage."

"Very well." But before I could go and sit next to the coachman, the maestro pulled me to him. He grabbed the front of my coat and pulled it tighter around my chest.

"You sound a little hoarse, Angelino," he said. "Take extra care of your voice. You will need it during the coming days."

I nodded and tried to overcome the butterflies in my stomach. I climbed up onto the box with stiff legs and looked round me. "At the end of this street we must turn right," I said to the coachman. "We are going right through the town."

Paolo was right: Fiesole was small compared to Florence. It didn't take long before Prince Ferdinando De Medici's posh carriage pulled up at the end of the Vicolo Porettana. Just a short distance from where, years ago, I had seen signore Guagli's carriage waiting.

At once people appeared from every nook and cranny to find out what such a stately carriage was doing in the simple street, and particularly, who was in it.

Still with that odd feeling in my stomach, I jumped down from the box. Now I was here, I no longer hesitated. What will be will be. If Mariana and my aunt wished to disown me, then so be it. I had to see them!

I ran as fast as I could to the simple house where Zia Ignatia and my sister had moved after the tannery had been sold. "Mariana!" I shouted.

Immediately, an excited voice came from behind me.

"Montegne?" I heard the astonished gasp. "Angelo?"

I turned round. "Ciao, signore Luigi! Ciao, signora Constanza! It is me!"

"Angelo! How are you?" Signore Luigi and a few other former neighbours came toward me with their hands outstretched.

"Good. And how are you all?" I also wondered why Zia Ignatia and Mariana's door remained closed. Was this a sign? Had one of them seen me coming and decided to keep the door shut? My knees were knocking.

"The same, the same...But boy, how you have changed! I recognise your black birthmark and you still have your mother's nose, but otherwise..." Signore Luigi shook his head.

I nodded toward the house. "Where is my sister?"

Signora Constanza butted in. "She works in the laundry. I'll send my youngest to fetch her. Mario! Get Mariana Montegne from the laundry! And quick about it!"

"Thank you." I stared at the house, which was just a few doors from our old house. It was smaller than I remembered from when I lived here myself. "And my aunt? Does she work in the laundry as well?"

"My boy." The men lowered their eyes. Signora Constanza placed her hand on my shoulder. "My dear boy…"

"What?" My eyes darted from the men to the woman and back again. "What's the matter?"

"Your aunt died in January. She was kneading dough and then suddenly…She fell over and that was that."

Zia Ignatia, who had lived in our house since I was born. Who had washed Mama when she died. Who had raised Mariana and me and comforted us when Papa couldn't manage it. She was dead?

"She had a very nice funeral," said signore Luigi. "And a grave near your father's."

"Yes," said signora Constanza. "It was beautiful. Hers was the only one that day, so the padre had plenty of time for her."

"Angelo?" I felt before I saw that the maestro was standing behind me. A hand was placed against my back. "Are you okay?"

I took a deep breath and searched for something to support me.

"Concentrate on your diaphragm," said the maestro. "Then you'll be able to get your breathing under control. It will become bearable…"

Somewhere signore Constanza screamed: "Giorgio! Fetch a bowl of thin beer for your old neighbour! Quickly!"

"Think about your breathing," sounded the voice of the maestro again. "Breathe in…out…in…" His voice slowly helped me calm down.

"Angelo?" From the distance came a woman's voice. "Is that you, fratello?" She ran to him, holding up her skirt. Behind her ran the small boy who signora Constanza had sent to fetch her.

166

Quickly I wiped my hand over my cheeks. "Ciao, Mariana! It is me!"

"Fratello!"

My arms opened to greet her. My sister. My darling sister!

"Brother," she whispered in astonishment. "Angelo!"

I held her tightly as I took a step backwards. "I've just heard about Zia Ignatia. Why didn't you write to me?"

Her mouth twisted into a bitter smile. "It costs money to hire a writer, remember?"

"And there wasn't any?"

She lowered her eyes and did not reply. It wasn't necessary. My gaze slid over her. She had aged considerably since I had seen her last! She had deep lines on her face and grey patches everywhere. Her hands felt rough; her skin was chapped. She saw me looking and quickly hid her hands behind her back. "I manage, little brother. Do not worry about me."

"We keep an eye on her," said signora Constanza. "If necessary, we pitch in."

"Angelino." Mariana took my face in her hands and stroked my cheeks, my hair, my forehead. "Little brother, how you have changed...you're so tall."

I felt my body stiffen. Was this the moment she began to suspect? Uncomfortably, I tried to laugh. "That's how it goes with little brothers, Mariana. They grow up."

"But so..." Her eyes slid over me. "So beautiful..."

Very slowly I relaxed a little.

"But what are you doing here?" she asked.

"I was in the neighbourhood."

"With that carriage?" She nodded at the carriage with its prominent coat of arms of the De Medicis.

I smiled. "Prince Ferdinando has invited me to sing for him."

"So you've become good have you? The padre who came to get you promised our aunt that you would be."

Immediately I felt sad again. "Zia…"

"She would have praised the Holy Mother for what you have achieved," said Mariana.

"Yes…" I didn't know what to say.

"Eh," began Maestro Perro. "Excuse me for interrupting, Angelo, but may I remind you that we must be leaving in half an hour?"

"Oh yes, of course…we don't have much time. Mariana, this is my teacher, Maestro Perro." I turned round to Paolo, who was waiting nearby. "And this is another fellow traveller."

"Come," said my sister before I could continue. "Let's go inside. I want you all to myself in the short time you are here." She waved at the people in the street. "My brother is here! Angelo, the singer!"

I winked at Paolo, who was holding his nose. Only then did I smell the stench that hung in the street. I hadn't noticed it as I had a few days ago in the tanner district in Florence. Perhaps I had instinctively felt that the smells belonged in my old street. In any case I was pleased that the maestro didn't show his aversion, not even when we entered the tiny house, which smelled of dust and damp cloths.

"Paolo, Maestro Perro," I said as soon as we were alone. "This is my sister, Mariana."

She dropped a curtsy. "Welcome, gentlemen."

Paolo walked up to her and bowed. "Young lady, it is both an honour and an enormous pleasure. If I had known that this young fellow had such a beautiful sister hidden away in Fiesole, I would have come sooner."

Mariana giggled and for a moment I recognised my sister of old. Overcome with all sorts of confusing feelings, I threw my arm around Paolo's neck and wrestled with him. "Be grateful that he did not discover you sooner, Mariana! He's the biggest troublemaker in the whole school. Tell her, Maestro. Am I lying?"

"I'm afraid I must agree with that," said Maestro Perro drily.

"Ah!" shouted Paolo. "Dear signorina Montegne, do not believe them! They mean that I have the finest voice in the whole of Florence, the whole of Tuscany even! I am sorry for your brother, but my voice is many times purer than his."

The maestro smiled and the dark mood was lightened for a moment.

Mariana made hot milk with honey and served homemade bread with it. I hardly ate anything. With each mouthful I thought: is this the food that she has for the week? Are we eating up her stores?

An enormous feeling of guilt flooded over me. I had allowed myself to be wrapped up in my own shame and had left my sister to her fate. I should have been there for her, should have known the condition she was in. How could I leave her alone again? Wasn't my place here, with her? But what about the prince? He was expecting us.

"Angelo?" sounded the voice of Maestro Perro. "The half hour must be over by now. We have to continue."

I sighed, took Mariana's rough hands in mine. "Listen. In a few days I will be travelling through Fiesole again. If I can, I will come to you. In the meantime, I shall think of a solution for you, all right? I do not want you to be so alone, to have to work so hard."

She shook her head. "Do not worry about me, fratello," she said again. "I would love to see you, but not because you are worried about me."

"But I shall still think about your future. You are my sister!"

She nodded and lowered her head, leaning it against my chest.

"Mother Mary must have sent you," she said. "This week, I have been longing for you to be here, and here you are."

"Perhaps I felt it..."

"Until next week, brother."

Paolo stood up. "We must be leaving, Angelo. Say your farewells. The maestro and I will be going."

I freed myself from Mariana's arms. It was terrible to leave her behind in such a condition. But I would return next week, even if I had to walk all the way back to Florence.

25

The rest of the trip took place in silence. I paid no attention to the scenery rushing past, but brooded about my sister and the impoverished circumstances in which she lived. Dependent on the charity of neighbours…my sister! How could I have allowed this to happen?

If only there was a suitor around, vying for Mariana's hand. As a housewife she would only have to worry about housekeeping and looking after the children. And she would bring in some money as well, if she sold her tiny house and moved into her husband's home.

But my sister had given no indication of a candidate, and I knew nobody in Fiesole who I considered suitable for her. Without the others noticing, I put my hands together and sent a prayer of intercession up to Heaven. *Holy Mother Mary, protect my sister! I implore you. She is all I have left in this world.*

The carriage drew to a halt in front of the imposing doors of the Pratolino estate.

"Shouldn't we use the servants' entrance?" Ill at ease, I stared at our splendid surroundings.

"What do you think?" The maestro pushed us firmly toward the double doors. "We have been invited here as guests, and guests do not use the rear entrance."

As if by magic, the doors swung open at that very moment. A liveried servant gave us a slight bow. "I bid you welcome. You must be the company from Florence."

"That is correct," said the maestro.

"Would you follow me?" The lackey led us to a salon, where Prince Ferdinando De Medici immediately sprang to his feet. He walked toward us with open arms. "Ah, there you are at last!" He kissed Paolo and me on the cheek and nodded at the maestro. "Did you have a good journey?"

He listened attentively to the maestro and Paolo. I said nothing. Not just because the others were speaking, but also because the sad face of Mariana constantly drifted before my eyes.

Apparently the prince noticed my silence. He gave me such a long stare that perspiration broke out and I felt myself shrinking back to the child I had once been.

"Well," he said finally. "I am pleased the journey went so smoothly. The prelude to it had enough bumps, wouldn't you agree, Maestro?" He smiled and I dutifully did the same. "Rooms have been prepared for you on the first and second floors," continued the prince in a business-like tone. "Tonight you will give your first performance. I have already informed my court composer and harpsichordist, Scarlatti, that there will be a rehearsal this afternoon."

My eyes widened. "Is signore Scarlatti here?"

The prince nodded. "You know him?"

"Yes. And his daughter, although it has been a long time since I met her." I thought about my singing practice in the altar boys' changing room and the girl who had sprung up like a jack-in-the-box.

"The composer's daughter acts as his assistant. She goes wherever he goes, so you are sure to meet her here."

I smiled. "That was how it was back then." The idea of seeing Rosa Scarlatti again caused a stab of excitement. My dark thoughts slid into the background.

"Not a man of half measures," whispered Paolo when the prince turned to converse with Maestro Perro. "Tell me that my ears did not deceive me...was he talking about *the* Scarlatti? The great composer whose works we've had to study?"

Maestro Perro was now beaming from ear to ear. "I had already heard that Scarlatti was in your service. That this honour should befall me! How fortunate that my students already perform several of his pieces!" An anxious look came to his eyes. "I only hope he can appreciate our performance."

I only half listened to the conversation taking place around me. Rosa Scarlatti! Was she just as skinny as she was four years ago? Just as cheeky?

At that moment, the door opened. A lackey stood silently in the doorway.

"Yes?" asked the prince irritably. "Why do you disturb me and my guests?"

"Excuse me, your highness. Signorina Scarlatti has asked permission to welcome the guests."

That answered my question. Just as cheeky as ever.

Prince Ferdinando waved his hand indifferently in a gesture of permission.

A young woman sailed into the salon. She must have been standing behind the lackey, awaiting permission.

"Ooh," sighed Paolo.

I would never have recognised Rosa if I had not heard her name. In the years since our previous meeting, she had flourished. Her fiery eyes glistened as if made of crystal, her cheeks had filled out slightly, and her posture was as upright and elegant as if she were of noble descent.

With a smile she walked toward me. "Angelo Montegne!" she said, as she offered me her hand. "As soon as I heard your name, I knew there could be no mistake!" She inspected me, and I saw that she understood how I too had changed. Fortunately, it didn't seem to bother her.

But we did not have much time to renew our acquaintance. Paolo had recovered and could not wait to be introduced to her. "Paolo Brunetti, Signorina Scarlatti. It is a tremendous pleasure to meet you."

She gave a brief lady-like curtsy. "Grazie, signore Brunetti. I met Angelo years ago in Fiesole, when he could already sing so beautifully. I understand that, vocally, he and you have developed even further."

"We shall let you hear this evening," said Paolo politely.

All this time, I could not take my eyes off her. I was eager to hear what had happened to her and her father. Whether she still sang and whether she wanted me to listen to an *Ave Maria* again, so that I could now honestly admit I found it wonderful.

But the prince gave an emphatic cough. "Signorina Scarlatti, would you mind returning to your father now?" The prince rang a bell and immediately lackeys appeared with salvers filled with delicacies. "I imagine you are ready for a small bite to eat," he said to us. He apparently did not doubt that Rosa would obey his command, for he completely ignored her.

"I shall see you later," she whispered quickly in my ear. "We have a lot to catch up on!"

Immediately after the meal, Prince Ferdinando had us shown upstairs. My room was on a wide hallway on the second floor. I could not believe my eyes when the lackey opened the door invitingly for me. In the middle of the room stood an enormous bed with a canopy of translucent material. Soft carpets covered the floor and a small table stood against the wall, on which a jug and basin had been placed. On the other side of the room was a table with a carafe and two glasses.

So this is how a nobleman felt. The luxury, the peace, the freedom: Never before had I had a room to myself.

I tiptoed into the room, scared to dirty the beautiful carpets with my shoes. If only Mariana could see this! If only she could feel this thick carpet under her feet instead of the cold floor in that stinking, dusty house in the Vicolo Porettana! If only she and Zia Ignatia could have seen where I was now! Ah, my dear aunt, that kind woman who had so often clasped me to her breast until I felt as if I was suffocating in that soft mass of flesh. The woman with whom I had always felt safe…

A knock sounded. I stiffened. Should I open the door? Perhaps there had been a mistake. Should I have been shown to a room in the attic?

Again there was a knock, louder this time. I opened the door slightly and peered through the crack.

"Rosa!"

"I had to see you." She turned and peered down the hallway. "Can I come in before somebody sees me standing here and starts spreading stories?"

I stepped aside and she slid past me. "What are you doing here?"

Triumphantly she raised her face. "Did you think I'd let myself be chased away by Prince Ferdinando? I want to hear all that's happened to you from the moment you were chosen to sing for Pope Clement. Did it go well? Did he compliment you? When did you decide to go to the conservatory? And…" She gestured to my waist.

I lowered my eyes. "Don't you know?"

"What?" She dropped into a chair and looked at me with wide eyes. "What don't I know? Tell me everything! What is the pope like, the one who forbids girls and women to sing? Is he ugly? Has he got black pimples on his face? Does his voice sound like a hoarse crow?"

"No idea. I didn't see him."

She frowned. "Didn't you sing for him? Were you ill? I know the pope visited Fiesole. I read about it."

I sat down opposite her. "It's a long story, Rosa. Are you sure you want to hear it?"

"Of course I do! Get on with it."

For the next quarter of an hour, I related everything that had happened to her since I won the competition to sing for the pope. I told her about the extortion that had cost us the tannery, about Papa's sudden death, and what had happened to me at the barber's.

Rosa listened in silence. Each time I looked at her, I saw the hazel-coloured eyes with the speckles in them that I remembered from long, long ago when everything was so different. Now those same eyes betrayed concern, sorrow, and indignation.

When I had finished, she punched the arm of her chair. "My father and I never knew that! If we had suspected…" She stared ahead for a moment. "You were far the better of the two, but that Gaetano was the one who sang the solo?"

I nodded. "Not that I gave a damn. When I first arrived at the conservatory, all I ever asked myself was whether singing was what I really wanted. I no longer thought of my voice as a blessing, even though my mother had always said it was."

"Those two priests were certainly prepared to do everything necessary to get you to Florence. And they were in a hurry. How old were you? Twelve?"

I nodded.

"Almost too late to prevent the change. But that chance…to perform for the pope." She sniffed. "All this time I've been wondering how you did. And now I hear you didn't even do it!" She shook her head. "Just wait until Papa hears this."

A silence fell. I saw her hand move over her knee in my direction. My mouth became dry.

"I saw immediately, by the way, that you were cut," she said, as if it were the most normal subject in the world. "I recognised your smooth skin, your height. Although, for a sopranist, you're not that bad. How tall are you? A head taller than me?" She narrowed her eyes and stared at me. "So what does it mean, actually? Are you capable of..." She hesitated for a moment. "...loving a woman?"

The flames engulfed me as if somebody had held a burning torch against me. "Loving? You mean..."

She stood up, towering above me, and pointing her fingers in challenge at my face. "I mean exactly what I say. I am not used to beating about the bush, or don't you remember that?" Her fingers caressed my forehead, my cheeks, the side of my neck.

I swallowed. Was this real? Was Rosa real? The room began to spin before my eyes. Was I dreaming this, on some early morning in the boarding school? Would Gregorio suddenly come running in?

"All these years I have dreamt of the boy with the golden voice who wanted nothing of me," I heard Rosa say. "I wanted nothing rather than to meet you again. And now you suddenly appear here...a gift from God."

I jumped up in total confusion. "Wait!" This is not how things were supposed to happen. Where was the romance? I, who was supposed to seduce the girl of my choice with sweet songs.

And why was I on fire from top to toe? Why was I shaking? Why did I want to flee yet, at the same time, reach out my hand to her?

With a start, I turned my back on her. "You should go," I mumbled. "Now. Please."

"Are you embarrassed?" I heard laughter in her voice. "No need."

She touched my back, allowed her fingertips to trace down my spine. Involuntarily, I closed my eyes and shivered.

At that moment, I heard Paolo at my door. "Angelo? Are you here?" He knocked. "Angelo! Do you need to rest your bones like some old man or shall we go and rehearse?"

"It's Paolo," I hissed.

Rosa shrugged. "So open the door."

"But "

Without hesitating, she opened the door. "Hello, Paolo."

"Oh," I heard him say. "Wrong room. *Scusa.*"

"I don't think so." Rosa took a step to one side and let him into the room.

"Angelo!" His eyes were almost bursting out of his head. "What's going on here?"

My head still felt as if it would explode at any moment. Inconspicuously, I shifted the doublet so that it covered the front of my trousers. "Rosa came by to reminisce," I mumbled.

"Oh, yeah?" I saw from his look that he didn't believe me. "Without a chaperone? In your bedroom?"

I shifted my feet. "So you wanted to rehearse?" I asked, trying to relieve the tension. "Are we allowed into the music room?"

"The prince said the room was ours when we were ready. I have rested enough."

"My father is still sleeping," said Rosa. "He needs longer afternoon naps these days."

"We can rehearse without the accompaniment of a harpsichord," I said.

"Apparently you two do not need accompaniment for anything." Paolo still did not seem recovered from his amazement. He looked directly at Rosa. "So, are you really the daughter of the great composer Scarlatti?"

"Indeed," she said. "We travel to many courts. We spent some time in Rome with the high clergy, then moved on to Naples for the viceroy of Spain. And now we are here with Prince Ferdinando. Papa is composing some pieces for him."

"We have studied music by your father," said Paolo. "*Caldo Sangue,* for example." He straightened his back and tried to impress Rosa with the first few lines.

"Papa composed that piece especially for cut ones," she interrupted him. "But women can also sing it." She sang the next few lines in a pure and stately voice.

I laughed and clapped. "She got you there, Paolo. She sang every bit as good as you!"

He wasn't bothered. "Perhaps we can sing together some time?" he asked bluntly. "Your voice and mine...We will sing the pants off everybody."

Rosa laughed but did not commit herself. Thank goodness.

"So you are still singing," I said, quickly changing the subject. "Despite the pope's prohibition."

She stuck out her chin. "What do I care about the pope? I sing when I want to. And if nobody wants to hear me, I do it for myself."

Paolo now seemed quite at ease with my unexpected guest. "That's what I like to hear!" He raised his hands in the air. "Praise be the men and women who despise rules!"

Was he trying to win her over, just as he did with the kitchen maids at the conservatory? "Do you want to rehearse or not?" I snapped.

"I have to get back to lay out Papa's clothes." Rosa opened the door, peered down the hallway and slipped away.

As soon as Rosa was gone, Paolo's attitude changed. "So." He dropped onto the bed. "Confess, my friend."

I took my music from my pouch. "There's nothing to confess," I said. "Come on."

Without waiting for him, I left the room. I quickly heard his footsteps behind me. "So she only came to 'reminisce'?" He grinned. "How quickly you've forgotten that stupid maid at the Verde house. Come on tell me..." He pulled at my sleeve. "Did you touch Signorina Scarlatti? Did she touch you? Was it as good as when you do it yourself?"

"Filthy monster!" I pulled myself free and quickened my pace. "Do you think the maestro has brought *Caldo Sangue* with him? Perhaps we can perform Scarlatti's piece this evening, if the maestro agrees."

"Don't try to distract me. I would never have thought this of you, Angelino!"

The worrying situation in Fiesole seemed far away when Paolo and I, wrestling and messing about, reached the music room which overlooked the estate's gardens. The room was round, with various entrances and a high, painted ceiling. Several musical instruments were waiting there: a couple of violins on stands, two harpsichords, a horn, and a trumpet.

Right in the middle of all these instruments stood another harpsichord, a particularly fine example made of dark lacquered wood with narrow, turned legs. The lid was open, and a man was bending over its interior.

"The technician?" I whispered.

"Must be," said Paolo. "In any case, he won't mind us rehearsing."

"Leave it to me," I said. "Signore..." No answer.

Grinning, Paolo gave me a nudge. "Leave it to *me*." Purposefully stamping his feet on the ground, Paolo went over to the musical instrument. "Signore!" he said loudly. "Signore, can you hear me?"

The man hit his head with a loud bump on the lid of the harpsichord. "Ouch! *Porca miseria!*" Scowling, he rubbed the back of his head.

Paolo grinned.

"We didn't intend to startle you," I said quickly. "We are students from the conservatory in Florence. Prince Ferdinando told us we could practise here for our performance this evening."

"He told you that?" The man's face turned glum. He turned to the instrument at his side. "And you really have to do it now? I would love to tinker further. Now that I'm this far."

"I heard the clock strike four," interrupted Paolo. "The afternoon is almost over."

The man gave a deep sigh. "Well, if that's the way it is…" He shuffled to a cabinet, fumbled around in it and pulled out two small pieces of cloth. "As long as you don't bother me," he said as he pushed the rags into his ears. He turned his attention back to the harpsichord as if we didn't exist.

"Crazy things are going on," said Paolo, softly. "You and that girl, this man acting as if he's gone off his rocker…"

"Like you're so innocent?" I said.

His eyes began to glow. "Well, I could tell you a thing or two, Angelino!"

"Not interested."

He smirked. "Of course not. You've got your own little darling hidden away here in Pratolino. And what a darling she is!"

I didn't react, but couldn't prevent myself from conjuring up Rosa's beautiful eyes in my mind. A shiver ran down my spine.

We moved as far away from the man at the harpsichord as possible and started practising our scales.

Halfway through our exercises, Alessandro Scarlatti came in. I recognised him immediately; he had hardly changed since the last time we met. Still just as flamboyant, he was a man you simply could not ignore.

Rosa was walking behind him. The provocative look in her eyes was enough to set my cheeks on fire, and I immediately turned away from her.

"Ciao, Angelo. Ciao, Paolo," said Rosa.

My friend grinned conspiratorially. "Ciao, *bellezza*."

"Are you going to sing?" Enthusiastically, she clenched her fists. "I'm so curious to hear how your voice has grown, Angelo! The pure sound of the little boy you used to be is still firmly etched in my memory!"

"I thought I had already heard the voices of these lads." Signore Scarlatti smiled. "Out in the hallway." He placed his folders on a table against the wall and turned back to shake our hands. "How wonderful that we should meet again, Angelo! Four years ago, who knew that we would have such an opportunity!"

"No, signore." I gave a slight bow. "I hope that you are well."

Right on cue, Maestro Perro came into the room. There was still traces of sleep on his face. He went straight over to Rosa's father. "Signore Scarlatti, what an honour! What an indescribable honour to meet a dignitary such as yourself. I am a great admirer of your work. I have taught several of your pieces to my pupils at the conservatory."

"You are too kind." Scarlatti bowed courteously. "Since we are passing out compliments, I would like to praise the training you have given these young men."

"Ah well..." The maestro smiled modestly. "The Florence conservatory does the best it can."

Scarlatti turned to the man with the wild hair who barely seemed to notice our presence. "Have you all met signore Cristofori?" asked Scarlatti. "This man will amaze the world with his invention." He walked to the harpsichord and placed his hand on the back of the man hiding under it. "Bartolomeo?"

Signore Cristofori again pulled his head from inside the instrument. He looked round in confusion.

Scarlatti laughed and pointed at his ears. Cristofori understood him immediately and pulled the rags from his ears. "Alessandro," he said apologetically.

"Bartolomeo, let me introduce you to two boys who I expect will possess the same virtuosity that you have."

"Hmm," mumbled signore Cristofori as he gazed as Paolo and me. "Haven't I seen you two already?"

"But then we had not been introduced." Paolo did not add that we had thought of the man as "nothing more" than a technician.

I put out my hand. "His name is Paolo Brunetti; I am Angelo Montegne. We are sopranists from Florence."

Instantly, Cristofori turned to face us. "Sopranists? Why didn't you say so at once! Are you going to sing?"

"Rehearse," said Paolo. "As we were doing just now."

"I am exceptionally curious about the suppleness of your voices," said Scarlatti. "Do you sing *Le Violette?*"

"But of course," said Maestro Perro. "The piece is perfect for sopranists."

"Then let us hear it." Scarlatti sat down at one of the harpsichords and placed his fingers easily and elegantly over the keys. At the maestro's signal, we began.

Cristofori stood listening with closed eyes. Halfway through the piece, his fingers began to move and his eyelids tightened and relaxed. It made me feel uncertain. What in heaven's name was the odd man thinking?

Immediately after our final note, Rosa burst into applause, her father gave a satisfied smile and Cristofori look at us in delight.

"This…" he stuttered. "…this is exactly what I want to capture!" He jumped up and rushed over to his instrument.

Confused, I stared at the inventor's back. Capture? What did he mean?

Cristofori began to hit the keys on his harpsichord as if he were not part of this world. His ear was bent toward the cabinet, he seemed to be listening very carefully.

After the first notes, I did that as well. My hair stood on end and a shiver crept up my calves, over my thighs and stomach, and into my neck. "What is this?" The harpsichord sounded different from what I was used to. Softer, much softer.

And then again louder. Much louder.

The maestro opened his eyes in amazement. "Is this…" He ran over to signore Cristofori's harpsichord and bent panting over the open cabinet. "This is that new instrument! I have heard talk about it! That I may see this. My God, what a day!"

"This, my boys, is the new keyboard instrument that master Cristofori has developed the pianoforte!" said signore Scarlatti.

Paolo stood looking at that thing as if in a trance.

"But it looks just like a harpsichord!" I squeaked in astonishment.

"Inside it's different. Come." Scarlatti pushed me toward the maestro. "Paolo, you too. Do you see the hammers there?"

It was difficult not to see them. Each time Cristofori hit a key, a tiny hammer would shoot up and hit a string. Sometimes softly, sometimes harder.

"Those hammers," said Scarlatti, "make the difference between the harpsichord and the pianoforte. That makes it possible to play sounds at different levels."

"And that," said Rosa triumphantly, "is exactly what the human voice can do. You demonstrated it beautifully, you and Paolo." She laughed. "Cristofori takes his inspiration from the human voice. And who masters that better than a sopranist? Do you now understand why he is so thrilled with you?"

"But I have never heard anything so incredible! It's like sorcery." Paolo stroked the dark wood of the cabinet with his fingers, as if he wanted to convince himself that the instrument actually existed.

"It is wonderful!" sighed maestro Perro.

"It is instrument of the future," summarised Scarlatti. "And Cristofori is still not completely satisfied. He tinkers with the mechanism day and night. At the moment, he is the only one who is able to conjure up such beautiful sounds. But whenever he allows me, I practise my touch. Prince Ferdinando has commissioned me to write a piece for the pianoforte." He licked his lips. "The most challenging assignment of my career!"

"Oh, and I'm so looking forward to hearing the instrument with your voices," swooned Rosa. "It must be splendid!"

"Let's begin," said Paolo immediately.

Without a moment's hesitation, we started *Le Violette* again, this time accompanied by the pianoforte. Soon we become so involved in singing the piece time and again, that we did not notice that Prince Ferdinando had entered. He was standing there, both hands leaning on a walking stick with a golden knob, looking at us all. As soon as Cristofori had played the last note, he turned round and left the room as he had entered it: in silence.

That evening, the practice room was transformed into a concert hall. Burning torches hung along the walls and they gave just enough light for reading the music. The instruments that we did not need had been pushed against the wall; only Scarlatti's harpsichord and Cristofori's pianoforte were left standing in the middle of the room. Fifty armchairs were lined up along one side.

The maestro paced nervously back and forth. "You can do it, boys," he kept saying. "This will be your breakthrough!"

Composer Scarlatti was not in the least excited. "Let us hope that my old-fashioned instrument will not disappoint the visitors," he sighed, while sweeping back his red cloak. "Once they have heard the pianoforte, I'll be done for."

Rosa was not there. Since she would not be performing and her father had, at that moment, no need for her, she was enjoying the banquet that the prince was offering his guests prior to the concert.

Strangely enough, I missed her. I constantly caught myself gazing at the entrance to the hall to see whether she had come in.

When the time of the performance drew near, Paolo and I took our places behind two heavily embroidered curtains separating part of the room. The space behind it served as a changing room and waiting area. We were wearing our conservatory clothing: the white cassock and over it, the blue choir smock. They had been washed and starched just before we left, and the shirt in particular felt like a rigid piece of rough wood. I ignored the scratching on my neck which gradually became more painful. In my head, I was already thinking of the music that we would be performing; at least, I tried to concentrate on it. Fortunately Paolo and I could fall back on our experience. We had sung the pieces we would be performing this evening so often that they were no longer a difficult challenge. But we hadn't had to sing them in front of an audience like this before one that had assembled especially to listen to us. That certainly made all the difference.

The heavy curtains were pushed aside. "Excuse me," said a lackey in a golden livery. In his hand was a tray with several gold-rimmed glasses. "His Highness Prince De Medici offers you a glass of wine from one of his own vineyards. He asks you to drink to the success of this evening." He handed us the glasses, bowed, and left the area.

At the stroke of ten, we heard sounds in the room. I peeped between the curtains and saw lackeys opening the double doors. Two others were showing the guests to their seats. The women were wearing magnificent gowns with wide skirts which made it impossible to sit easily in one of the armchairs. They had to be assisted by the gentlemen accompanying them.

Between the guests, I spotted the upright figure of Rosa. She had pinned up her hair and was wearing a green dress that left her shoulders bare and revealed the soft curves of her breasts. Again I had that feeling in my stomach. What would have happened this afternoon if Paolo had not knocked on the door? Rosa had said she desired me. Me!

Slowly, a realization dawned on me. In the years past, I had thought of her. Dreamed of her. Just as I had of the other pretty girls I had met over the years. But to say that I had only desired Rosa in all that time? If I had expected to meet her again, yes, then perhaps. But how could I foresee that? She and I led such different lives.

I stared at her again. A smug fellow with a long, dark wig smiled intrusively at her and touched her for a moment. I had to suppress the urge to jump up and hit away his hand.

Why? What was the matter with me?

"It is nearly time, boys," said Maestro Perro. "Stand over here." He positioned Paolo and me next to each other. "Breathe deeply. Stretch your back. Place your hand on your diaphragm, feel where the air is coming from. *Nn-oooh.*"

We sang after him, although we didn't really need the exercise to find our voices. It was rather a way to make us concentrate on the concert. And perhaps I needed that more now than ever. My head was full of the events of the last few days.

Signore Scarlatti performed first, playing several of his compositions. All that time, we stood behind the curtain, waiting our turn. My hands felt wet with perspiration. I tried to listen carefully to what the famous composer was playing.

Then it was our turn. Amidst loud applause and excited murmuring, we strode to our places. When the sounds had died down, we began to sing and the world stood still. I no longer heard the accompaniment on Scarlatti's harpsichord nor the singing of Paolo, where we sang different parts.

In the deep silence that fell at the end of our performance, signore Scarlatti stood up. He bowed to the audience and made way for Cristofori. The hall filled with a surprised muttering. The guests apparently knew the status of the composer and were astonished that the celebrity gave way to that singular figure with an eccentric hairstyle. As the pianoforte was moved to the front and Cristofori checked the purity of the keys, I had time to look into the audience.

Rosa was breath-taking. She sat on the edge of her chair, chatting to her neighbour, blushing with pride, and gesturing enthusiastically with her beautiful, slim hands. A few men nodded approvingly at Paolo and me, and a woman farther along pursed her lips seductively when I looked at her. Quickly I turned away.

My gaze was caught by Prince Ferdinando. He was staring at me with half-closed eyes. When he saw that my attention was directed at him, he took a deep breath and tightly closed his eyes again. His index finger, with a conspicuously large ring on it, slid to his mouth and made circular movements.

I feel uncomfortable at that gesture and was relieved to see Maestro Perro giving me the sign that Cristofori had completed his preparations.

The piece we had practised that afternoon, accompanied by the pianoforte, caused surprised exclamations from the guests. Several stood up and pointed in amazement at the instrument, just as we had done this afternoon.

Prince Ferdinando said nothing. He listened to us in silence, but as soon as Cristofori lifted his hands from the keyboard, he leant back with a proud, satisfied smile on his face.

Calmly, Paolo and I accepted the compliments. We bowed again and again, until I lost count. Cristofori had disappeared without a trace; apparently the applause meant nothing to him.

When it was Scarlatti's turn to take a bow, we disappeared behind the curtain.

"Did you hear that?" beamed Paolo. "That was for us, Angelino! We've made it!" He jumped with joy. "I knew it! Be warned, you big bad world; Paolo Brunetti the magnificent is coming!"

I smiled, lifted my choir smock like a girl and curtsied. "What an honour, Paolo Brunetti the magnificent, that you wanted to stand at my side."

Maestro Perro was also delighted. "Wonderful!" he cheered. "I am enormously proud of you! When they hear about this in Florence...Let me embrace you!"

The curtain was pushed aside again. A lackey entered, once again with a tray in his hand. This time it carried a folded note.

"Signore Montegne." He bowed deeply and offered me the letter.

"For me?" I turned to the maestro in surprise.

"Take it, boy. Take it!" he said, encouragingly. His voice almost broke with excitement.

Carefully, as if it could turn to dust in my hand, I took the piece of paper. People had not often sent me letters. And none like this, on such fragrantly perfumed paper! I lifted the folded note to my nose. From Rosa?

"What does it say?" called Paolo.

The maestro tried to read it over my shoulder, but I turned so that nobody else could see its contents. This letter was for me! For nobody else!

With some effort, I deciphered the ornate letters.

Angelo, il mio amico, all the qualities I would possess, you have in one single body. Grant me the indescribable honour of entertaining you this evening in the privacy of my chambers. Il Principe.

My mouth became dry. From the prince? For me? Disappointment and confusion fought in my mind. Not from Rosa…but from Prince Ferdinando?

He invited me? Only me? What did it mean?

"Show me." Paolo tried to grab the letter from my hands. "Who sent it?"

Quickly I pressed the paper against my chest. "Nobody," I mumbled. "It is nothing."

"Ha!" Paolo grinned. "I bet it's from Signorina Scarlatti. That's why you are blushing!" Proudly he looked round. "You didn't know, did you, maestro Perro? The castrato and the composer's daughter!"

"Shut your mouth!" I wanted the ground to swallow me. Fortunately, just at that moment, a second lackey appeared with glasses of ruby red wine, and Paolo and the maestro fell on them greedily.

As they toasted the evening's success, I pulled off my choir smock and cassock and slipped out of the room to my sleeping quarters.

26

I paced up and down my room in my undershirt and knee breeches. What did the prince want from me? Why had he invited me? Only me?

Restlessly, I took a mouthful of wine that had been placed in my room. Under other circumstances, I would have fully enjoyed the sweet, intoxicating drink, but now...

Something hammered against the back of my temple, as if my feeling was warning me. But why? What did it have to do with the prince? I had felt it from the moment he had kissed Paolo and me in the Verde house. Something unmentionable.

But shouldn't I be grateful to him for what he had given me? Had I not experienced more today than I had in four years at the conservatory?

Again I swallowed a mouthful. Thank goodness they had left a full carafe; I needed drink, a lot of drink. I wanted to numb the confusion swirling around inside my brain. First Mariana and the death of Zia Ignatia, then Rosa and the pianoforte, and now the invitation from the prince...

What should I do? Accept it?

Could I refuse?

I paced around like a caged animal. To the wide window with the draped curtains, to the bed, to the table with the washbasin, to the table with the carafe of wine.

I could creep into the canopied bed and pretend I had fallen asleep. Or slip outside through one of the many doors and wander around in the park. The weather was fine. Why not? And only come back inside when all the candles in all the rooms had been extinguished.

My heart almost stood sill when I heard my name being called in the hallway. "Signore Montegne?" The polite voice of one of the lackeys.

I held my breath. Perhaps he would leave of his own accord if I did not answer.

"Signore!" Some fiddling with the door.

Holy Mother, he came in! I was suddenly bathed in sweat. "Yes," I mumbled in a sleepy voice. "Who's there?"

"Signore Montegne, the prince has sent me to fetch you."

There was your answer. No request, no choice. I was being fetched.

"I am very tired. Can you offer my prince my apologies?"

"Nobody keeps the prince waiting, signore."

I dropped to my knees, threw my arms round my head and rocked back and forth. Oh, God! The pounding in my head grew worse.

"Signore."

"I'm coming!" I called. "Give me time to put on my clothes." I stood up, my limbs as heavy as lead, and started preparing myself for a private visit to the prince.

The lackey did not leave my door until I had joined him. He almost grabbed me by the arm and pulled me through one hallway after another. I felt like a prisoner, not a guest in a princely residence.

After we had descended two flights of stairs, we arrived at the rooms of Prince Ferdinando. "Please go in, signore." He showed me into a salon and walked over to closed door and knocked on it. "Your highness, your visitor has arrived."

The door immediately swung open. Had the prince been waiting behind it? "Angelino, *il mio amico!*"

I gave a deep bow and waited for a sign that I may stand up again. I felt a hand on my shoulder. "Please feel welcome, Angelo Montegne," said the prince softly.

At first I hardly recognised the prince. He wore a shiny house gown over loosely fitting clothing and had countless wrinkles on his face which I had never noticed before. He also looked shorter, but that was probably because he was not wearing his tall wig.

"I am honoured that you have accepted my invitation," he said.

I could hardly say that I would have preferred to drink a mug of soapy water, so I thanked him.

"Please sit down." He gestured to a chair near a burning fire. "A glass of wine? Some thin beer?"

"Wine, please," I said, as I perched myself down on the edge of the chair.

The prince served me himself; there were no lackeys in sight.

"It is a pleasure to make your acquaintance personally." The prince sat down opposite me. "As soon as I heard you singing after the funeral of…" He fell silent and did not complete his sentence. "Then I felt that I wanted to hear and see more of you. And my feeling was correct. I drew intense pleasure from this evening's performance." He raised his glass and clinked it against mine.

"Thank you, my prince."

He smiled. "It's incredible that you are still only a pupil! Your voice already sounds so mature. And yourself." His gaze slid over me.

Uneasily I shifted in my chair. "We have already completed more than half of our training. My contract will end in three years" time, and Paolo's in less than that."

The prince's eyes glazed over with that look that I so detested. "I would prefer not to talk about your friend," he said slowly. "I do not think you comparable. Not only is your voice better, but also your presentation. Your back is straighter, your movements are…more professional."

"Thank you, your highness. As far as I am aware, you are the first to remark on that. Paolo and I always perform together."

"Incomprehensible!" He shook his head. "You should think about going on alone. When your careers start, you will certainly be separated. Your talents are too disparate. Concentrate on your own career, Angelo-mio. I foresee a golden future for you." He shifted toward me.

We were sitting as close together as Rosa and I this afternoon. Then that had filled me with a delightful confusion. And now? I didn't dare move.

"I could offer you a wonderful future, Angelo," whispered Prince Ferdinando in my ear. "I could take you into my house, as I have with signore Cristofori, signore Scarlatti, and many other great talents. What would you say to an annual stipend of 2500 florins?"

What was wrong with me? Was I hallucinating?

The orange-yellow flames in the fire flickered. Outside, an owl hooted. It was a long time since I had heard one; it must have been in Fiesole.

"I offer you a life in great wealth," said the prince. "With all the musical support you could wish."

I swallowed and forced myself to answer. "I feel…honoured, your highness." As inconspicuously as possible, I slid back a little. "But as I just mentioned, my contract at the conservatory still has three years to run, I…"

"I can buy off that contract."

"That would be a great honour." I searched for words. "But I have considerable faith in my teachers. If they think that my training is not yet complete."

"Think about my proposal, Angelo. I can introduce you to the most prominent courts in Europe, hire the very best orchestras to accompany you, have an opera written for you."

Each word made me feel even more uncomfortable.

What he was offering me was something you could only dream of as singer. He was offering me the world! But what would it cost me? Would my father have refused this as well, claiming that the price was too high?

Again Prince Ferdinando brought his head close to my ear. I felt his breath on my cheek and from the corner of my eye I saw his lips approaching.

I thought of Mariana, who had seemed so desperate and needy. *Perhaps this is the solution you are seeking for her problems,* whispered my mind.

I could support her. She could stop the tiring work in the laundry and no longer be dependent on the generosity of the neighbours.

My thoughts again turned to Rosa, seated on my bed this afternoon. Full of interest for my life as castrato, full, too, of desire for me. At least, so it seemed.

The prince's hands slid up my arm and stroked my cheek, my chest, my stomach...

I endured the caress as if drugged. Something moved in my groin. Quickly, I shifted my position. My miserable, deformed body! It was betraying me, even as I was disgusted by those hands. Would it not even grant me my pride?

Suddenly, I felt terribly nauseous. I swallowed the expensive wine in one gulp and almost choked. "I do not know what to say about this great proposal, mio principe," I stuttered. "It is too much."

"You are worth it," he whispered with his eyes closed. "Heavens, how smooth your skin is."

I jumped up. "Please forgive me, your highness. I wish to think about your words. But my head...The performance and the journey here have tired me."

"You disappoint me bitterly, Angelo." The prince sat up straight. The desire on his face was quickly replaced with coldness. "Bear in mind that I shall not repeat this proposal. After your last performance the day after tomorrow, I shall expect your answer. Here. In this very room." He stood up and turned his back on me. He tugged at his satin dressing gown, pulling it straight. "Do not throw away your future. You will be making the choice between a glorious career and a future as church singer in a second-rate bishopric. I wish you wisdom."

I bowed deeply and remained standing until I heard the door close behind the prince.

I was so confused that I got hopelessly lost wandering through the second-floor hallways. A lackey who fortunately came out of one of the rooms saw my confusion and accompanied me back to my quarters.

"Can I perhaps offer you a warm honey drink?" he asked before he closed the door. "It will calm you down."

I accepted his offer gratefully. Seated on the edge of my bed, I drank it with small sips. The soft honey slid inside and eased my throat but not my mood.

If only I could talk to somebody about what had happened to me today. Who could I trust? To whom could I reveal my fear and doubt?

When the first rays of light penetrated through the gap in the curtains, I crept into bed. My fatigue, the soft mattress, and the warm blankets finally lulled me to sleep, my head resting on the place where Rosa Scarlatti had sat that afternoon.

27

It didn't seem much later when I woke with a start. My first thought was that everything had been a dream. Light filtered into the room through a gap in the curtains and gave everything a pink glow. From a table near the door came the delicious smell of freshly baked bread. Jugs with thin beer and juice, and all sorts of delicacies invited me to get up.

I awoke in a dream world. And in that dream world I thought: and why not? What had I to lose?

Yourself, said a voice in my head. Don't be so naive. You know what the prince expects.

Don't you want to get to know Rosa better? asked another voice. Don't you long to feel her arms around you?

Perhaps Rosa wouldn't want me at all, I tried to convince myself. Who can say whether she was just playing? But if I were to stay in Pratolino, I would see her every day. I would sing with Cristofori's mighty instrument and perhaps I would go down in history as the first sopranist for whom a piece with pianoforte accompaniment was written. I could insist that Mariana received an annual stipend, or even support her financially myself.

You would be at the mercy of the prince's whims, said the first voice again. Rosa would have to keep her distance. Is that what you want?

Immediately, that heavy feeling in my breast returned. What did I really want?

There was a loud knock on the door.

"Angelo!" I heard Paolo calling. "Lazybones! Are you alone this time?"

I quickly got up and opened the door for him. "Shhh…"

"Sleep well? I never want to leave here." Paolo pursed his lips. "Alone in a room, no panting boys around you. Delicious food." He waved his arms around. "This is the world I deserve, my friend!" His gaze fell on the untouched food. "Not eating that?" He did not hesitate for a second, walked over to the rolls, and stuffed one in his mouth.

As I watched him, a thought occurred to me. Prince Ferdinando had made it clear that he preferred me above Paolo, but if I really insisted on going back to the conservatory, wouldn't he make do with Paolo? He seemed so happy to be here that he would probably say yes without a second's hesitation. And the Prince's other wishes? Would Paolo have as much of a problem with them as I did?

Honestly speaking, I didn't know. Of course he played around in the dormitory, with himself and with others. I had seen him in someone else's bed often enough. Sometimes he made suggestive remarks to other boys or imitated movements in a way that left little to the imagination. And he was renowned for his adventures with the kitchen maids, sometimes with more than one at a time.

No, he certainly wasn't innocent. In any case, less innocent than I was. That *could* imply that he would be open to the prince's advances.

As I got dressed, I racked my brains. Did I want to sell myself, body and soul, for a sparkling career? For my sister? Or should I try, despite my mutilation, to carry myself with pride, worthy of my father's name? And if I did indeed decide to turn the attention of the prince from me to Paolo, how would I do that?

After our morning lessons and lunch, the maestro granted us permission to walk in the park surrounding the estate. He didn't have to tell us twice.

The prince's park seemed endless, much larger than the grounds of the estate of signore Verde. Next to the house there was a wonderful herb garden, featuring mainly kitchen herbs. I recognised the basil, thyme and rosemary Zia Ignatia used to use.

Terraces had been laid in various other places in the park. Here and there, fountains played in the air, each grander than the next, and there were enormous statues. It was a fantasy world with all sorts of strange creatures.

Just as we were admiring the gigantic statue of a squatting man on the edge of the water, I heard, much to my surprise, my name being called.

"Aha, your little sweetheart." Paolo laughed. "Shall I chaperone you or would you prefer to be alone?" He raised and lowered his eyebrows in a suggestive way.

"I have nothing to hide," I said. "Do whatever you wish."

Panting, Rosa caught up with us. "I've looked for you everywhere. I was hoping that we could sing together this afternoon."

"Together?" asked Paolo mockingly.

"I think it would be wonderful to let our voices sound at the same time," she said without false modesty. "I do not often get the chance of singing in parts. I am, of course, assuming that you have not suddenly become strict believers who object to women using their voices in any way other than for raising children."

"I am not the pope." Paolo made the sign of the cross. "Thank God."

"Of course we would like to sing with you," I said. "But we were actually just looking around these magnificent gardens."

"Thanks for the invitation," she said. "I would love to join you." She lifted her skirts and began leading the way. Stupefied, Paolo and I remained motionless.

"Did I miss something?" asked Paolo.

"No." I stared after her. "But she lets nobody stand in her way."

Rosa continued walking without looking to see whether we were following. "Have you already visited the maze?" she called back to us over her shoulder.

"A maze? Here?" Paolo's voice rose in excitement and he rushed after her. "I've always wanted to visit one."

Rosa led us to the west side of the park, where tall hedges formed the side walls of four paths which, from a central point, led deeper into the greenery. "Each of these paths has turnings which do not allow you to see where you are going. If you choose the correct route, you will arrive at the centre of the garden and find a surprise awaiting you."

"What is it?" I asked.

"You'll have to find that out for yourself."

Paolo's eyes sparkled. "What shall we do? Each of us take a different path?"

"That'll be the most fun," said Rosa. "Whoever reaches the middle first will wait there for the others. Agreed? I'll take a path I've not tried before to make it more exciting."

I would rather have searched for the surprise with her, but she had already walked off.

"I'll take that entrance," said Paolo pointing. "That leaves those two for you." He waved farewell and set off.

I took the far left path. All four looked the same. What difference would it make if I took the far left path or the other one?

At first, I could still hear Paolo. He called, sang, and whistled until his voice gradually grew softer and finally faded.

The hedges on either side of the green path towered at least three feet above me. There were the sounds of bids singing and rustling in the greenery. A few times, a frog sprang off in front of my feet; there must be water somewhere near.

All in all, the lonely walk through the maze was an odd experience. The sounds calmed me down. As I listened carefully to the bird song, I was able to recognise the various species and their different pitches. Together with the croaking of the frogs, they formed an almost playful composition. If I had been in Florence, I would have asked our composition maestro whether the sounds of nature had ever been a source of inspiration for a musical work. Perhaps he would even have helped me compose such a piece myself.

I would have liked to lie down somewhere and allow all the sounds to wash over me, but I couldn't do that of course. Rosa and Paolo would be waiting for me. So, without hurrying, I turned one corner after the other. I had no idea whether I was walking toward the others or away from them.

After the umpteenth corner, I suddenly came face to face with Prince Ferdinando. He was leaning motionless against the trunk of a cypress tree and looking at me.

"My prince!" I almost fell on my face when I tried to bow. "What a surprise..." Was this what Rosa had meant by the surprise in the middle of the garden? If only I had known!

"The pleasure is all mine," said the prince. "In fact, you pay me a compliment when you enjoy my gardens. I was actively involved in every detail of their design."

"They are beautiful," I said, to hide my confusion.

Prince Ferdinando looked round. "Where is your friend?"

"Paolo and I each chose our own path. Signorina Scarlatti is also walking around somewhere." In the depths of my heart, I was hoping that Rosa would suddenly jump out from around a corner, especially when the prince began to walk toward me with that brooding look in his eyes. I had to suppress the urge to back away.

The prince stopped right in front of me, his eyes boring into mine. "So, the young lady is also one of the party," he said slowly. "You two get on well, do you not?"

"Rosa and I have a lot to talk about."

He nodded and kept staring at me. My cheeks began to burn

"They're waiting for me, my prince," I said quickly. "If you will permit me…" I gestured toward the path.

He nodded. "Then I wish you a pleasant stroll." With his hands clasped behind him, he walked past me and disappeared among the greenery.

The meeting drained all the pleasure from the walk. I was happy when I finally arrived at the fountain in the middle of the maze, where the others were awaiting me.

28

The concert on the second evening went even better than on the first. Once again we had a surprise. During the rehearsals that afternoon, Rosa had impressed everybody with her songs. Her father and Maestro Perro immediately agreed to have her sing that evening with Paolo and me, and to let her sing a solo. After all, there were no clergy among the guests who could object.

Although the audience was initially just as reticent as when Cristofori appeared the evening before to play his pianoforte, the guests soon fell under the spell of the singing beauty. They jumped up and applauded at the top of their voices.

When the last guests had left, the prince invited all of us, including Rosa, to attend him in his room for a small meal. That turned out to be an enormous table, overflowing with the finest delicacies.

Paolo nudged me. "Do you remember?" he said. "All those snacks at the Verde family's house? That seems ages ago."

"Yet it was actually only two weeks." I again saw Carola before me and again felt a flash of pain at the memory. Quickly I pushed it away. "Now there's nobody telling us not to eat the food," I said. Strange, I thought, that life could so quickly take such a turn.

Prince Ferdinando took the tray from his lackey and offered each of us personally a glass of wine. "Ladies and gentlemen," he said. "First of all, let me sincerely congratulate you on what we have achieved in the past days, and what you will demonstrate twice again tomorrow. I am deeply impressed by your voices…" He raised his glass toward Paolo, Rosa and me. "…and by your compositions…" He raised his glass to the composer. "…by your conducting…" He looked at the maestro. "…and by your remarkable invention!" he concluded, with a glance toward signore Cristofori, who modestly bowed his head.

"As a token of appreciation, I have brought a gift for each of you. Signorina Scarlatti, would you please come forward?" A lackey held out a gold tray, draped with a dark, soft fabric. On that soft fabric were six boxes, containing the most beautiful jewels I had even seen. Rosa was given a golden rose set with rubies, which perfectly matched her radiant face. For Paolo there was a tiny violin with fine strings that could produce real sounds. For signore Scarlatti, Maestro Perro and signore Cristofori there were miniature pianofortes, and finally, for me, an oval golden pin with the image of the Greek god Apollo.

"The Greek god of music," said the prince as he pinned it to my doublet. I was deeply embarrassed; all I saw was the nudity of the deity. The others clearly noticed it, too. Paolo had a strange expression on his face and Rosa frowned. She studied the faces of the prince and me as if she was trying to understand something.

Only the three elderly men acted as if nothing was amiss. "To the prince!" called Scarlatti. "To the patron of music!"

Everyone followed the composer's example and all the tension seemed to evaporate. But I couldn't relax. My hand constantly went to the pin, in an attempt to hide Apollo's nudity.

I didn't think I would ever wear the pin again after this evening.

During the rehearsal next day, there was no trace of Rosa. Before I could ask her father where she was, I read the annoyance in his face.

"Lord Almighty," he grumbled. "Where has she left that damned penknife? And the new music paper, where is it? Good heavens, why did she need to leave for Florence!" Impatiently, he fumbled among his writing equipment on the desk in the rehearsal room. "Would it have been too much of an inconvenience to wait a day?"

"She's gone to Florence?" asked Paolo. "She said nothing about it last night."

"Last night, she wasn't planning to go!" grumbled Scarlatti. "And nor was I! But if the prince orders something, well, who are we humble creatures to say that it is not convenient? That we have to prepare a wonderful finale for this evening, and also have to perform something this afternoon as well? That our assistant is indispensable for all that?" He threw down a couple of pages of music on his desk with such anger that they fell to the ground.

"We won't see her again today," said Paolo, casting me a sideways glance.

If he thought I would react, he was mistaken.

"Probably she won't return until late this evening," said Scarlatti. "If the trip goes to plan, that is. But no matter what, she won't be singing with us today." He took a deep breath and resumed his professional pose. "Well, boys, let's get back to business. Your maestro and I would like you both to sing one of my solos this afternoon, which I have written specially for sopranists. It is not too difficult. You should be able to learn it in a couple of hours."

"Wonderful!" Paolo beamed. "Then I can finally let the prince see what I am capable of, without my friend here constantly screeching next to me. May I read the piece?"

"Please." Maestro Perro handed it to us.

I was not really paying attention. Paolo's words had sown the seeds of a plan in my mind. In my mind, I saw the prince's brooding look, heard the desire in Paolo's voice. He knew exactly what he wanted: to make a career in a royal court. He would accept whatever was necessary to reach his goal. Even if that meant having to endure the prince's embraces.

Couldn't I persuade the maestro to let Paolo sing a charged solo? One which would certainly appeal to the prince?

"Maestro…" I cleared my throat. "My voice…"

Maestro Perro immediately started wringing his hands. "No… " he groaned. "Please do not tell me you have problems with your voice! Please don't do that to me."

"I have asked the kitchen for some hot water with honey." I couldn't remember ever having deceived the kind maestro, but it did not cause me any problem to alter my voice.

The maestro began pacing back and forth. He had a deep frown on his face. "Dear, oh dear, oh dear…"

Signore Scarlatti sat watching, a slightly amused grimace on his face. His moaning voice had apparently completely disappeared. "What are you worried about?" he asked. "You possess two magnificent voices. If we keep Angelo's role small this afternoon and look after his voice, we can depend on him again this evening. And Paolo can sing another solo. My piece can wait."

That signore Scarlatti! He was worth his weight in gold!

"I know what piece Paolo should sing," I said. "Do you remember the praise he received at the conservatory with *Dovrb dunque mollire* by Caccini?"

The maestro pushed me to one side. "You look after yourself, Angelo. Ask the kitchen if they can make an infusion of oregano, three-coloured violet and rosehip. Quickly now! And tie a cloth around your neck and chest. You must be ready to sing this evening!"

And so I had an unexpected free morning and Paolo rehearsed a piece that would hopefully seduce Prince Ferdinando De Medici to invite him to take a special place at court. Hopefully, my roommate would make good use of the chance to place himself in the spotlight.

That whole morning, I hung around in the park. I had taken my music with me and because there was nothing really the matter with my voice, I tried to practise for that evening's performance. Our last concert was to be the climax of our visit to Pratolino. The room would be crowded with guests of Prince Ferdinando: people were expected from Florence, Melta, and even from Cesena and Urbino. Most would spend the night in the prince's guest rooms.

It promised to be a wonderful evening. An evening when we would emphatically prove our talents to all the dignitaries from near and far. An evening on which we would make our names as masterful singers. Signore Scarlatti had heard that perhaps there would even be a royal music master from the Spanish court in attendance.

But above all that hung a sharp-edged sword, over my head: the prince's proposal. He would be expecting my answer after the concert.

I had slept badly in recent nights. I would constantly awake with a start, my head full of questions. And each time, the quickly fading faces of Mama, Papa, Zia Ignatia and the fatigued Mariana would dance before my eyes. And the face of Rosa Scarlatti.

I would see her before me longer than all the rest: first, the face of that skinny child that I had met long ago in the church in Fiesole and who couldn't care less about anything or anyone, and next the face of the beautiful young woman she had become. The face of the woman who had awoken my desire and given me the attention I had longed for all these years.

Could I exchange the arms of this girl around me for the arms of a prince and an opera written especially for me?

A shivering crept up my legs to my neck when I thought of it.

I wanted to hear a woman's voice whisper sweet things...not a stubbly chin that pricked my skin and a flat chest against my own.

But what about Mariana then? Could she get a job at the conservatory? In the kitchen, perhaps? When I thought of the way the other students treated the girls, about the pregnant kitchen maids, the thought did not agree with me.

Was there another possibility?

I took my music folder again. Tonight we were to sing pieces by signore Scarlatti, alternating with pieces by Palestrina, Carissimi, and Monteverde. The maestro would accompany us on the violin. I knew he would be nervous, despite all his experience, and to that I had added the concern about my voice. Probably he was at that very moment still restlessly pacing back and forth in the music room.

I did not feel at all guilty.

What would Paolo make of his solo this afternoon?

It was true what I had said: when he had sung the Caccini piece before during an evening recital for the benefactors of the conservatory, he had received nothing but praise. Listeners had tears in their eyes and he was asked to repeat a small piece so that they could experience it again.

If anything could transmit a feeling of desire to the prince then it was the passionate music of Caccini.

Dovfo dunque morire
pria che di nuovo io miri voi, bramata cagion?
 Must I then die
without having seen you again, the source of my desire?

Would Prince Ferdinando allow himself to be entranced by a passionate Paolo? After this afternoon, would his proposal to me no longer be valid? In any case that would mean I would not have to bother about whether or not to accept his inviting promises. But what would I be giving up?

Again I imagined my sister before me. This time she was wearing a dark blue conservatory apron tied around her waist. And I saw Paolo's filthy hands accidentally touch her to attract her attention. Had his eyes left her for as much as a moment during our visit to Fiesole? And what about the other boys with their wandering hands?

Again I tried to concentrate on the music for this evening. Far behind me, I heard the rattle of cart wheels bringing new provisions for the kitchen. There were also carriages arriving with early guests who would also attend the afternoon concert.

I stood up, closed my folder, and walked to the concert room to listen to Paolo rehearsing.

Later that afternoon, I was prouder of Paolo than ever. He put his whole heart into his *Dovrb dunque morire* for the prince. He did everything except go down on his knees, but there was no doubt about it: he directed the plea in the love song to the man with the black wig on his head and the elegantly expensive clothing.

Even I, who knew what I could expect, felt the emotion prickling my eyes. Several of the guests sniffed. Others jumped up after the last note had faded away and started to applaud loudly.

I kept my gaze on the prince. I sat at the side of the hall and had a good view of his face. During the whole piece, a pleasant smile played on his lips. His eyes gradually narrowed as the song continued, and his attention was totally directed at Paolo.

Somewhere deep inside, it hurt slightly that Paolo seemed to be moving toward his goal. Certainly when, after the piece was finished, he took a few steps toward the prince, made a deep bow and presented him a red flower. The prince reacted by gallantly placing the hand holding the flower against his heart and nodding at him.

The rest of the afternoon, Paolo didn't stop beaming. "The world is at my feet!" he cheered. "Did you see his reaction?"

Not exactly the world, I thought, ambushed by my own jealousy. At the most, Prince Ferdinando De Medici! As if that wasn't enough. Did he not provide the entrance to the world of musical and noble celebrities?

Just before the start of the evening concert, Rosa rushed in like a whirlwind. "Papa, I'm here! Have you found the right clothes? Are the pieces for this evening in the right order?"

I could not suppress a smile. I noticed that everybody changed as soon as Rosa was around. Even the absent-minded Cristofori reacted more frequently to what was happening around him. Now and then I caught a smile on his lips although from his posture you could never tell whether he had heard what Rosa or one of the others in the room had said.

Signore Scarlatti turned on his stool. "Daughter!" he said with warmth in his voice. "I'm so pleased you have managed to get here on time."

She laughed. "You should have heard how I bullied the coachman! I kept on hanging out of the window to ask him to hurry up. I have never passed through the villages at such a speed before!"

"Then we may count ourselves fortunate that you are still alive," said her father. I thought the same. The images of a coach thundering through Fiesole appeared clearly in my mind. Could it have gone faster than the one I saw in my childhood?

Rosa kissed her father lovingly on the cheek. "It wasn't all that dangerous, Papa! We never once took a corner on just two wheels." Remorsefully she began straightening his coat. "I'm sorry I didn't have any time to lay out your clothes. We left so suddenly!"

Signore Scarlatti frowned. "Is something wrong with my clothing?"

"Well." She took a step backwards and looked at him appraisingly. "I would have given that shirt a little more starch."

Her father turned back to the harpsichord. "It'll do," he said. "Basta! What about getting changed yourself? The performance will begin at eight-thirty precisely."

"So! You think you can get by without my help?" Offended, she turned round. "Is that why I nearly drove the coachman to death?"

Signore Scarlatti winked at me. "Women! They always think the world will end if they are not around."

Paolo laughed. "Strange. I had the idea that the world would end when she came rushing in." The nervous tension before the performance was again broken by a moment of frivolity.

Only Cristofori did not join in the laughter. He was preoccupied with adjusting the mechanism of his pianoforte.

"Gentlemen," called the maestro. "Time to disappear behind the curtains."

For the fourth time that week, we stood behind the curtains, listening to the laughter of the guests arriving, the clattering of heels on the marble floor, the rustling of the wide skirts of the fashionable ladies.

"Do you think Rosa's dressed?" Paolo grinned as he whispered into my ear. "I can hardly imagine that in such a short time she can transform herself from a windswept, brutal street urchin into a princess dressed in silk! Don't women always need loads of time and a hairdresser?"

"There's no time for the latter," I whispered back. Various chamber maids and hairdressers had accompanied the guests. But it seemed to me that now, just before the performance, they all had their hands full. "Perhaps she will appear with that same windswept hair-do." I smiled at the idea. It would not surprise me if she paid little attention to any idea of beauty. That was exactly what was so fine about her: that she always remained her own insolent self.

Paolo crept up to the curtain and pushed it open slightly. "It's fuller than the other evenings!" he sighed. "And just look at the prince."

I huddled up close to him. Prince Ferdinando De Medici had never seemed so radiant. The wig on his head was combed up even taller than ever, his cheeks were powdered pink, and the coat he wore was embroidered with gold. The light from the many candlesticks and chandeliers seemed to set him ablaze. He made a truly radiant centre point.

"Are you ready, boys?" asked the maestro.

"Well, what do you know?" said Paolo, totally ignoring the maestro. "She's made it!"

I followed his gaze. Rosa was just entering. Despite the little time she had had, she had managed to twist her hair into an elegant style. Two sky-blue feathers arose from it.

"What a woman!" Paolo panted passionately. "And she offers herself to you? I know exactly what I'd do! Heavens above!"

With a dry mouth, I watched how Rosa walked through the room, looking for a place. Apparently there was no seat reserved for her as there had been on the previous evenings. There was no free place on the front row. When she passed the prince and politely nodded at him, he turned his head in the other direction.

She was sent off on purpose, I suddenly realised! She was not supposed to be here this evening. Why not in heaven's name?

I was deeply touched when I saw her searching all alone, without any of the gentlemen politely offering her their seat.

Finally, Rosa walked to the back of the room and sat down on a bench between several members of the court. She held her head proudly and leant sideways to exchange some words with her neighbour.

The prince raised a lace handkerchief and turned to look to the rear as he dabbed his nose with it. When he turned back again, a satisfied smile played on his lips.

Bastard, I thought. You're punishing her! Why? Because she is my friend?

"Boys!" hissed Maestro Perro. "You really must prepare yourselves now. Just a few more seconds. Take a deep breath, straighten your choir smock…"

Unable to concentrate, I followed the maestro's directions: I drew in my breath and slowly breathed out. In the meantime, I gazed at signore Scarlatti, who apparently was unaware that at that moment his daughter was being treated like one of the serving girls.

Apparently my attempt to shift the prince's attention to Paolo had not succeeded.

"Get ready! Paolo, Angelo, I will give you a sign from the hall. Keep your eyes on me."

Signore Scarlatti was the first to pass through the curtain. He took his place at his harpsichord and played a short piece by Palestrina. Then the maestro came on. His violin part began, soft and small, but soon took a dominant position beside Scarlatti's harpsichord. Then, to wild applause, it was our turn. I entered the room with lead in my shoes. I had the feeling that I disappeared into nothing next to Paolo, who strode in with a straight back and a proud look in his eyes.

Uncertainly, I searched for the maestro. He nodded at me encouragingly and I started precisely with Paolo with Ave Maria.

From that moment, I lost myself in the music and forgot all my worries.

As soon as I had sung the last notes, a shiver of satisfaction ran through me. For a moment, I had been miles away from everything bothering me. I had a mist before my eyes and the first thing I saw when that dispersed was the proud and glowing face of Rosa who stood applauding wildly at the back of the hall.

Other people stood up. Yet it was her blushing cheeks and the sky-blue feather that held my gaze captive.

I bowed deeply. Paolo bowed too and we backed off the stage behind the curtain.

"So!" Paolo clenched his fists and doubled over as if he had been punched in the stomach. But his face did not show any expression of pain. Quite the opposite; it was one of pure delight. "Did you see those faces, Angelino-mio? Did you hear them?"

At the same moment, the maestro entered, followed by signore Scarlatti who pulled Cristofori with him behind the curtain. "Young gentlemen," he said. "We have worked wonderfully well together!" He released Cristofori and grabbed first my hand, then Paolo's. "A storm rages in my heart," he said dramatically. "I feel euphoric after the concerts of the past few days, but also deeply sorrowful that after this evening those will be a thing of the past. My boys." He opened his arms. "Come here, *figli-mio.*"

Signore Cristofori watched, somewhat bewildered.

"Will you not miss it just a tiny bit, my friend?" asked Scarlatti.

"Of course," mumbled Cristofori. He was saved by Rosa, who entered through the curtains with her arms outstretched. "You were fantastic, yet again!" The feathers in her hair stuck out triumphantly above her head. "I am so proud of you!" She looked happily at me. "Although I naturally knew, all those years ago, that you were heavenly."

I smiled. Somehow I was relieved that it was over. Only that conversation with the prince…it weighed heavily on my mind.

"Are you going to take off your choir clothing?" she asked Paolo and me.

Paolo's eyes gleamed. "If that's what you want…" He began to raise his surplice.

"Joker." Rosa gave him a swat on the shoulder. "No. I mean that everyone is waiting for you, the respected students of the Florentine conservatory, and the other gentlemen in the salon."

Oh yes, that as well. The prince had sent word that he would be organising a party for us. Quickly Paolo and I took off our choir smocks and pulled on a jacket.

"Gentlemen?" came the voice of a lackey. "Will you follow me?" He pushed aside the curtain with his back and accompanied us into the salon, where the audience was still applauding.

"Ah, my stars! Scusa!" Prince Ferdinando quickly took his leave from his guests and came over to us. I bowed slightly, just like the others.

"A brilliant performance!" said the prince. "You have really moved my guests and myself." He made an extravagant gesture to the lackeys who were walking around with trays laden with delicacies. "I imagine you are ready for a small bite to eat. Please do not hesitate to help yourselves."

Without paying any special attention to me, he turned back to his guests.

"I haven't eaten anything since lunch," said Rosa next to me. "I want that whole tray-load."

"You'll never eat all that," said Paolo with a sideways glance at her slender figure.

She looked at him as if considering whether or not to prove him wrong.

Quickly I intervened: "Shall we start slowly?" I beckoned to the lackey, who immediately offered us his tray. I had come to appreciate the kitchen in the villa in Pratolino more every day.

But Paolo and I did not get the opportunity to indulge ourselves. Guests were constantly interrupting to pay us their compliments and to ask questions about our extraordinary singing voices. The ladies in particular approached us; the men remained at a distance, listening, and some threw us sympathetic looks.

Paolo monopolised the conversation. He boasted how high he could get with his voice, flirted seductively with the most beautiful women, and gleamed with pleasure from all the compliments.

When the first guests slowly left for their bedrooms, the prince's major-domo came over to me. "Signore? May I accompany you to your appointment?"

Rosa, who was standing next to me, looked at me in astonishment. "Appointment?"

"Ah yes," said her father quickly. "An evening like this is not simply for pleasure, but also for doing business. In this case, it would not surprise me if the young gentlemen from the conservatory were immediately contracted." He took his daughter by the shoulder and hauled her over to a cardinal who had been looking at him for some time.

If I had had the nerve, I would have asked Rosa to accompany me. But I did not have the nerve. And now it was too late: I saw only her back as she started talking animatedly to the man in the vermillion cassock.

The major-domo led me into Prince Ferdinando's study. I had not noticed his highness leave the salon, but there he sat, still dressed to the nines, in his chair.

"Be seated," he said to me. The major-domo left the room

without a sound. "May I first pay you my sincere compliments for your performance on this memorable evening? I am still convinced that you are the better of the two, although that beautiful piece that Paolo Brunetti sang this afternoon was utterly charming."

I already felt ill-at-east, now I also felt embarrassed. "Thank you. Paolo has never before…"

He immediately interrupted. "In memory of this evening, I have had a small gift made for you."

My face felt as if it would burst into flames when I took the tiny box.

"*Il mio principe*," I stammered. "You are too generous."

He smiled in satisfaction. "You are worth it, my friend." The prince watched as I opened the box and removed a beautiful ring set with rubies. I couldn't prevent myself from giving a gasp. I had never seen anything as beautiful as this, let alone owned it. I could not tear my eyes from it.

Before I had fully recovered, the prince said: "This afternoon, my envoy paid a visit to the Vicolo Porettana in Fiesole."

I looked up with a start. "What?" I forgot at once all norms of politeness.

"Your sister Mariana asked him to convey her love to you."

I opened my mouth and then shut it again. I felt myself growing angry. What, in the name of the Holy Mother, did this mean?

"My people provided her with fresh produce from our gardens. It seemed a nice gesture toward the only sister of the best singer of Florence and surroundings. I shall send her a visitor with some regularity to estimate her needs and to satisfy them. Tomorrow, the daughter of my cook will be leaving for Fiesole. She will take over the housekeeping from your sister so that she has some relief."

Poor Mariana. She most probably almost died with fright from such an esteemed visitor. Had it been the stately coach with the six bulbs that had wormed itself through our tiny street? What had she thought when she suddenly saw the vegetables and herbs on the table? Did she really want a replacement for Zia Ignatia?

Of course I understood what the prince was doing. He was like a spider who had trapped me in his web. He was beguiling me more and more, with his gifts and his attention and the visit to my sister. The question was whether I could still free myself. "I thank you, il mio principe."

"Now," said Prince Ferdinando. "Let us turn to the heart of the matter. I imagine that you have given my proposal some thought?"

I looked at the ring in my hands. "Indeed, mio principe." I looked for a way to postpone matters. I still had not reached a decision, and now I first had to process all this news.

The prince bowed forward, brought his head close to mine. "Do not keep me in suspense, Angelino. Tell me you have chosen me."

Him. He didn't beat about the bush. I looked at his large hands so close to me, the manicured nails on the fingers that flicked up and down as if they were playing the harpsichord.

I had to make a decision. Now!

"I will arrange the dissolution of the contract with the conservatory," whispered the prince. "Think of all the chances you will get. I shall introduce you to the European courts, have an opera written for you. I shall cherish you and overload you with gifts. I shall send your sister assistance and money so that you need never have any concerns about her…"

That proved decisive. "Il mio principe…" I whispered. "I thank you for your generosity. I am pleased to accept your proposal. Only…"

The prince did not give me the chance to say anything. He jumped up and pressed his head against my shoulder. "Tell me," he insisted. "I shall do everything for you! Everything! The heavens be praised. Thank you, Holy Mother, for this great gift!" His wig shifted on his head and for a moment I asked myself whether I could change my mind. I imagine Rosa's accusing look when she heard of my association with his man. What had I done? God, to what had I allowed myself to be seduced?

But the prince gave me no chance to retract my words. His lips pressed against my cheeks, my chin, my nose.

"My prince," I whispered, "allow me to finish this year at the conservatory. Let me become accustomed to the new situation. Please be patient with me. I…"

He took my face in his hands. "Your yes is enough for now. I shall control myself, temper my love. Tomorrow I shall commission Scarlatti to write a magnificent opera for you. I will give you the time until the opera is ready. From the première, you will be mine, in heart and soul. Can you agree to that?"

I bowed my head and nodded. I couldn't claim that the prince did not do everything to try to please me.

As soon as I entered the salon, Paolo stormed over to me. "What did he want with you?"

I took a sip of my juice and avoided his gaze. "What are you talking about?"

"The prince! What did he want with you?"

"Whatever makes you think I was with the prince?"

"Do you think I'm stupid or something?" He clenched his fists and for a moment I thought he would punch me. But he tried to control himself. "Who else orders the major-domo to fetch somebody? And completely by coincidence the prince was suddenly nowhere to be found. I heard guests asking for him, but he was in his private quarters and could not be disturbed." He narrowed his eyes. "Tell me, what scheme are you cooking up?"

I took a deep breath. They'd all hear about it at the conservatory any way. "I don't know whether I will be continuing my training for much longer."

"You have a contract with the conservatory! Wasn't it you who reminded me of that?"

"It's not that I want to leave…" I continued awkwardly.

"What then?"

"The prince…he was rather insistent that I should build up my career from here." I did not dare look at Paolo.

"So." He was stuttering. "So you are being given the chance that I deserve? He's buying off your obligations?"

I wrapped my arms around myself. Cold…

"Do you think I asked for it?"

"Well didn't you?"

"No."

He stared at me, as white as a sheet. "Why did you act as if you were ill this afternoon? Was that when you worked out your miserable plan? Did you seduce the prince with your absence so that he would desire you more than ever? Or did you use the time to be with him?" He scoffed. "Did you think I didn't know that there was nothing wrong with your voice? Filthy Judas!"

"No!" I gasped. "No, Paolo, that's not the way it was! Believe me."

"Angelo? Paolo?" Rosa apparently had the habit of appearing at exactly the right moment. "What's the matter with the two of you?"

"He calls himself a friend!" Bitterly, he turned his back on me. "A devious traitor, that's what he is!"

More and more of the guests still present turned toward us.

"Shhh…" Rosa pulled us into a corner. "What has made you so angry, Paolo? Have you forgotten that you are the stars of the evening?"

He pointed angrily in my direction. "Ask him why I'm so angry! I will never say another word to him. Never."

She turned to face me. "Angelo?"

I saw the lights in her inquisitive eyes start to shine. How could I tell her I had sold myself to the prince?

"Well?" she insisted.

"It's nothing," I mumbled.

"I don't believe you." She narrowed her eyes and her inquisitive look swept over me. "It can't be as bad as that."

"It is." I hesitated. "The prince wants me to work for him, just like your father."

The concern in her eyes gave way to a relieved grin. "Are you serious? You're coming to Pratolino?"

"Don't you understand? Are you really that stupid?" Paolo threw her a look that spat fire.

She stuck out her chin. "Are you jealous?"

I shifted my feet. I would have liked to run away. Now he would say it out loud. Rosa would hear what I had done. What I would do.

Paolo's head turned deep red. Then he turned round. "Forget it!" He strode out of the salon with angry strides.

"What's the matter with him?" Rosa looked after him in astonishment.

"He did his best to attract the attention of Prince Ferdinando and now I am the one to get the chance." I felt so hypocritical when I said the words, but I didn't have the heart to tell her the truth.

But she was not stupid. "Is there…a catch to the prince's offer?" She waited, took a deep breath. "Is the catch the prince himself? Is that what's bothering Paolo?"

I lowered my eyes.

"Fine." Her tone could have frozen water. "I get it. The prince does not want just your voice. He wants you. That explains the Apollo pin." She nodded. "I assume you know what that means?"

What could I say? I kept my eyes on the ground.

"I will have to stay well out of your way, that's for sure. But perhaps that is what you want and in that case I wish you much happiness." Just like Paolo, she turned around abruptly. Her skirts rustled and her heels clicked on the marble floor as she strode off.

I opened my mouth to call after her, to swear to her that I had chosen for my sister and not for the love of the prince or a sparkling career. That I would have been pleased if Paolo had won the prince's favour. That I had not betrayed him.

But her rigidly straight posture told me she was not interested in any explanation, even if I could have found the right words.

When signore Scarlatti came to me a little later and offered me a glass of wine, I apologised. "I have to be up early tomorrow." I bowed briefly. "If you will permit me…"

"Of course," he said. "Most sensible." He looked round, perhaps for his daughter. Then he gestured in the direction of the doors. "Do not let me detain you, young man. I will look for our host and then I will follow you and the others. Hopefully we will be able to say our farewells tomorrow. If not, please know that it has been a great pleasure to work with you. And that also goes for signore Cristofori, although he would not say so. In the past few days, he has tried ceaselessly to capture your voices in his instrument. I am sure you have made a contribution to the development of the pianoforte." He bowed toward me.

"Thank you, signore." And I took my leave.

That night one thing became very clear: the stay in Pratolino had not been good for my night rest.

29

The following morning, the coach left for Florence under a heavy cloud. Paolo was still furious. Since we met that morning, he had not looked at me once or said a single word to me.

How should I react? I had made a choice, but it was a choice between two evils and it didn't make me any happier.

Fate had taken over the course my life and there seemed to be little I could do to change how it unfolded. If I had not been castrated, I would have been a tanner, just like Papa and Nonno. Probably I would have married some neighbour's girl or other within ten years and would have had a few children with her.

But things had turned out differently. My parents were dead, the tannery in Fiesole had been sold, and I would never marry or have children.

What more could I do for Mariana than ensure she could lead a carefree life?

And myself? I had also adapted to life as it presented itself to me. Whatever lay before me, I could handle it. Couldn't I?

The maestro sat in the carriage looking straight ahead. He must have gathered, in some way or another, what was happening. Probably he was worrying about how he could explain to the conservatory that I would be giving up my study shortly in exchange for a life at the court of Prince Ferdinando De Medici. Padre Orvieto would tear his hair from his head, regretting that he had granted permission for us to go to Pratolino.

The carriage slowed down. The footman knocked on the

window. "Gentlemen?" he called. "Should we stop in Fiesole?" The maestro looked at me. "Well?"

I shook my head. I didn't dare look Mariana in the eye. How was I to explain the attentions of the prince? I would send her a letter from Florence telling her that there had been no time for a visit, but that I was aware of the help from the prince.

Partly thanks to the angry glances from Paolo and the silence of the maestro, the journey seemed to last an eternity, and I was happy when the carriage finally stopped in front of the conservatory's main entrance.

At that moment, the change-over between lessons was taking place, and the carriage attracted the attention of the students. They pointed at us from behind the windows.

"Paolo! Angelo!" Josepho rushed outside, his eyes gleaming with excitement. "There you are! Come on! I want to know everything. Everything!"

Paolo grabbed his bundle from the hands of the footman, acknowledged nobody and stamped passed Josepho into the building.

"What's the matter with him?" Our young roommate gazed after him in amazement.

I clapped a hand on his shoulder and forced a smile onto my face. "You'll hear about it later. Is everything all right here?"

"Quiet, as usual. Except, of course, for the sound of the instruments and the bleating of the baritones and tenors."

"So you missed us a little?"

He shook my hand from his shoulder. "That depends. Did you put in a good word for me so that I can come with you next time?" His look was almost imploring.

"Is that what you really want?"

"What do you think? It's fine to sing in the church for a bit, but my future lies elsewhere." He placed his fists dramatically against his chest. "I feel it."

"Your future is certainly in a palace," I said. "Or a big villa, an estate perhaps…"

"Exactly! The people here think the biggest honour is when you may sing for God and the pope. Well, I've never seen either of them, and they've never told me that I am any good. We are decoration, nothing more. We stand there, singing our hearts out "

I interrupted him. "Did you take over our parts in the church?"

"Oh yes. We took turns at the solos. But I didn't think much of it. Nobody saying you did well. No applause." He grabbed my arm. "Tell me they applauded you! And cheered!"

"Angelo!" called Maestro Perro. "Take in your things!" He placed my bundle on the ground in front of me.

"Of course they did. What did you expect?" I placed my hand for a second on the bag under my shirt, containing the pin and the ring, and asked myself what Josepho would say if he knew we had such valuable things as souvenirs of our journey. "Come on." I picked up the bundle. "We are sure to be doing more for the prince in future. Perhaps you can come with us."

"Wonderful!" Josepho could hardly contain himself. "You'll tell me everything, won't you? Every hour, every second that ticked away there."

"Of course," I lied. "If you carry my bundle inside."

Paolo may have been giving me the silent treatment, but he certainly wasn't holding his tongue with the other students. The news of my imminent departure reached the staff and the students of the conservatory within a couple of hours. The maestros did nothing to disguise their disapproval and before the day was over, I was summoned by Rector Orvieto.

"Be seated." Once I had sat down, he began. "I have heard that your journey was a great success. In particular for you."

"For both of us," I said. "We were applauded as famous singers and we performed with the composer Scarlatti. We brought honour to the conservatory."

The rector smiled briefly. "So I understand. Maestro Perro beamed with pride when he gave us his report several hours ago."

My lips twitched. I wanted to join in the laughter but nerves took hold of my throat.

"Naturally, I am very grateful to you for that." Padre Orvieto pushed his spectacles up his nose. "But that is not why I sent for you. I have learned that, during your visit to Pratolino, you decided not to complete your training here."

I lowered my eyes.

"Is that true, Angelo?"

I nodded. "I was made an offer I could not refuse."

"We can talk about that offer later." He leaned toward me. "Do you realise what the consequences are if you end your contract prematurely?"

"I will receive a fine."

"Not only that. You will never be able to return here or receive any assistance from the conservatory in any way whatsoever."

I said nothing. What could I say?

"Are you sure that this is what you want, Angelo? I have placed a lot of confidence in your future."

"I know that."

"You will graduate in several years. The name of our institute opens doors in the world, both sacred and secular."

"The name of Prince Ferdinando opens those same doors," I said. And perhaps even better ones, I added in my mind.

Rector Orvieto sighed. "Yes, his name too. But that is not always a positive matter." Again I remained silent.

"There has been no message from the Prince De Medici, but I assume I can expect one?"

"I asked whether I could in any case complete this year."

The rector's look softened. "If I am correct, you do not find it easy to leave."

"No, Padre."

"Why are you leaving then?"

"The prince has promised to provide for my sister."

"Ah, that explains a lot." He looked at me thoughtfully. "Are things not well with her?"

Everything came out. "My aunt, who did the housekeeping, has died. Mariana lives alone. She works in a laundry. She isn't married, doesn't even have a suitor." I swallowed. "Her hands were rough and chapped when I visited her, and neighbours sometimes had to pitch in to give her a meal."

"And the prince promised to relieve all your worries?"

I nodded.

"And in exchange for that, you have to offer him your services?"

I hesitated. Did he know what those services entailed?

"Well?" he insisted.

"Yes, Padre," I whispered.

"And you're prepared to do it?"

I thought back to my castration. "Yes…"

He sighed again. "Personally, I have considerable difficulty with your choice, and the same is true of everybody here. But I also have some understanding for it. You are becoming an adult. I must say that there is not much more to improve in your voice. As long as you keep singing and do your daily exercises…You are one of the greatest talents of recent years."

"Thank you."

"When will you be leaving?"

"The prince is having an opera written for me by signore Scarlatti…" I hesitated slightly, fearful that the statement carried an inadvertent note of boastfulness.

"That is wonderful," said Padre Orvieto, encouragingly. "Quite an honour."

"When it is finished, he will send for me. I hope it takes a long time."

The padre placed his hands together. "I am not annoyed at you, Angelo. Of course a fine must be paid, but it seems as if the prince is prepared to do that. Let us await the moment when he sends for you. Until then I expect you to act like a normal student."

"You can be sure of that," I said.

"In each life, there is a moment when difficult decisions must be made, when we must cut the cords," said the padre. "But sometimes we do not realise what those cords are binding together and we have to wait and see whether the world falls apart. But if you never cut them, you will never know if life will continue as you want it. God's ways are incomprehensible."

I felt a wave of relief rush over me. He was not angry; he was letting me go. "Thank you, Padre Orvieto," I said. "I shall never forget this place, no matter how old I get!"

He smiled. "That's good to know, Angelo. I am convinced that we shall not be given the chance to forget you. Presumably God has a great future for you in mind."

Even though the rector had reacted more calmly than I had dared to hope, the events awaiting me put me under enormous pressure. I was restless and still slept badly. Furthermore, I felt a distance arising between me and my roommates.

Paolo didn't speak to me. If he wanted something from me, he asked others to ask me.

His behaviour was completely over the top. He seduced every girl who set foot in the conservatory and dropped them just as easily. He even got a passionate cleaning maid fired from the conservatory by claiming that she had offered him her virginity. Later I discovered that the girl had been Paolo's sweetheart until he had lost interest in her. Rumour had it that she had put an end to her life by jumping into the Arno.

One of the young bass student followed Paolo around like a puppy. The boy, a head shorter than him but twice as heavy, obeyed everything he said. He saved his meal in a handkerchief so that he could take it to Paolo later, and if Paolo asked him to run an errand in the city, he risked a severe punishment by slipping out of the conservatory for him.

Paolo was anything but reticent in his love life. Josepho said that he had caught him and Silvio in a passionate embrace. They were both half undressed and panting as if they had run across the city.

The rumours about Paolo and Silvio grew. Although the two of them never visited each other in the dormitory more than was acceptable, I sometimes caught glances that clearly betrayed the intimacy between them.

The rumours also reached the staff. Gregorio made more frequent unexpected visits to the dormitory or peered around the door, his glance first going to Paolo and Silvio.

I could not fathom Silvio. I assumed that Paolo had let off steam to him about me, for the slender castrato only ever looked at me with disgust on his face.

I couldn't care less. I had my own little disciple: Josepho followed me everywhere. Of course I did not take advantage of this; I regarded him more as a pupil. I remembered only too well how I had sometimes felt alone in my first years at the conservatory, how uncertain I had been about myself and my voice. Padre Matteo Battista and Padre Alonso had often made it clear that they had chosen me because my voice was exceptionally pure. But just suppose that it had turned out that my voice had suffered from the operation? That in retrospect my performances had proved disappointing?

In Josepho, I saw myself. The shyness and doubt that were suddenly revealed in his words and actions. How he was searching for his place in the hierarchy of the sopranists...

One day I was just returning from my music rudiments lesson when Josepho rushed up to me, agitated and bathed in sweat. "Come, Angelo! Come quickly!"

"Calm down, Josepho. What's the matter?"

"Paolo..." he panted. "He's been caught with Silvio by Gregorio and Padre Matteo Battista!"

I closed my eyes. Please don't let it be true, I prayed. God, what an unbelievable idiot! "What exactly do you mean?" I was scared of the answer.

"They were doing it again. In the cupboard where they keep the music stands. Gregorio heard noises and fetched the padre."

We could have expected something like this. Everybody knew that Paolo and Silvio messed around whenever the opportunity arose. "And then?"

"Padre Matteo Battista naturally pulled open the door." Josepho gasped for breath. "They were completely naked, Angelo! Can you imagine it? Their choir smocks and cassocks were in a pile on the ground! We could just see them before the padre and Gregorio blocked our view. They must have thought we didn't know what was going on in there. Come on!" He dragged me up the stairs by my arm. "You can prevent him being expelled!"

"Wait a bit." I pulled my arm away. "What do you mean, expelled?"

"Ooh," he groaned. "Don't you get it? They were caught playing with each other's peckers! They're bound to get kicked out. The padre thrashed Paolo and Silvio. I saw it!"

Of course I knew the consequences. Paolo and Silvio weren't the first and they wouldn't be the last. I bit my lip. Would I mind if my oldest friend at the conservatory had to leave?

I didn't have to think long about the answer. I would be devastated. Paolo had helped me when the others had ignored me. He had told me in detail what the padre and the barber had done to my sex, and he was the first to let me listen to the older sopranists. If Paolo hadn't been there, I don't know how I would have survived those first months. Of everybody here, he had shown himself most as a friend. Until the Prince De Medici came between us.

I set off at a run. "Come on!"

Near the cupboard on the ground floor where the music stands were stored there were only a few baritones and basses hanging around.

"Where are they?" I asked.

"What difference does it make to you?" asked the bass who followed Paolo everywhere. "You screwed him, didn't you?"

I ignored him and looked round. "Anybody know? Was he sent straight to the rector?"

A baritone shrugged. "I think so. Padre Matteo Battista said it was over for those two. Good job, too. Castrati cause nothing but trouble."

Before he had finished, Paolo's friend attacked him.

There was no time to intervene. I turned round and ran to the rector's room. Through the closed door, I heard Padre Matteo Battista ranting. "Filthy pig! You are a disgrace in the face of God!"

I entered without knocking; nobody would have heard it

anyway. In the study, a furious Rector Orvieto stood facing Paolo and Silvio, who had lowered his eyes. Paolo did not show much remorse. He stared insolently at the rector.

"Rector," I said, trying to be heard above Padre Matteo Battista. "Padre Orvieto, please, listen to me."

"Piss off," snarled Paolo as soon as he saw me.

For once Padre Matteo Battista agreed with him.

His round head went from red to deep purple. "Be off, Montegne! What are you doing here?"

"Padre Orvieto! I ask your forgiveness for Paolo and Silvio! Please give them another chance. Their voices are among the finest in the conservatory, as you well know. And outside these walls they have never brought you or the conservatory into disrepute."

"These boys have committed a sin in God's eyes!" Padre Matteo Battista gave both Paolo and Silvio a clip round the ears.

"Padre Orvieto," I tried again. "I know that what they have done is wrong, but please, give them a chance…"

"Be quiet, all of you!" Never before had I heard the rector adopt such a cold tone. "Padre Matteo Battista, I agree with you. These boys have committed a terrible sin, and the punishment for this transgression is clearly stated in our charter: expulsion from the school. That you should throw away your careers in this way, my boys." He shook his head.

I didn't give up. "But Padre Orvieto…"

Precisely at that moment, Maestro Perro stormed in. "What on earth is going on?"

"Calm down, Perro!" Padre Orvieto placed a hand on his shoulder.

The maestro shook it off. "More problems with one of my best singers! What has got into you?" He looked at Paolo and me. "First such wonderful performances, and now that your bright future is coming closer, we have all this…"

I felt the need to say that in this case I had nothing to do with it, that I was only here to defend Paolo and Silvio, but it seemed as if nobody had any interest in that information.

"What difference does it make what you think of me?" screamed Paolo. "I'm nothing but a second-rate singer. Everything revolves around him there!" A finger jabbed in my direction. "He got the prince to fall for him with his hypocritical face and his friendship with the Scarlattis!"

"That's not true," I protested.

"We can also hear you if you adopt a more normal tone, giovani Brunetti," said the rector. "You know that you are all equally dear to us and that we do not have favourites."

"Have I ever expressed a preference for one of you?" asked Maestro Perro.

"What has that to do with defying God's laws? *Madre di Dio!*" Padre Matteo Battista literally spat with fury.

"Padres, Maestro, please listen to me," I tried again. "I beg you, forgive Paolo and Silvio this one time. Please! Paolo, Silvio, say that you're sorry!"

"I'm sorry," said Silvio quickly.

"I'm not," said Paolo. "What business of yours is it what I do with myself?"

"Paolo!" exclaimed the maestro. "Do you not wished to be saved?"

"It doesn't matter much to me," snarled Paolo.

Things were beginning to look bad, I thought. And even worse when Gregorio suddenly came in and handed two pouches to the rector. "Excuse me, venerable Padre," he said to the rector. "I found these under the mattress of Paolo Brunetti."

"What is it?" asked Padre Orvieto.

"See for yourself!"

I had already recognised one of them. It was mine; I had placed it under my own mattress.

Padre Matteo Battista pushed closer to the rector to view the contents of the pouches. The maestro apparently had little interest in them. Probably he already knew what they contained.

Carefully the rector teased apart the knots in the cords around the pouches. He tipped the contents into his hand: a golden pin in the shape of a violin with real strings, a pin with the image of the naked god Apollo and a beautiful ring, set with rubies.

The others gasped when they saw the treasures. Even the maestro. "Where did that ring come from?" His eyes were wide with amazement. "What is Angelo's ring doing under Paolo's mattress?"

"Do you recognise it?" asked the rector.

"Indeed. In any case the image of the Greek god and the pin with the violin. They were gifts from the Prince De Medici. But that ring."

Paolo had turned pale. His shaking hands crumpled the fabric of his choir smock.

"Master Brunetti?"

"I received that ring from the prince after I sang to him."

"After the *Dovrb dunque morire?*" asked the maestro. "I didn't see you get it. It must be worth a fortune! And the pin. Wasn't it given to Angelo?"

"The prince appreciated my ode." Paolo's eyes darted back and forth. "He was extremely generous."

"It's actually a little different," I said as calmly as I could. "That Greek god of music is mine, and so is the ring. I was given it by the prince when he invited me to live on his estate. I first kept the things hidden under my own mattress, but later I gave them to Paolo to look after."

The rector's eyes darted from me to Paolo. "He had to look after them for you?" he asked in disbelief. "Why?" The maestro also looked at me as if I had gone mad. He was fully aware that the friendship between Paolo and me had cooled since our journey.

"I don't believe a word of it." Padre Matteo Battista raised his hand and gave Paolo another slap on his head. "So you're a thief as well!"

"Is what Angelo says true, Paolo?" asked the rector. "Or is the padre right and you stole these items?"

"You have already made up your mind. Why should I bother trying to change it?"

"I am asking you," said Rector Orvieto. "To whom do these jewels belong?"

"To me."

"Angelo?"

"The violin belongs to Paolo, the ring and the pin are mine. But he is looking after them for me." I turned toward my old friend. "Why don't you just tell them? That you're looking after them for me because I'm scared I might damage them during a restless night? And that I can have them back again when I ask for them?" *Say it, idiot,* I thought. *Save yourself!*

"Maestro?" said the rector. "What do you know about this?"

"I saw Angelo receive the pin of Apollo from the hands of the prince. It has to be his. But isn't it his right to give them to a friend for safe keeping?" He must have suspected the truth, but like me, he was making a last attempt to save Paolo.

The rector took a deep breath. "Good. Gregorio? Go with Angelo to the dormitory and look under his mattress."

I followed Gregorio from the study and up the two flights of stairs to our dormitory. Everywhere students were talking excitedly. The conservatory was in a turmoil.

"Angelo?" hissed a few students. "Do you know anything? Is he staying?"

"Get rid of the filthy castrato," whispered another, precisely loud enough for me to hear but not Gregorio.

Josepho clamped onto me. "Tell me that they're staying," he said, begging almost.

"I can't," I said. I no longer knew whether I wanted him to stay. Why had Paolo stolen from me? Jealousy? Had he thought he could get away with it?

Gregorio sent everybody out of the dormitory. "You have no business here during the day," he said, angrily. "How often do I have to say it?"

The students left grumbling. They all had to pass Gregorio, who stood there with his arms folded waiting until everybody had left.

In the meantime, I had walked over to my bed. Under the mattress there was nothing, of course, except some dust, which had probably been there for ages.

"And?" asked Gregorio.

"Gone," I answered. "I said so, didn't I? Paolo was keeping them safe for me"

"You can con the old man," said Gregorio. "But not me."

Downstairs, Padre Matteo Battista had again entered into discussion with the maestro about the consequences of Paolo and Silvio's intimacy.

"What are your findings?" the rector asked Gregorio. He simply shook his head.

"So the jewels belonging to master Montegne are no longer under his mattress? And this is the only Apollo that there is, and this the only ring?"

"No, Reverent Padre. Yes, Reverent Padre," said Gregorio.

I felt myself growing impatient. "That's what I said. I gave them to Paolo for safe keeping!"

"Silence," commanded the rector. He turned to Paolo. "What have you to say about this?"

Paolo glared through his eyelashes in my direction and shuffled his feet. "Nothing. Except that they're mine."

He wanted to be expelled, I suddenly realised. The stupid little idiot!

Rector Orvieto sighed. "I cannot believe that, Brunetti." His gaze stayed on Paolo for a long time and then on Silvio. "You realise that you have sinned against God's rules and against those of the Florentine conservatory?"

Silvio nodded. Paolo continued to look down with a surly expression.

"Under the present circumstances I have, to my inexpressible regret, no option but to expel you from our school, giovani Brunetti."

Despite his big mouth, Paolo staggered when the axe finally fell.

My legs shook too. Was Paolo not my companion in our fate, my oldest friend here?

"Paolo!" Instinctively, my hand reached for his.

He pushed it away roughly. "Knock it off!"

"Silvio, for you I will allow mercy to rule over the law," said the rector.

"How can you?" shouted Padre Matteo Battista.

"Have you forgotten who is in charge here?" asked Padre Orvieto.

Padre Matteo Battista sniffed, turned round, and left the room.

"That means that this is your only chance to return to the straight and narrow," continued the rector, imperturbably. "You, giovani Brunetti, will be given the jewel that belongs to you. Go to the dormitory, take off your conservatory uniform and place it on your bed. Then you may go to the kitchen for a piece of bread and some cheese, after which you will close the doors to our school behind you forever." He placed a hand on Paolo's head. "Giovani Paolo Brunetti, let me pray for you." He closed his eyes and began to recite a prayer.

I saw a shiver pass through Paolo's body. It seemed as if he shrank by inches.

When the prayer was finished, Padre Orvieto made the sign of the cross on Paolo's forehead. "Go now," he said softly.

We all stared after Paolo as he walked away. I could swear there were tears in his eyes before he turned away. But he gritted his teeth and said nothing. And now? Would he return to his family? Become a baker's boy, even though he was once so delighted that he had been spared that fate?

Maestro Perro placed his arm around my shoulder. "I am so sorry, my boy. I wish I could have prevented this."

That was the moment I felt something break inside. I put my hands before my eyes and felt the tears flowing.

"Go to your room, Silvio," said Rector Orvieto. "Remain there for the rest of the day. Ponder your sins and place them before your confessor. Tomorrow you will start afresh."

"Thank you," mumbled Silvio.

I did not wait for permission to leave the room, but turned and followed him out.

30

I lay with my eyes wide open until sleep finally overcame me. It was three days since Paolo had been expelled from the conservatory and I kept replaying his sorry departure in my mind.

Where was he? What was he doing? What would his future bring?

I turned onto my side. The wall was a large grey area, dimly lit by the tiny beam of moonlight that shone into the dormitory.

Was it my fault? Could I have prevented him from being expelled?

No, said something inside me. He messed things up for himself. Was his glowing career over for good at the moment the prince's eye fell on me? Of course not.

I sighed. I had heard somewhere that failed castrati were never fully accepted back into the normal world. They were always viewed as deformed creatures, and they were best off if some parish or other took them in. Then they sang in one or more churches and lived the life of a reclusive cleric.

Would Paolo choose that? I had my doubts. Wide awake still, I turned onto my other side.

How could I tell Rosa that Paolo had been so angry that he had done everything forbidden by God and the staff of the conservatory? Was she still angry at me?

I felt my blanket being lifted. A cool draft of air swept over my legs and back. A warm body slid against mine. Had I fallen asleep after all? Was I dreaming sweet dreams?

"You're tossing and turning," said a soft voice in my eye.

"Josepho?" I whispered. "What are you doing?"

"You've been restless like this for night after night," he said. "I've come to bring you rest." He put a thin arm around me and began to stroke my chest. "Close your eyes and let yourself go."

This mustn't happen, I thought. I'm three years older than him. But I closed my eyes and concentrated on his hand, which stroked me so lightly that he hardly touched the skin of my body.

Stop him, I thought. *Make him stop. This is a sin in God's eyes! We'll find ourselves on the street!*

But I couldn't. For the first time in a long while I felt myself growing calm. My legs and stomach began to tingle and my eyes closed.

And after a while, I forgot everything…

31

The expulsion of Paolo did nothing to close the gap between my roommates and me. The other castrati took the side of Silvio and constantly ignored me.

Or perhaps I put myself on the sidelines. I felt no real need for contact with the others. Only with Josepho that was enough.

After that first night, he often crept into my bed. He would slip under my blankets and nestle his chest and stomach against my back.

I would always see Rosa's crystal eyes in my mind when I felt him against me. I imagined that they were her small hands gliding over me and caressing me. More than that, I longed for her closeness, her perceptive remarks and her slender, elegant body. All too often, I felt an erection when Josepho's hands caressed me, but I would never turn over, would never give in to my desires.

I would satisfy myself when Josepho left for his own bed as morning drew near. Then my hands would slowly take possession of my body. I would touch the spots that gave me a good feeling and would think of Rosa, my Rosa. I loved her, I now knew that for certain. She did not leave my thoughts for a moment. Josepho was only a substitute. But thanks to him, I had never felt so rested since I had left for Pratolino. I was enormously grateful to him.

My roommates must have known of Josepho's visits. There was no way they couldn't. Yet I never heard anyone talk of it. It was as if, since Paolo's departure, the unwritten rule that what took place in the dormitory stayed in the dormitory applied more than ever before.

"Master Montegne!" One of the conservatory's messengers came to me with a letter in her hands.

"For me?" I asked, without much enthusiasm.

"Would I be standing here otherwise?" the girl snapped back.

I smiled. I found more and more pleasure in girls with a quick tongue. They reminded me of the impudent girl I loved. "Why not?" I answered. "Perhaps I excite you." A remark that Paolo could have made.

"Pooh." She held up the letter provocatively. "Well? Are you going to take it or not?"

With a bow, I accepted it from her. "Grazie." I held the paper to my nose. If it smelt of expensive perfume, I would not open it. Then it would be from the prince, declaring his love for me for the umpteenth time and informing me in great detail about the progress of the opera. Each letter brought my departure from the conservatory closer. The only reason I opened them in the end was because I searched between the lines for news about Rosa. But the prince never mentioned her name.

Most of all, I feared the letter in which I would read that the opera was finished and that the prince would be expecting me in his mansion. It would not only be difficult to say farewell to the conservatory and my teachers, I was also dreading the moment when the prince would take me in his arms and tell me that I was now his. My stomach turned over, simply at the thought.

This time the letter did not smell of expensive perform but of the bone glue with which it had been sealed. I opened it as I walked.

"Angelino," it said at the top.

From Mariana? I stopped in my tracks. She was the only one who called me that, but she could not have written the letter herself. Had she hired somebody to send me this message?

Quickly I read the letter.

Angelino,

I am sorry to have to tell you that your darling sister is seriously ill. There are fears for her life. Come home as quickly as possible.

Constanza Morelli

I lowered the paper in bewilderment. Mariana? Ill? What was wrong with her? My mouth became dry. Was I going to lose her as well?

I leant against the wall for support. Why hadn't I visited her on the way back from Pratolino? I had broken my word. Holy Mother, if only I had suspected that it may have been the last opportunity to see her!

Maestro Perro appeared next to me. "Is something wrong, Angelo?"

"My sister..." I had the feeling that at any moment I would burst into tears. Mariana, who looked so like Mama...

"Mariana? What is the matter with her?"

Silently I handed him the letter from the neighbour in Fiesole.

"That is terrible." The maestro took my hand. "You must go to her as quickly as possible, that is obvious. Go to Rector Orvieto."

"The letter was sent several days ago, perhaps..."

He shook his head. "No 'perhaps.' There is no time to lose! Shall I come with you to the rector?"

I nodded mutely.

He threw his arm around me and took me to Rector Orvieto's study. "Padre?" He pushed open the door. "Excuse me for intruding. Angelo Montegne has received a message. He needs permission to take leave as soon as possible."

"Oh yes?" The rector's footsteps came to the door and he pulled it open so that he could see me. "Montegne? Come in. There is a chair. It looks as if you need it."

I immediately explained the situation. "My sister is very ill. The neighbour thinks…" I had to swallow. "She may not pull through," I continued softly. "I must go to Fiesole. She is all that I have left."

"Your sister?" A sympathetic frown appeared on the rector's forehead. "That is terrible, my boy." He folded my hands in his. "I suggest we pray for her recovery and for strength for you."

Although I knew Padre Orvieto and could have expected a prayer, I felt ambushed. I wanted to leave. Now!

Despite everything, I reverently bowed my head. What else could I do?

For minutes on end Padre Orvieto churned out Latin prayers for my sister. As he did so, my thoughts went to my sister and the family into which I was born. To the time when Mama was still alive and Papa was the hub of our family. Always cheerful, always ready for a romp. Enjoying life, enjoying his home, his work. And Mama. I tried to conjure up her face in my mind, but I did not succeed. I couldn't even remember the voice she always used to whisper sweet words in our ears.

Would Mariana's face also slowly disappear from my memory?

She is not dead, I said to myself. Stop. Stop!

All at once I noticed that the rector had turned from Latin to Italian. "…protect you in your hour of sorrow and worry. May God Almighty bless you: God the Father, God the Son, and God the Holy Spirit." He made the sign of the cross over my head.

"Amen," said the maestro.

"Amen," I repeated.

"Well, then, Angelo Montegne," said the rector. "So you want to leave to visit your sick sister?"

"With your permission."

"Of course you have my permission. I hope you are on time. Go quickly and pack your cloths."

"Thank you, Padre." My knees were shaking and I wanted to turn round.

"Maestro?" I heard the padre say. "As long as the young man is our pupil, he must be accompanied on long journeys. I would like you to go with him."

"Padre?" said Maestro Perro in astonishment.

"You will understand we cannot allow him to travel alone."

"Yes, of course, Padre, but…"

"I do not think you have any time to lose, Maestro."

Maestro Perro gave a deep sigh. "I shall go home to collect the necessary things."

"I'm sorry," I said as soon as the door to the study was shut behind us.

"Don't worry about it, my boy. You cannot help it."

No, I couldn't help it, and in some way I was pleased that he had found me in the hallway and not Padre Matteo Battista. Imagine having to travel with him!

I did not remember much of the trip in the hired coach. Only when I walked into Vicolo Porettana did I come to my senses. Don't let it be too late, I prayed silently. Let my sister live, Holy Mother. Please! Take me in her place!

The door of Mariana's tiny house opened when we were still a few yards away. Mistress Constanza was just about to step into the street.

Without thinking, I pushed my bundle into the arms of the maestro and ran to her. "Neighbour!"

She looked round in surprise. "Angelino!" She spread her arms, but quickly held them close to her body when I went to embrace her.

It surprised me, but I didn't take the time to ask about it. "How is Mariana? Is she inside?"

A worried look came to the face of the neighbour. "She's alive, Angelino, but it is good that you came so quickly. She has a high fever and keeps on calling your name."

The maestro had remained standing at a distance. "What is it?" he asked directly. "Something contagious?"

Mistress Constanza bowed her head. "It looks like the pox. The surgeon has not been here, but I have heard of other cases in the city."

The maestro turned pale. He gave me my bundle and said: "I'll find lodgings at the nearest inn, Angelo. Now that you are safely among friends, I can return to Florence tomorrow."

I didn't understand. Hadn't Padre Orvieto ordered him to stay with me? Mistress Constanza saw my confusion and sighed deeply. "Dear Angelo," she said. "You should know that your sister has an illness that can be passed from one person to another. I seem immune to it since I had it myself, but others…" She fell silent. "The girl from Prince Ferdinando took off when the first signs appeared. Since then, only vegetables and herbs have been sent here from Pratolino."

"I can't be with her?" I interrupted her. "Is that what you are saying?"

"You will be taking a risk." A deep crease appeared in her forehead. "I've racked my brains, but I can't for the life of me remember whether you had the disease as a toddler. Do you remember?"

I shook my head.

"And as student?"

"No." I had been seriously ill just after the castration, but nothing after that. But I couldn't care less that the pox might infect me. "My sister needs me," I said. "I came here for her."

"It is good that you did so."

The maestro patted me on the shoulder. "I hope to see you as quickly as possible back in Florence, Angelo. I shall pray for you and your sister."

Silently Mistress Constanza and I stared at him as he left.

"Perhaps there is a way to prevent the illness," she said when he had turned the corner. "I've asked around."

"I will do everything to prevent myself catching the disease, but I am going to my sister, no matter what."

"Listen, there is an old-fashioned method that was used when the Black Death raged in our country. The barber-surgeon would wear a cap over his head when he went near the sick, with a sort of beak before his nose and mouth. Apparently there were herbs in it which purified the air. Those surgeons were often spared, I have heard. Perhaps..." She raised her hands. "You place your life in God's hand for your sister. But perhaps in that way the danger is less."

Suddenly a thought crossed my mind. Didn't the barber who cut me all those years ago belong to the umpteenth generation of barber-surgeons in the town? Did he still have his shop?

"I'm off to find a beak," I said. "Wait for me."

32

Although it had been years since I lived in Fiesole, I found the way to the barber without difficulty. The man had grown visibly older since the last time. His back was bent, and most of his hair had fallen out. "Buon pomeriggio," I said in greeting.

"Ciao, young master." His eyes studied my body. "Can I be of service? A trim, perhaps? By the look of it, a shave it not necessary."

I went and stood in front of him. "Do you know who I am?"

"Should I?" He raised his head to study me. "Are you perhaps Mario, son of the old Di Alma? You have his build and his nose."

"So that's all the impression I made." Bitterly, I gave him a shove. "Perhaps you castrated Mario as well, just like me. And there may have been others. In any case, you made an indelible impression on me."

He placed his hand under my chin and turned my face from left to right. "Angelo Montegne?"

"Do you know you still give me nightmares? I have never forgotten what happened that night."

"But my boy…" He shook his head. "It was ordered by the padres themselves! And it was in your own interest. Your future. I do not blame you that you didn't realise it at the time, but by now you must…"

"In my own interest?" I wanted to grab him by the doublet and shake him until it got through to his stupid brain exactly what he had done to me. "I never asked to be castrated!" I screamed. "I wanted to sing. Nothing else!"

"Well," he said. "I did what I was ordered."

My hands itched. If only I could place that same tape measure around his neck and let him feel the fear of God! But I needed him. "I am looking for a surgeon's beak," I said. "Do you have one?"

"A surgeon's beak?" The barber looked at me in amazement. "It has been a long time since I heard that word. What do you need it for?"

"It doesn't matter. If you have one, I would ask you to give it to me. Or must I turn your shop upside down?"

He fixed his gaze on me for several moments, then he seemed to give in. He trudged to a large cupboard in the corner of the room. "It must be here somewhere," he said. "I have never used it. My father did, during the last epidemic of the Black Death. That was last century." His arms pushed aside all sorts of objects. "Where is that thing?"

I now only saw his backside and his legs, the rest of his body had disappeared into the cupboard. "Hurry up, man!" I urged him on.

"Calm down, you brat!" came the muffled reply. "You may be head and shoulders taller than me, but I can still give you a good hiding!"

"If you don't have it, I don't want to waste my time."

"I'll find it. At least, if you show a little patience."

After a long while, the barber came upright. "Here it is." He wiped off some dust and dirt. "You can keep it. I don't expect to need it again."

"Thank you." I grabbed the thing from his hand and left the shop without taking my leave. Would the beak mask protect me against the pox? Did I even care?

The Vicolo Porettana was deserted. Mistress Constanza was nowhere to be seen. Probably gone to her own family.

At the door of Mariana's house, I put on the mask.

"Mariana?" I called to announce my arrival. "It's me, Angelo."

The house smelled musty and smoky. A few cinders glowed in the hearth. The shutters in the room were closed and I could hardly see a hand before my face. "Mariana?"

A groan sounded from the bed.

"It's me, Angelo," I said again. "Don't be scared, I look strange." But I was startled by the form in the bed. Was that Mariana? Despite the darkness, I saw large sores on her face, her neck and her shoulders. Several had burst open and fluid was dripping onto the mattress.

"Angelo?" Mariana's eyes blinked. "You came."

"Of course I did. What did you expect?" Although I had to force myself to ignore the sores, Mariana must have noticed my shock, for she slid as far away from me as possible.

"No closer, Angelino…" Her voice was almost inaudible. "Dangerous…"

"I am prepared," I answer. "Do not worry yourself. I have come to be with you."

Her mouth formed into a weak smile. "Glad…"

"That's good." I looked round. "I shall open the shutters a little so that the smoke can clear. It is stuffy in here." Before I did so, I pulled the blanket further over my sister.

"Where is Mistress Constanza?"

"She's popped out," I said. "She'll be back in a while. Can I do anything for you?"

"I'm thirsty…"

"I shall brew some herbs." I got up. "The prince has sent some, hasn't he?" Perhaps I could also put some of them into my beak. Hadn't Mistress Constanza said that that was the idea?

From that day, Mistress Constanza and I took turns in caring for my sister. Mariana grew sicker and sicker. At some moments, she no longer seemed conscious of the world around her. Then her mind would wander, calling for our mother. The sores on her face spread and fluid continued to seep out of them.

"That doesn't matter," said mistress Constanza. "The more filth that leaves her body the better." Without hesitating, she wiped up the fluid before it dirtied the mattress.

I boiled herbal mixtures from the fresh greens that Prince Ferdinando had sent and which mistress Constanza had brought from the market. Sometimes I tried to feed her a thin gruel, into which I would beat an egg. Gregorio did that when anybody at the conservatory was ill.

Strangely enough, I did not miss my training one little bit. There, in that room with my sister at death's door, a wonderful peace fell over me. I thought about the life I had led in this very street. My mother, who wanted me to continue singing for the honour and glory of God. Would she be pleased with what I had achieved? With the contacts with the prince and with such a famous composer as signore Scarlatti. Or would she feel shame because of the boundaries I had crossed.

And Papa?

In the silence in Mariana's house, I began to understand how lonely he must have felt after Mama died. How he had fought to keep the tannery. And why he had so firmly refused to allow me to go with the padres from Florence. He knew about the castration, I was sure of that now.

Naturally I also thought about Zia Ignatia, who had sacrificed her own life to assist her brother's family.

Each time I wiped a cloth over my sister's face, I understood more and more how happy I should be with the people who had surrounded me in my early youth. And each time I thought how much I would give to drag my sister back from death's door. I didn't want to lose her as well.

After a week, a clear look appeared for the first time in Mariana's eyes.

"Hello," I said.

"Little brother."

"How are you?"

She sat up a little and reached for her face.

"Don't touch," said mistress Constanza. "Let me."

"You have fewer sores," I said. "When I first arrived, I hardly recognised you. You were so covered with sores. Now you look more like my sister."

She smiled. "You don't look like my brother with that crazy thing on your face."

I smiled back. "That is a precaution."

She took my hand. "I'm hungry," she whispered.

"I'll make you some soup." Mistress Constanza placed a hand on my shoulder. "Let us not celebrate too soon, but it seems as if the worst is behind us."

"Will she live?" I asked so softly that hopefully Mariana would not hear.

"I think so."

I would have liked to run to the arena and sing a song of praise to our Heavenly Father!

In the days that followed, Mariana gradually gained her strength, and I used the moments when our neighbour was with her to wander around my hometown.

During one of those walks, I found myself at the church where I had enjoyed my first years of singing in the choir. Curious as to whether Maestro Alonesi was still in charge of the choir, I entered the building. Immediately I heard the tender voices of a boys' choir. They were singing a piece by Monteverdi: *Vespro della Beata Vergine.*

As quietly as possible, I walked down the nave to the front pews. Breathlessly I listened to the almost perfectly pure singing, just as breathlessly I stared at the awkward movements of the maestro, which I knew so well.

When he brought his fingers and thumbs together at the conclusion, I stood up to applaud.

Maestro Alonesi narrowed his eyes and stared in my direction. "Who's there?"

I gave a small bow. "Buonasera, Maestro."

"Buona…" He raised his hand to his mouth. "Angelo Montegne? Is that you?"

"Yes, Maestro. It's me."

He sprang from his platform and rushed over to me. "My dear boy!"

"How are you, Maestro?"

"Fine, my boy. Fine. As long as I can do what I enjoy most." He embraced me, grasped my hands, and squeezed them so tightly that it hurt. Then he turned to his choir. "This, boys, is a former pupil whom you should take as an example, Angelo Montegne. The greatest voice I have ever had the privilege to train." He pulled me by the arm to his music stand. "Let us hear something, Angelo!"

For a moment, I was completely disconcerted. I had not expected such enthusiasm. Perform something? What?

"Something by Scarlatti?" suggested the Maestro. "You must have practised that at the conservatory."

Le Violette I could do it in my dreams. I closed my eyes and took a deep breath.

Rugiadose Odorose

Violette graziose...

When I finished, the maestro embraced me again. But from the corner of my eye, I saw the boys in the choir nudging each other and pointing at me.

"Well?" The maestro turned to his pupils. "Is that not magnificent? Which of you will follow in his footsteps? Marcello? Aurelio? Luciano, perhaps?"

They all giggled.

"Not me!" Aurelio was apparently the cheekiest of them all. "Not if I get a body like that." Now the giggling turned into laughter. Some boys turned away, embarrassed.

"Ah," scoffed the maestro. "These louts don't understand such things, Angelo-mio. They have never seen a sopranist before. Please excuse their insolent behaviour."

But it had been a long time since I had been laughed at because of my elongated body, and I was not armed against the boys' behaviour. A knot formed in my stomach. Quickly I placed my hand on my stomach in order to regain some control. "It was good to see you again, Maestro," I said, as composed as possible. "Now I must return to my sister."

In the time that I cared for Mariana, I had regularly thought that I could perhaps return to Fiesole. I would leave the prince and my accursed musical career behind me and live here together with my sister. We could care for each other, maintain our parents' graves, and lead an almost normal life. Perhaps I could earn a living as church singer.

But my visit to the maestro and his choir brought me roughly down to earth. People would stare and point at me. No wife, no children, no family of my own. What would I do if Mariana ever found a lover? What sort of life would I then lead? That of an eternally deformed, eccentric failure whom children and even some adults would avoid like the plague? Who would call after me and curse me from a distance?

Never!

There was no other choice. I had to leave for Pratolino and join Prince Ferdinando De Medici.

33

I stayed with Mariana for another two weeks. I thought as little as possible about my future and enjoyed being with my sister. Her recovery was slow. You had to look carefully to see that the colour was returning to her cheeks, and listen well to notice that the conversations became deeper and deeper and lasted longer.

Each morning I went to the market to buy what we needed. It was really a woman's job, but it was my way of thanking mistress Constanza for everything she had done for my family. On the market, I would listen to the sounds that hung in the air: quarrelling women, merchants praising their goods, shouts from customers who noticed that pickpockets had been at work, and the lanky boys who begged for rotten fruit and vegetables with which they pelted the prisoners in the stocks in the middle of the square.

One day, the wheels of a carriage clattered into Vicolo Porettana. I was just entering the alley with a basketful of food and immediately recognised the sound. For a moment, I thought of turning round and running away, but in the distance I saw the door of the carriage open and a dainty woman's shoe step out.

"Thank you," came the clear voice of Rosa Scarlatti, as the footman offered her his hand.

Rosa? I stopped in my tracks. Delight and fear fought together for priority. Rosa!

I ran to her. "Rosa! What are you doing here? Don't you know the pox is raging?"

A broad smile spread across her face. "Hello, Angelo. Good to see you again."

I wanted to embrace her, hold her, cover her with kisses. But I checked myself. "It could be dangerous for your health!"

"When I have ever allowed danger to stop me?" She took a basket from the footman and handed it to me. "Here, be a gentleman and carry this inside for me." She threw me an impatient look. "Well? Let's get going. I have brought fresh vegetables for your sister and even practised making a spicy soup for her." She threw a look at the basket in my hands. "Although I understand you do not exactly lack vegetables."

"Oh, this..." I felt so stupid. "I was doing some shopping for the neighbour. But really, Rosa, you cannot enter my sister's house. She is ill. You could contract her illness."

Impatiently she put the basket on the ground. "I know that your sister has the pox, Angelo. The cook told me in detail. But if she has survived, it must be almost over by now. What's more, half of my family had the pox when we were living in Naples, and the pox has never got me. Believe me, I don't just rush into a nightmare." She grabbed the basket again and pushed it into my free hand. "And now I would like to go in."

"Scusa, giovane donna," said the footman respectfully. "When will you expect us again?"

"Around noon, please," said Rosa.

There was no other choice but to let her enter my sister's house.

It was as if I was entering it for the first time. Suddenly I saw how small the room was and how gloomy, even with the shutters open. Perhaps because I tried to look with Rosa's eyes? She seemed completely indifferent to everything. She went straight to Mariana's bed and pulled up a stool.

"Hello, Mariana," she said cheerfully. "I am Rosa Scarlatti. I have already met you, but probably you no longer remember. It was a long time ago!"

Mariana did not seem at all overwhelmed. She sat up and pulled her sheet over herself. "Buongiorno, signorina. Where was that?"

"In the church near here. Do you remember when Angelo heard the result of the competition against the mayor's son?"

"You're the daughter of the composer," said Mariana. "Now I remember."

"And now I live with my father with Prince De Medici. That's where I heard of your illness."

"The maid the prince sent me was scared." My sister's gaze shifted. "I understand that, of course."

"Me too," said Rosa. "But if you ask me, the prince should have sent her back some time ago."

"Now you're here," I said softly. I could hardly keep my eyes off Rosa.

"Little brother, give our guest something to drink."

I jumped up. "Of course." There was some diluted wine in a jug the neighbour had brought last evening. I didn't know whether I could offer Rosa that. Otherwise there was only water, which I could boil with some herbs in it. I decided to do the latter. In Rosa's basket I found mint, and I brewed a fragrant warm drink from that.

"I am getting better," I heard my sister reply to a question from Rosa. "I will recover fully. I can feel it."

"I think so too." Rosa tapped the sheets in encouragement. "My brothers and one of my sisters have also had the pox. None of them succumbed, heaven be praised. When they started to recover, they looked just like you."

My sister improved visibly from the visit, but it also exhausted her. Toward noon, Rosa look her leave. I followed her outside.

We had hardly taken a few steps when she pulled a letter from her sleeve. "The prince asked me to give you this," she said.

I sighed and hesitated to take it. "The opera…"

"Yes," said Rosa. "Would you like to be alone when you read it?"

I shook my head. "I know what it says."

"Here, take it." Rosa pushed the letter into my hand. "My father says the opera is perfect for you. I have heard fragments as he was composing and I think he is right."

"What is the name of the opera?"

"*Arminio*. Do you want to hear the story?"

I shrugged. "I couldn't care less about the whole opera. With all respect for your father."

"Don't let him hear that. It is not very polite to say something like that to somebody who has done his very best to make you the centre of attention."

Again, I sighed. "I'm sorry, I did not intend to insult your father. But…" I looked at her, unsure of myself. "You understand don't you? I mean…you understand why Paolo was so angry with me on that last evening in Pratolino?"

"Of course I understand what the prince wants with you." Rosa waited for a moment. "Listen, Angelo, I am only seventeen and hardly an adult. But I have lived at royal courts for so long that I am quite used to things. I know you are not the first and also not the last person in the prince's life. And there are certainly disadvantages that he has set his sights on you. But the opera that Papa has written for you may very well become world famous. Kings, princes, dukes and other members of the nobility will worship you, and your name will be chanted in opera houses at home and abroad. All thanks to the love of the prince."

"And what will it cost?" I asked bitterly. "What woman would ever love me, would want to share my bed when I have been the lover of the Prince De Medici?"

Rosa pursed her lips. I did not know whether she was laughing at me or whether her smile showed understanding. I felt regret that I had been so honest.

"You know," said Rosa. "Physical love is greatly overestimated. A few caresses here, a kiss there…a small sacrifice when you think of all the advantages it will give you."

"Signorina?" Amazed, I lapsed into formality.

She turned to me, serious again. "I know what I'm talking about, Angelo, it happens everywhere. Not only among men, but also among ladies."

I felt myself getting nauseous. I didn't want to know this, hear it. Where was the romantic love immortalised in countless pieces of music? "I'm going back to my sister," I said.

"I did not mean to confuse you, Angelino. But that's the way it works, unfortunately."

Angrily, I walked back toward the house. What good was such knowledge? I didn't want to be the prince's lover. *Basta!*

Rosa Scarlatti ran to catch me up. "Read the letter, Angelo. Choose for your future and learn to live with the consequences. You will see that it is worth it. But if you don't want to?" She waved her arm. "I won't be annoyed at you. Although I would regret it."

Behind us, the carriage of the Prince De Medici turned into the alley. Rosa remained where she was. "Do you want an answer to your question, Angelino Montegne?" She didn't wait for my reply. "I will," she said so loudly that I was afraid the whole street could hear it. "I will love you when the prince has had enough of you. Me, Rosa Scarlatti!"

34

She wanted me! Had I understood her? Did she really want me? As her lover?

My body was burning and I wanted to run, spring, and shout to find some way to release the energy I suddenly felt.

Did I still dread leaving for Pratolino? In any case, the decision to go felt a lot lighter. As long as I did not have to leave my sister alone.

Filled with feelings of guilt about my sudden elation, I sat down a little later on Mariana's bed.

"She's nice, Signorina Scarlatti," she said after she had stared at me for a while. "Fresh vegetables are always welcome."

I felt my face get warm and saw from the gleam in her eye that Mariana had noticed my embarrassment.

"Rosa is very nice." I shuffled my feet. "She also brought me a letter."

"A letter?"

From the prince De Medici…" I took a deep breath. "He has had an opera written for me."

Her eyes widened in astonishment. "An opera? For you?"

"I am supposed to be singing the main role."

"And Signorina Scarlatti came here to tell you that?"

"No, I already knew her father was working on it. But now he has finished."

"And?"

"I think the prince will ask me in the letter to come to his estate to study it."

"You think…?"

"I haven't read it yet," I confessed.

"Fetch it," she commanded. "How can you leave a letter from the prince unread?"

"But it would mean I will have to leave here!"

"Then so be it. I must try to get back into the daily routine. I will manage, with the help of mistress Constanza and the Holy Mother."

Hesitantly, I pulled the letter from my doublet. The strongly perfumed envelope had absorbed the heat of my chest. I turned it over and over until my sister slapped my hand. "Stop that, fratello! What's wrong with you?"

I could not put it off any longer. I unfolded the sheet of paper and started to read.

My heart,

The Holy Mother is merciful to me! With the greatest joy in my heart, I send you notice that signore Scarlatti has completed the opera dedicated to you.

I shall come to fetch you next Friday, so that you still have some time to spend with your undoubtedly loving sister before you become mine. Know that I look forward to seeing you with a heart filled with desire.

Il principe Ferdinando

I hung my head. Friday! The day after tomorrow!

"Angelo? What does it say?" I took a deep breath and straightened my shoulders. "Tell me!"

"In two days, they will collect me and take me to the court of Prince De Medici."

"But that is wonderful! What an honour!"

"Yes," I muttered, as the image of the passionate prince came into my mind. "A wonderful honour."

My sister threw me a curious look. "What's the matter, Angelo? Why are you not as happy as you should be?"

"Because…I must leave you behind," I invented quickly. That was, of course, true, I would have preferred to stay until she had completely recovered.

"I have already said that you need not worry about me, little brother. I can manage. You should be happy that you will again be near the daughter of signore Scarlatti." She did not look at me. "She has beautiful eyes and speaks without fear."

"I will not pretend that I have not noticed her."

"I wouldn't believe you if you did." I saw a smile on her lips. "You kept on looking at her."

"Did I?"

"Ha!" She slapped my leg. "Didn't you notice it yourself? You are in love, little brother."

I sighed. "Oh yes?"

Mariana took my hand. "Listen, Angelo, stop worrying about me and just leave for Pratolino. When you are there, take your chance to find happiness. You have my blessing."

I did not dare confess that the church would never allow me to marry. My happiness would always remain a forbidden fruit, and naturally the prince was that as well.

"Come," she said. "Help me up. If you poke the fire and fetch a blanket for me, I will sit in the chair for a while. I have lazed around enough."

35

That Friday afternoon, the carriage of the Prince De Medici drove into Vicolo Porettana for the second time in one week. I heard the carriage arriving long before it stopped in front of the door because of the voices calling out.

"That will be the carriage." Mariana wrapped the blanket tighter around her shoulders. I did not stand up. With a feeling as if a pile of stones had been piled on my chest, I listened to the sounds from outside.

Angelo!" My sister's voice sounded urgent. "Go and welcome our visitors!"

Slowly I stood up. I shuffled to the door, just in time to open it before there was a knock.

"My dear boy!" Prince Ferdinando opened his arms to me, pulled me to him, and kissed me on both cheeks. I felt Mariana behind me watching on in amazement. "I have come to get you," said the prince. "The opera is finished, the composition is extremely promising. I am looking forward to the moment when you sing it for me."

Behind him, the neighbours huddled together. Birds circled above us, the wind blew, a stone rolled from a roof and bounced on the street.

"Angelo," hissed Mariana behind me. "Answer him. Have you packed your things?"

"Ah, signorina Montegne!" Prince Ferdinando pushed me to one side and entered the room.

Mariana immediately slipped out of her chair in an attempt to kneel.

"No, no, signorina. Please don't do that!" Politely he helped her up. "I am delighted to make your acquaintance," he said, without paying any attention to the fact that she was hardly wearing anything. "Your brother has told me much about you."

I hadn't done anything of the kind. Everything he knew he had learned from the spies that he had sent here himself. And perhaps from Rosa.

But there was no time to worry about his bragging because he quickly turned to me again.

"The conservatory…" I said quickly. "They do not yet know that I am not returning."

"Do not worry, il mio amico," said the prince. "I have informed the rector. There is no problem whatsoever."

"And my sister…I cannot leave her alone. Not yet…You can see she is not fully recovered."

Prince Ferdinando immediately turned and took Mariana's hand. "Signorina Montegne, I invite you to accompany your brother. He shall need an assistant to help him with his costumes and his music. Who better to take on such a task than you, his dear sister? Please, accept my offer."

"Me?" Mariana pulled the blanket even tighter around her shoulders. "Il mio principe."

"If you feel well enough, of course. Miss Scarlatti informed me that you were recovering."

My legs felt weak. If my sister came with us, I would no longer be able to conceal my humiliating position from her. *No!* I wanted to shout. *Say no, Mariana!*

"Nobile signore," she stammered. "I do not know what to answer to that."

"Of course," he replied without hesitation. "I understand that my offer is unexpected and that you must make arrangements. Let us say that my carriage will come to fetch you in one week."

She bowed her head. Her face had turned red. No idea whether she would have voluntarily accepted his offer, but it seemed as if he would not take no for an answer.

I yet again gave up any resistance. "I am grateful, my prince," I mumbled. "Will you permit me to fetch my pouch?"

He gave me a smile and nodded affably. "Go, my friend."

A short while later we arrived at the prince's home. Someone must have been on the lookout, for the major-domo came hurrying outside as soon as the carriage rolled up the drive.

The prince threw him his coat. "Prepare a small meal for us," he ordered. "And take signore Montegne's luggage to his rooms. Come, my darling." He took my hand and pulled me into the mansion. "Let me show you the apartments I have had prepared for you."

I hardly had time to think about what has happening to me. I stumbled along after the prince who moved hurriedly along corridors and doorways on the ground floor until he pushed open two double doors. "Here are your rooms, my heart." He stepped aside to let me through.

My mouth dropped open even wider when I saw the rooms in which I would live in the time ahead. The bedroom was furnished more luxuriously than I had ever seen. The enormous bed of carved reddish wood was covered in blankets with golden tassels at each of the four corners. The De Medici family crest was precisely over the centre. The sheets peeping out slightly from under the blankets seemed to invite caresses, so soft. Like the skin of a baby. On a table in front of the window stood a carafe of wine and a dish full of juicy fruits.

Behind the bedroom were two other rooms. One of them had

a long tall table on which there was a washbasin with fragrantly perfumed water. The basin was flanked by dozens of elegantly decorated bottles. The washroom had a separate entrance, through which a servant could apparently enter to refresh the water without me noticing it in the bedroom.

In the other room there stood racks with the most magnificent items of clothing. "I hope they fit you, my dearest," said Prince Ferdinando. "I had my tailor make them especially for you." His fingertip glided over the birthmark on my cheek. "So seductive," he whispered. "Delicious…"

I suppressed the urge to step away. "For me?"

"My people asked the conservatory for your measurements. After all, the costume for *Arminio* had to be made. It goes without saying that a suitable wardrobe will be prepared for your sister."

He again took me by the elbow and pushed me toward another door. "See, my treasure, here is the entrance to my private rooms. Nothing or nobody need disturb us when we are together."

I quickly turned round. "I am not worth all this, il mio principe."

"Nando," he said. "Call me Prince Nando."

"Prince Nando…I do not deserve this…"

He gave me a tender smile. "You will prove to be worth all this, my little treasure. You will not disappoint me." Fortunately, at that moment there was a knock at the door.

"Sì!" snarled Prince Ferdinando.

"Your meal is served," said the major-domo respectfully from behind the door.

"Ah, buono. My friend, I shall leave you alone to clean yourself up. I shall have you fetched in a few moments." He turned and left my apartment through the connecting door.

Immediately after he had left, I fell on the bed with my face in my hands. Holy Mother, how could I escape?

Rosa and the other guests in the mansion were nowhere to be seen during our meal. There were silver chandeliers on the table, deliciously tender veal, soft cheeses and bright red wine in crystal glasses which were constantly filled by servants who appeared behind us from nowhere.

I enjoyed the food, until I noticed that Prince Ferdinando hardly put anything in his mouth. His eyes were pinned on me with a hungry look and my appetite left me.

The prince noticed and took it the wrong way. As I slowly cut a piece of meat, he placed his hand against my cheek.

"I no longer have any interest in this meal," he said slowly. "And I see that you feel the same. Let us go."

"Prince?"

He stood up. "I passionately desire you, my sweet, beautiful sopranist!" He placed his hand over his heart. "Come." His voice sounded hoarse.

I wanted to grab the table and collapse on the spot, but I had no choice but to follow him. Beads of perspiration broke out on my forehead, my heart thumped against my rib-cage.

Too quickly we reached the corridor leading to our apartments. My legs grew heavier with each step. If only I could turn to stone. Or have the building collapse on top of us…

Next to me, Prince Ferdinando was breathing shallowly. His steps were short and urgent, as if he were almost running. "Come, my darling, come." Impatiently he opened the door through which a lackey had shown me so long ago.

Almost before he was inside he took off his tall black wig and placed it on its stand. What remained was a middle-aged man with a bald head. More insistent than ever, more passionate.

More disgusting.

He pushed me onto the sofa and began touching me. I wanted to push away his hands! He was everywhere: at my ear, my neck, under my doublet, at my waist.

Again that damned body of mine reacted. My sex rose and betrayed me. Unreliable, accursed, devil's organ! Why, Mother Mary, did they not cut away everything? Why did the Holy Mother do this to me? This disgrace, this treachery!

I squeezed my eyes shut, kept my body limp and imagined that I was in the Roman amphitheatre near Fiesole. I saw an eagle high in the air, circling in search of its prey, rabbits scuttling innocently among the tall grass. I heard birds singing and crickets chirping. Behind my closed eyelids, my gaze went to the centre of the arena. To a beautiful young woman, her figure slender and elegant, her eyes fierce and loving at the same time. Rosa! She reached out her arms to me, pulled me to her. Her hands pushed my doublet upwards until it almost reached my armpits. Her soft fingers caressed me.

"Yes…" I whispered. "Yes."

"Darling…" Rosa pressed her lips against mine. She licked me, covered me with kisses.

I wanted to feel her. My fingers ran down her back, pushed their way under her dress. Her skin, so soft and smooth. Her hips.

"Rosa…" I groaned. "Rosa…"

Immediately the caresses stopped. "What did you say?" said an indignant voice.

With a shock I was returned to reality. My eyes opened and saw the indignant face of Prince Ferdinando above me.

"Rosa? Did I hear you properly? Rosa Scarlatti?"

"My prince…I'm sorry…" I stuttered. "I don't know what came over me."

He shot up, his clothes crumpled and raised. "Never in my life have I been so insulted!" Beads of spit shot from his mouth. "Leave!" he thundered. "Leave me alone!"

With long strides he stormed out of the room, leaving me behind, dumbfounded.

36

Dazed I left the prince's apartment, taking the same route by which I had come. My own rooms were close by, but I couldn't stand being that close to the prince. I didn't want to think about what had happened in his rooms. I didn't want to think about his fingers on my body, his breath in my neck. I was filthy. Dirty. Vile. Tainted.

If only I were in Florence, on the banks of the Arno. I could throw myself into the purifying water of the river. What difference would it make it the water dragged me under? If I drowned?

Why should I live? With that filthy, unfaithful, mutilated body of mine?

Groggily I wandered through the corridors of the mansion, searching for something I recognised, a place where I felt safe. And that place could be none other than the concert hall where I had enjoyed so many fine moments with Paolo, Rosa, signore Scarlatti, Maestro Perro, and signore Cristofori.

The door was not locked. Two smoking candlesticks on the wall threw a dismal light through the room.

The pianoforte was still standing in the middle of the room. The lid was closed and a soft cloth lay over it, Exhausted, I sat on Cristofori's stool and placed my hand on the cloth. The miraculous, majestic instrument that produced such beautiful sounds did not comfort me. It only supported me. I laid my head down on it. My eyes stared into nothingness. I did not want to think, did not want to be. I still felt dirty, sullied by the prince.

How I longed for soft, comforting arms! For a safe breast to lay my head against!

Where was Rosa? Why had I not yet seen her? And her father, where was he? Had they left?

Impossible. Earlier today, the prince had spoken with pride about the opera that had been written for me, the opera composed by signore Scarlatti.

*Arminio…*strange name…

What was it Rosa had said about the libretto? Had I given her the chance to say anything about it? I no longer remembered.

The flickering candles were calming. Slowly I fell into a condition of bare consciousness.

"What are you doing here?".

"Huh?" I lifted my head in a daze. Immediately, I felt the stiffness in my muscles and groaned.

"Yes," muttered Cristofori. "You'll have cramps if you laid the whole night like that." That was also the last thing he said to me. He pushed me from the stool and studied his instrument to see whether there was any damage where I had laid my head.

Standing there, with my back against the wall, I tried to gain control of myself. What had happened the day before?

Much too quickly, my consciousness returned. And I wanted to crawl away. Crawl away into a deep hole in the ground, away from all the misery that awaited me when I had to face the prince again. Could I just run away before the court awoke? Go back to Fiesole?

But the door was pushed open. "Buongiorno, amico," came the cheerful voice of signore Scarlatti. Then he saw me. "Master Montegne!" he said in surprise. "Up so early?"

There was no need to ask myself whether he knew what had been facing me last night. I saw it on his face. He came closer, his gaze taking me in. "I had not expected you yet."

"It all went terribly wrong." I raised my hands to my face. "I insulted him."

"Come, come, it can't be as bad as that."

"No!" I burst out. "It was as bad as that. I wish I could return to Florence and just get away from here!"

Signore Scarlatti sighed. "What happened, my boy? Did you reject his advances? Reject *him*?" He did not wait for an answer. "No, Angelo. Do not tell me. I do not need to know what takes place behind the doors of your apartments."

I wouldn't have told him. How could I? What words could I use to explain that I had been fantasizing about his very own daughter? That I felt her hands when the prince caressed me?

"What now?" I whispered. "Should I leave before he appears? Perhaps I could still return to the conservatory. Padre Orvieto wouldn't…"

"Be quiet, Angelo. Why would you do that? The prince is bound to see things differently once he has calmed down. Perhaps he will realise that he approached things badly with you. That you are a thoroughbred who needs more careful treatment than he permitted last evening." Scarlatti tried to adopt a frivolous tone. "They say that passion can be fanned by rejecting a lover."

Rejecting? I had called out the name of another a woman during his caresses!

Signore Scarlatti brushed some dust from my doublet. "First return to your rooms. Eat some of the delicious breakfast that has undoubtedly been served, dress in something comfortable and come back here. Music heals everything, you'll see. Let us start the rehearsals of *Arminio*!"

What else could I do but follow his advice? Perspiring with fear, I left the safety of the music room.

When I returned as quickly as possible, Rosa had come in. She rushed over to me as if she had not seen me in years and hugged me. Had her father told her about my problems with

Prince Ferdinando? Uncertainly, I pushed her away from me.

"My dear Angelino!" she said. "How good that you have arrived safely." She said nothing about the fact that I had arrived the day before or about what I had done in the meantime.

"How is your sister?" she asked.

"She is healing well." Neither of us knew how we should act. All the thoughts I had had of her shot through my mind. My face burnt and I didn't know where to look.

Fortunately, her father intervened. He pushed a score into my hands. "There are you, my boy. *Arminio.* Let us run through it together. Rosa, if you would be so kind as to…" He pushed her away.

"I understand." I had the idea that she was relieved. "I shall go and do your shopping."

Scarlatti had already forgotten her. Standing next to me, he leafed through the piece, pointing out certain parts in the music and humming some melodies. He also told me the story of the love between the German Prince Arminio and his wife Tusnelda. How the Roman general Varo tried to tear the two apart in order to be able to marry Tusnelda himself and how Tusnelda's father played a treacherous double role. He showed me where the key scenes could be found in the music.

"There are, of course, several roles," he said. "I would like to discuss with you who should sing them."

"Would you like to use students from the conservatory?" I asked.

"That is my preference," he said. "I have good experiences with you and Paolo."

"Paolo is no longer a student. He was expelled from the training."

Abruptly signore Scarlatti lowered his papers. "What did you say? I had imagined him with his blond curls and blue eyes next to you in one of the most important roles."

"A lot has happened." I sighed and forgot my own misery for a moment. "It ended when Paolo was caught in a cupboard with another boy. They were committing…" I hesitated to say the words out loud.

"Oh so," said signore Scarlatti thoughtfully. "What a terrible waste of such a beautiful voice." He thought for a moment. "But we have nothing further to do with the conservatory. What would think of visiting him in Florence and asking him to come to Pratolino?"

Again I hesitated. "Towards the end, we didn't get along very well. But I always enjoyed working with him." I wouldn't desert him here. Perhaps this was a last chance for him to save his career.

"Good, then I'll have people look for him. And the rest?" asked signore Scarlatti. We need more voices."

We discussed voice types, roles and the singers available at the conservatory for some time. I was even able to include Josepho. Although he was not that old and his voice was by no means mature, his enthusiasm would have a positive effect on all of us.

If Rector Orvieto gave his permission, there was no need for the singers to come to Pratolino immediately. The first rehearsals could, suggested signore Scarlatti, be held at the conservatory under the leadership of Maestro Perro. Scarlatti had sufficient confidence in him.

We were so deep in concentration that we did not notice that Prince Ferdinando had entered the room until he suddenly was standing before us.

"Ah, my prince…" said signore Scarlatti.

Prince Ferdinando said nothing. It seemed as if he was staring at me, but I wasn't completely sure. I kept my eyes on the ground.

The shame at the treachery my body had shown was still too great. How could I ever look the prince in the eye again?

"We have started going through the score," said Scarlatti, trying to lighten the mood.

But there was no reaction from the prince. The silence in the room became increasingly awkward. Cristofori apparently also felt it; I heard him nervously shifting his stool.

Just as I had decided to offer my apologies in public, the prince broke the silence.

"Signore Scarlatti. I would like to speak to you in the salon."

The composer gritted his teeth. "Of course, my prince," he said. "I will walk with you."

But the prince had already left the room.

"Oh…" I whispered.

"Don't worry," said signore Scarlatti reassuringly. "It's most probably a business matter. Wait here for me."

Of course I would. I was bursting with curiosity about what the prince wanted of Scarlatti. And I was scared to death that it had something to do with me.

The composer returned in next to no time. He fell into the chair beside me with a dejected look in his eye. "Dismissed! Immediately!"

"What?"

Scarlatti leaned forward and placed his head in his hands. "Sent packing, banned from Pratolino…"

"Why?" But I already knew.

"My work is no longer up to standard, he claims." Scarlatti shook his head in disbelief. "Why did I not learn of this before? I have received nothing but compliments. Praise, gifts…and now… Rosa and I must leave the mansion by Monday."

Rosa. Of course she was the real reason for signore Scarlatti's dismissal. It wasn't about the composer. She had to be got out of the way. For what I had uttered in my heated hallucinations!

"I'm sorry…" I wiped my face with my sleeve. Don't cry, no tears. But I could hardly keep them inside.

"I'm sorry too!" Scarlatti sighed deeply and bowed his head for a moment. Then he suddenly shot up and grabbed the score of *Arminio* from the table. "So what? Let the man get the pox on his cheeks! That red painted peacock with his foot-high wig and his effeminate airs! There are enough people waiting for my talents!" He stamped through the room, riffled through the papers that lay everywhere, threw what he did not need onto the ground. "If he thinks I'll be leaving my compositions behind my opera, the rest of the things I composed here…I will leave nothing behind!"

"I cannot believe what I am hearing, my friend!" said signore Cristofori, dazedly. How can you be leaving us?"

"I have to." I had never seen signore Scarlatti so angry.

"But why?"

"The saints in Heaven may know!" Scarlatti flung a pile of papers against the edge of a chair. "The Viceroy of Spain has offered me a position at his palace in Naples. I could have joined him in a snap long ago. I only remained here because of the innovative ideas that are born here. Almighty Lord!" Angrily he stamped his foot on the ground. "I suppose I cannot persuade you to go with me, Bartolomeo?"

The person he was addressing looked round in confusion. "Me, Alessandro? Go with you to the Marquis Del Scarpio?" He shook his head. "I belong here, my friend. I would never be able to settle in Naples."

"I would like to go with you," I said to my own amazement. "If you think there is work for me at the court of the viceroy."

"You?" Both looked at me in surprise. For the first time I had the feeling that not as much escaped Cristofori as I had thought.

Scarlatti shook his head. "The prince would not let you go, my boy. He has been yearning for you for far too long."

"I will not remain here on my own." I looked at the composer square in the eye and set my jaw. "If you leave, along with your daughter…What would I do here all alone? I shall pay for the journey myself, if that is what worries you. I can sell the ring that Prince Ferdinando gave me."

"It is not about the money," said Scarlatti. "You are not alone here, Angelo. The prince is here and I have heard that your sister will be coming too."

"Yes," I mumbled. "The prince."

The composer now turned completely to me. "Listen well, my son, let me say this very clearly: with your phenomenal voice, you can reach the heavens if you stay with Prince Ferdinando."

I fiddled with the sheets of the score in my hand. "I will never reach the heavens if I stay with the prince," I said. "I will lose myself."

"And what about your sister?"

"Couldn't she come with me to Naples?" For me there was no longer any question about me going. What would I do without Rosa?

Signore Scarlatti gave a deep sigh. "Very well. I won't stop you. At least, as long as the Viceroy of Spain assumes your debt to the conservatory. In musical matters, the marquis Del Scarpio is somewhat more conservative than Prince Ferdinando, but then, with all those talented people he hires…And I shall, of course, introduce him to the newest developments in the world of music."

"And my sister?"

"If you become a great star, you will need an assistant," said signore Scarlatti. "Of course we will take her with us."

"Then we can pick her up on Monday when we leave here," I said.

"You have made up your mind, I see." Signore Scarlatti shrugged his shoulders in resignation.

"God, oh God," muttered signore Cristofori from behind his pianoforte. "The prince will curse you all."

I may have reached my decision without any hesitation, but I had no idea how to tell the prince. And so I tried to avoid him. That didn't prove all that difficult, since it seemed he had decided to do the same.

"He will be waiting until we have left," said Rosa. We were sitting on a bench in the park. "As long as Papa and I are around, he'll keep out of the way." She bent toward me and placed a hand on my leg. A deliciously sweet perfume filled my nose. "What exactly happened between the two of you, Angelo? Why is he so furious?"

What could I say? The truth? I looked into her almond eyes. The specks seemed more abundant than before. I couldn't do it. I could not confess to her that thoughts of her had taken over me as the prince made love to me.

"No idea," I muttered.

She slid closer toward me, "I don't believe that. I have never known the prince be so unpredictable."

I fidgeted with my doublet. "Please do not force me to tell you," I whispered.

"Is it really so bad?"

I nodded.

For several moments, we both fell silent. Rosa's hand lay motionless on my thigh. Without being able to prevent it, the skin in my crotch began to tingle. My penis awoke and began to grow. God! I thought. Not again. Not now!

Rosa's fingertips moved slowly along my leg. I nervously

tightened my every muscle in a vain attempt to prevent my body from giving in to the moment. In my thoughts, I begged Rosa to stop, but at the same time I begged her to continue.

My vocal chords had stopped working the singer had no voice.

"Now I finally have an answer to my question," whispered Rosa as she shifted her hand to my crotch. "You are clearly capable of making love to a woman."

Don't speak, I thought.

"Was that it?" she asked. "Did you not react to him in the way you do to me?" Her hand slid under my doublet, touched the naked skin of my stomach, my chest.

I could no longer control myself and gave in. Precisely like in my dream, my hands sought their own way. They pushed up Rosa's skirts, stroked her thighs to the edge of her undergarments.

"I want you, Rosa," I heard myself whisper. "I want you. You!"

37

On Monday, just before I was about to leave the mansion of Prince Ferdinando De Medici with Scarlatti and his daughter, I had myself announced to the prince. I could not avoid it any longer.

"Show him in!" I heard his voice in his study.

The lackey stepped aside and bowed.

I paid him no attention. My stomach felt as if it would explode at any moment.

The prince arose from his chair as I entered. "My friend," he said politely. "I have been expecting you. I am happy I finally have you with me."

The irony of his words made my head spin. If he only knew what I had come here to do! "Il mio principe…" I whispered awkwardly.

"After today we shall be together. You will see how pleasant the future is that lies before us."

He truly doesn't suspect anything, I suddenly realised. Oh, Holy Mother.

"Unfortunately, the opera that Mister Scarlatti wrote will leave Pratolino with him, but I shall invite the finest composer I can find to write a new leading role just for you."

"My prince."

"I hear there is a very talented young man in Northern Germany, a certain master Handel. I shall invite him to come here."

I gathered together all the courage I could find. "My prince, I am leaving with signore Scarlatti for Naples."

"What?" Prince Ferdinando narrowed his eyes. "You're leaving?"

I bowed my head. "I am sorry."

"Nobody leaves here without my permission. And that includes you."

"Il mio principe."

"Have you not understood?"

"My place in the carriage has been booked."

"Then cancel it."

"No." How could I make him understand? "Prince Ferdinando…" I took a deep breath. "I must leave!"

"You must do nothing! Remember, it was at my insistence and only at my insistence that Padre Orvieto gave you permission to leave the conservatory. The conservatory will not tolerate you leaving here!"

"I shall inform Padre Orvieto of the reasons for my departure."

"The foundation for your future is being laid here in Pratolino, for a worldwide career as one of the best sopranists ever! I can offer you everything that it takes for that!" Without realising it, the prince had begun speaking to me as an equal.

"You have already offered me much."

"Offered you much? I have invested in you! Have you any idea how much it cost me to have *Arminio* composed for you?" His breath came in gasps. He reached for his walking stick and squeezed it as if he wanted to reduce it to dust. "I have sent a maid to your sister, have had costumes made for you, had an apartment furnished for you. And now you think you can turn your back on me just like that?"

"I have no choice…"

"I will not let you leave!" he bellowed. "What are you thinking?"

"My decision has been made, Prince Ferdinando…" I whispered. "I shall repay the money you have spent on me."

"The money? The money?" A carafe hit the ground and broke into pieces. Splinters hit my legs. "I do not want a cent from you. If you leave, I will destroy you! Do you hear? Never will you be accepted anywhere!" He raised his arm and took several paces toward me. For a moment I thought he was about to attack me. Quickly I raised my head, steeled myself.

"Il mio principe." He must have seen that he could do nothing to change my decision, for suddenly he turned away from me with a jerk.

"Be gone." A voice as cold as ice. "Be gone from my sight. You no longer exist for me. There are dozens where you came from. Dozens? Ha! Hundreds!"

"I am sorry, il mio principe." I hesitated for a moment to see whether he changed his mind, but his back seemed resolute. His shoulders moved up and down as if he were panting.

"I thank you for everything," I whispered to his back. "For the opportunities you offered me. Farewell."

As I took the first steps along the corridor after leaving the study, my departure played on my mind. Could this farewell not have been more dignified, without screaming and threats? Could I have announced my departure more carefully?

No. The prince would never have accepted my departure, no matter what I said or did.

I thought back to the funeral of Innocentio Verde where it had all begun. The meeting with the prince, which would mean a turning point in my life. In his own way, he had been benevolent to me and I was, despite everything, grateful. I hoped he wouldn't make good on his threat of revenge. Did he have the power to destroy me?

I took a deep breath. There was no point in worrying about it now. I had made my decision. It was a good decision. And I would never change my mind, never in a hundred thousand years. My future lay ahead of me. And what would that future bring? Well, Rosa Scarlatti, in any case!

With each step I took toward the concert room, my concern and agitation faded into the background. In their place came an overwhelming feeling of relief. I felt the urge to skip, to echo through the high corridors of the princely mansion.

Never! Never again would I allow things to be forced on me which I did not want. My life was my own. Mine, and mine alone! And as long as the Heavenly Father gave me my life, it was for me to decide what would happen to it.

Halfway down the hallway to the concert room where my bundle was waiting, Rosa came running toward me, her skirts raised. I saw two elegant feet, beautiful ankles, and calves as strong as solid oak.

"Are you ready?" she asked. "My father is waiting in the carriage." The specks in her eyes sparkled at me.

"Yes," I said. "I'm ready."

CPSIA information can be obtained
at www.ICGtesting.com
Printed in the USA
BVOW08s2019191216

471148BV00028B/198/P